C00 996 049X

D1614434

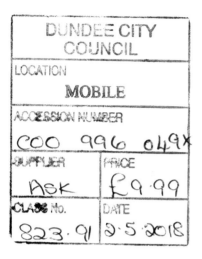

DUNDEE CITY
COUNCIL

LOCATION
MOBILE

ACCESSION NUMBER
COO 996 049X

SUPPLIER
ASK

PRICE
£9·99

CLASS No.
823·91

DATE
2·5·2018

© Copyright Rachel Amphlett 2015
The copyright of this book belongs to Rachel Amphlett
No reproduction without permission

The names, characters and events in this book are
used fictitiously. Any similarity to actual people
living or dead, events or locales is entirely
coincidental.

National Library of Australia Cataloguing-in-Publication entry
Amphlett, Rachel, author.

Three Lives Down

ISBN: 978-0-992-26859-6 (paperback)

A823.4

Three Lives Down

Rachel Amphlett

Chapter 1

Captain Matt Ryan sat with his back pressed against the hard surface of his jump seat in the back of the Mk9 Lynx helicopter, ignoring the queasiness at the pit of his stomach as the aircraft banked sharply to the right.

He didn't usually worry about being sick on a flight – all of them had been there, done that at some point – but the medic who sat across from him was new to the team, young and inexperienced in battle. The last thing he'd need to see would be his commanding officer throw up into the aisle between the seats.

Instead, he lifted his head and smirked at the man in front of him. 'Nervous yet, Thompson?'

If the medic turned any paler, he'd be invisible. He wiped his mouth with his sleeve before shouting over the noise of the rotors. 'Just a bit, sir.'

Matt winked. 'You never get used to it,' he yelled. 'I usually throw up before we land.'

'That's why none of us sit opposite him!'

The shout came from a large soldier who was squeezed into a seat further along the fuselage, and the men next to Matt dissolved into laughter.

THREE LIVES DOWN

Pleased, he noted the young medic joined in and silently
thanked Sergeant Simon Blake for lightening the mood.

'Five minutes!'

The call over his headphones pulled him back to the job
in hand, and the fuselage fell silent as each man began to
rehearse the plan in his head one final time.

They'd been flying dark for the past hour, the sun
slipping over the horizon minutes after they'd left German
airspace, the pilot using the full capabilities of the aircraft's
night vision compatible cockpit.

The aircraft began a rapid descent, and as Matt's ears
popped, his experience told him they'd just crossed the
border.

Last chance to turn back.

Instead, the helicopter surged forward, its engines
powering the craft through the night and he imagined its
camouflaged form hugging the landscape, churning its way
over the mountains that led a path to their destination.

He'd spent the past forty-eight hours poring over the
topology maps and then the building's blueprints, planning
the mission with his superiors, discussing the risks,
describing his tactics for both the worst and best-case
scenarios.

At one point, the Major General had stepped away from
the window he'd been staring through, the grey outline of
the *HMS Belfast* on the river beyond his silhouette.

'Is it worth the risk?' he'd asked.

A second man had pushed his chair back from the desk, and Matt had seen the cold steel glint in his eyes before he'd replied.

'Yes. It is,' he'd said. 'We're under threat, and he's been compromised. We need him back here. Now.'

The meeting had concluded two hours later, the plan finalised.

Matt's stomach lurched instinctively as the helicopter began a fast, sickening descent.

'Two minutes!'

'Get ready to saddle up!' Matt yelled.

Last minute nerves threatened, as always, despite the knowledge that the Lynx had diffusers fitted to its exhaust to thwart enemy radar attempts to track its infrared signal, as well as the capability of disrupting its own electronic signature.

They were flying in as silently as possible, in one of the Army's fastest aircraft.

Adrenalin began to course through his veins, the reality of the mission all too clear in his mind.

Get him out. Get him back to London. Alive.

'Dead is not an option,' the mysterious man at the briefing had said as he'd fixed his glare on Matt. 'Is that understood?'

'Yes, sir.'

Matt had stood as the man had risen to leave, before turning to his superior as soon as the door had closed. 'What's going on, sir?'

The Major General had shrugged. 'Fuck if I know, soldier. I know as much as you.'

Which is next to nothing.

Matt shook the thought away and concentrated on running his hand over the equipment strapped to his clothing.

At the order of the mission commander, all their insignia had been stripped away. Even the camouflage they wore belonged to a foreign state.

'Just doesn't feel right, not having Her Majesty's crown on me,' Blake had grumbled. The team had laughed, but Matt knew what he meant. He'd been involved in a couple of secret missions before, sure, but there was something different about this one.

All this for one man? And what if something went wrong?

When he'd posed that question to his commanding officer, the older man had glared at him.

'Failure is not an option,' he'd said.

Matt exhaled, closed his eyes for a moment, and stretched his neck, psyching himself up for the imminent attack. He consoled himself with the thought that at least they *were* landing, not jumping out with parachutes.

'Sixty seconds!'

He heard the Sergeant pull back the starboard sliding door of the fuselage, then the port. The wind whipped through the gaping holes, and when he opened his eyes, they began to water. He slipped goggles over his face, and then stood and nodded to the medic. 'Come on, Thompson.

Time to dance,' he shouted, the roar of the engines whipping his voice away as quickly as he'd spoken.

The young man nodded and leapt to his feet, his eyes wide.

Matt turned to the rest of the team. 'Okay, you've rehearsed this enough times over the past twenty-four hours. Now it's for real. Everyone knows their job. Get on with it. Get out. Get back here. Understand?'

'Yes, sir!'

The men lowered night vision goggles over their faces, and then reached above their heads for the hand straps dangling from the airframe as the gunner aimed his weapon towards the building that loomed below them.

Matt leaned forward until he could peer out the starboard opening and got his first glimpse of the granite-hewn prison they were about to break into.

The two lookout stations that had once towered over the prison walls were now derelict, crumbled from decay and exposure to the frigid elements, whilst the perimeter walls appeared deserted.

Evidently no-one expected anyone to break out – or break in – from the desolate location.

As the helicopter dropped from the sky, its wheels bounced on the ground, the pilot executing a textbook manoeuvre before he slowed the rotors.

'Go, go, go!' Matt urged as he stepped from the aircraft, keeping his body hunched over from the rotor wash above him.

The helicopter had landed in a large walled area, which Matt knew to be the exercise yard of the prison. His feet scuffed up dirt and small stones as he ran.

He didn't look back – he didn't need to. He knew his men would be right behind him, falling into position, covering him and the aircraft while he led the smaller team, including the medic, towards their target.

There was room in the cabin for one stretcher patient only.

The freezing temperature turned his breath to steam as he ran across the bare earth, his fingers already turning numb in the thin mountain air. He flexed his hand around his weapon and brought it up to his chest before he threw his shoulder against the far wall, turning to provide cover fire if required.

As Blake slid to a halt next to him, he glanced over towards the abandoned guard towers positioned along the perimeter and frowned.

'Do you see anything?'

'Negative, sir.'

Matt tapped the microphone he'd stuck to his body armour with black electrical tape. 'Alpha One, confirm area appears deserted, per intel.'

'Copy that.'

'Where is everyone?' hissed Blake.

Matt covered his microphone. 'It's an old Soviet prison,' he murmured. 'The CIA was using this for extradition purposes until they got caught. Intel suspects that someone's been using this for their own agenda ever since.' He dropped his hand back to his weapon, the familiar surface a comfort under his grip, checked the lead to the camera on his helmet, and then took a deep breath. 'Okay,' he said, turning to the men beside him. 'Stay sharp. Let's go.'

They ran single file along the length of the wall until Matt slowed and held his fist in the air. He recalled the blueprints, pleased that his superiors had, at least, managed to get the details right – so far.

Beside him, a solid metal door barred entry to the building. He beckoned to Blake, and then stood to one side as the man pulled out a line of det cord from his vest and began fixing a small explosive to the door. He waited until Blake stepped back, then joined Thompson by the side of the building and turned his head.

The explosion was short and effective.

The lock on the door disintegrated under the force of the plastique, and the men entered the building one after the other without incident. Matt ordered the last of the men through the door to pull it shut and stay on guard.

'We're in,' he murmured over his comms link. 'Heading towards the cells now.'

'Intel says he's on the inner block. Blueprints show a flight of stairs to your six o'clock position. Two levels down.'

'Copy that.'

'Down!'

Matt ducked, the urgency in Blake's tone leaving no room for argument, dropped into a crouch, and spun on his toes, raising his rifle to his chest.

Gunfire echoed off the enclosed space, and he saw a shadow drop to the floor, the sound of metal on concrete reaching his ears as the victim's gun fell from his hands a moment before his body collapsed.

Matt's attention snapped to Thompson, who was standing, his rifle still raised, his face pale.

'Good work, soldier,' he said. 'Stay focused.'

'Sir.'

'Stairs,' said Blake. 'So there must be more people somewhere.'

Matt ran through the building's plans in his head, recalling the layout that he'd pored over in the room above the River Thames.

After the first flight of stairs, there was a room that intel believed was being used for storage. In the old days, prisoners would have been kept there, although that was supposed to have come to an end twenty years ago.

The real fun and games would begin on the second level.

Blake led the way, with Matt bringing up the rear as they descended.

Reaching the bottom of the stairs, Matt pushed his night vision goggles up onto his forehead and peered along the dimly-lit corridor over Blake's shoulder.

A bare, unpainted wall, its surface slick with damp, ran to their left flank. On the opposite side, a series of heavy steel doors remained closed, the dark paintwork chipped and peeling.

'Which one?' hissed Blake.

'Fourth,' said Matt. His attention snapped towards the far end of the corridor. 'Incoming!'

All three men dropped to a crouch, spreading out and raising their weapons at the two figures that had emerged from the shadows of the basement cell block.

Matt flinched as brickwork sheared off the wall while their enemies' gunfire filled the enclosed space.

He squeezed the trigger of his own rifle and felt a moment's satisfaction as one of the guards dropped to the floor, clutching his leg.

Next to him, Blake fired a rapid burst at the second guard, and the man's silhouette spun with the force of the bullets before crumpling to the ground.

The first guard had begun to crawl towards his discarded weapon, one hand wrapped around his leg.

Matt stood, sighted his rifle, and fired.

The corridor fell silent; Matt signalled to Blake to cover their rear and then ran towards the fallen men.

He didn't expect to find any identification on them, and he wasn't disappointed. He left the bodies and jogged back to Blake and Thompson, pointing at the fourth door.

Blake pulled out a second line of det cord from his pocket, but Matt tapped him on the arm and held up the keys he'd taken from one of the dead men.

'Quieter this time. And less chance of damaging the goods,' he said and gently jangled the bunch of metal in his hand.

'But also less fun,' grumbled Blake, standing back.

It took two attempts before Matt found the right key and then twisted the handle and pushed the door open.

All three men took an involuntary step back at the stink emanating from the gloom.

'Jesus,' said Matt.

He swept his gaze across the floor in the dull light from the corridor until he located a bundle of ragged clothes, a pair of large feet sticking out from the far end. As his eyes travelled up the form, he picked out a pair of hands that clutched at a bare chest, the skin blotched and scratched, and then finally a face, bruised and battered, eyes half closed from the bruises that surrounded the man's cheekbones and eye sockets.

Blake swore under his breath, and then returned his attention to the corridor, his rifle sweeping left and right.

Matt moved his fingers along the wall of the room until he located a light switch, but it failed to work, and then he noticed the fitting hanging from the ceiling of the cell, stripped of any light bulb.

He swallowed. Evidently, the prisoner's captors were determined not to let the man take his own life. At least, not until they were finished with him.

'Come on,' he murmured to Thompson. 'Let's see what we've got.'

Matt crouched down next to the curled-up form and beckoned the medic towards him.

'Assessment. Quickly,' he said. 'Can he be moved?'

Thompson joined him and pulled out a small flashlight from his vest, shining its beam over the man, who blinked through swollen eyelids and raised his hands to protect his eyes from the sudden glare.

The medic ran his hands over the prisoner's body, checking for major injuries that his blood-stained clothing might hide.

Matt reached into his webbing and pulled out a small rectangular-shaped electronic device and switched it on. The screen flashed once, then a swipe screen on the front of it illuminated, casting a green glow across his face.

He reached out, turned the screen towards the man, and gently lifted one of the prisoner's hands until his index finger rested against the swipe screen. He held the man's hand steady until a low *beep* sounded from the device, then turned the screen and checked.

The man's fingerprint had been captured, the whorls and folds of his skin scanned and evaluated.

Confirmed.

Matt flinched at the cuts and bruises on the man's face as he switched off the device and tucked it back into his webbing, and wondered if the prisoner could walk or needed to be carried.

Blake moved closer, his rifle aimed at the open cell door. 'Is it him?'

'Yes.' He leaned towards the medic. 'Well?'

The man turned, sweat pouring down his face. 'I can't find any compound fractures, sir. I can't vouch for internal injuries. There appear to be cigarette burns on his legs. These cuts on his arm have had bleach or something poured onto them.'

'Right, we're going.' Matt stood and gestured to Blake. 'Help me. Grab him. Let's get out of here.'

He ducked under one of the prisoner's arms, waited until Blake had done the same, and then staggered for a moment as they adjusted the man's weight between them.

'Ready?'

'Go.'

'Cover our backs, Thompson.'

'Sir.'

Matt stepped sideways through the open cell door, fumbling to keep his rifle steady in his right hand as he moved.

Their progress was going to be slower than he'd have liked, but there was nothing he could do about it, so he gritted his teeth and instead kept a constant watch on the other cell doors as they passed.

A trickle of sweat began at his forehead as he wondered who else was being kept behind those locks – and whether anyone was coming to rescue them. He blinked to clear the thought and had begun to turn towards the concrete stairs that led back to the exercise yard when Blake shouted.

'Hostile, left!'

Matt swore.

The guard had appeared out of the darkness – on his blind side. If Blake hadn't shouted, they'd have been cut down without a chance. Stuck behind the rescued man, Thompson had no angle by which to shoot. Instead, Matt reached for his rifle, hell-bent on taking the guard before he could fire.

He cursed.

The comms lead had slipped down his arm during the extraction and was now entangled around his wrist, preventing him from turning his rifle towards the guard. The seconds passed by in slow motion as he kept his eyes on the guard, the man already reaching for his own weapon.

Matt gritted his teeth and tried to reach his weapon, all the while desperate not to drop the rescued man to the floor. He swore with frustration, cursing under his breath that he'd made such a rookie mistake in his haste to get the prisoner and his team to safety.

A tug at his arm caught his attention, and he looked down as the prisoner reached out, wrapped his hands around the rifle, and then swung the muzzle towards the guard and fired a quick burst.

The guard twisted where he stood, his face a mask of agony as he spun towards the floor.

The prisoner grimaced and relinquished the weapon.

'Take it,' he hissed before passing out.

Matt didn't need a second invitation. He ripped the comms equipment from his neck, looped the loose wire, and then shoved it down his vest.

He turned to Blake and Thompson. 'Let's get out of here before we're ambushed.'

They climbed the stairs, their progress hampered by the dead weight of the man they carried between them.

Matt could hear Thompson's breathing, heavy and laboured. He frowned, almost ready to question the man's fitness, until he realised the young medic was terrified. Matt glanced over his shoulder.

Sure enough, the man's face was pale, sweaty, as he covered their rear.

Matt turned his attention back to the man whose arms were looped around his. Thompson would have to learn to live with the terror if he wanted to remain part of the elite group – same as they all did.

A dull light began to pierce the gloom as they neared the top of the stairs, and Matt squinted until his eyesight grew accustomed to the brightness compared to the underground complex.

Their team mate stood at the doorway, relief spread across his face as the team reached him.

'Good to see you, sir.'

'Likewise,' said Matt. 'Take him.'

He swapped places with the man, and then once he and Blake were heading towards the waiting helicopter as fast as they could, Matt turned his attention to the doorway.

Thompson was peering back into the gloom.

In a heartbeat, Matt cleared the space between them, pulling the young medic to one side, a split second before gunfire exploded up the flight of stairs.

Bullets sent chips of the concrete doorway flying past them as they huddled to one side.

Matt waited, keeping still until silence pierced the air, their attacker pausing to reload.

'Go, go!'

He pushed Thompson towards the helicopter. 'Don't stop. Don't look back,' he ordered.

He made sure the young medic was on his way, then swung his rifle up and fired a short round down the staircase. Next, he reached for one of the grenades fitted to his body armour, pulled the pin, and tossed it down the stairwell.

A loud curse in a foreign language echoed up from the depths of the prison, before it was carried away by the explosion.

Dust and smoke chased heat up the stairs towards Matt, and he leaned back, closing his eyes against the blast wave, before he spun around and launched himself towards the helicopter.

The rotor blades began to increase in speed as he approached, and Blake leaned out of the aircraft, weapon steady as he waited for him.

As he drew closer, he saw Blake swing his rifle to the left, before a shout reached his ears.

'Down!'

He hit the dirt.

He felt, rather than heard, the bullets as they ripped through the air above his prone body.

A cry from the direction of the building behind him carried across the wide expanse of the exercise yard, and then was cut off by another round.

'Go!'

In an instant, he was on his feet and running once more.

He glanced over his shoulder and his heart fell. Armed guards were pouring out of a roof access and running towards the top of the prison, taking up positions around the yard.

'Move!' he yelled.

The helicopter began to rise in the air, the downforce hampering his progress, slowing him down.

He gritted his teeth, dug deep for another burst of energy, and pumped his arms. The gap between him and the aircraft closed.

Blake leaned out, his arm outstretched as the helicopter's wheels left the ground. He yelled encouragement at him as Thompson leaned over his shoulder with a rifle, providing cover fire.

And then he was there, being hauled up into the aircraft as it turned and lifted into the air at a sickening speed.

His men thrust him to the centre of the fuselage, before they turned their attention back to the guards on the prison roof, firing short bursts until the helicopter plunged below the line of the mountain and out of range.

Matt crawled towards the open door and peered out as the landscape rushed past beneath them. He signalled to the man next to him to close the door, then stood on tired legs and made his way towards the front of the helicopter where

Thompson and Blake were strapping the unconscious prisoner into a seat.

As he approached, the rescued man opened his eyes and raised his head, his eyes taking in the fascinated stares of the team, before falling to Matt. 'Who the hell are you? What's going on?' he rasped.

'Captain Matt Ryan,' said the team leader, 'of Her Majesty's British Army.'

The man frowned. 'Where are you taking me?'

Matt's answer was interrupted by the pilot's voice over the radio.

'We're clear of their airspace.'

The aircraft erupted with the roar from Matt's men as they celebrated. He high-fived Blake and then turned his attention back to the rescued man and grinned.

'You're going home, Dan Taylor.'

Chapter 2

Three weeks later

Northumberland

Jack Halligan swung the door to his office open and
hurried across the car park to the four-wheel drive vehicle
that had been left within the secure compound.

His site office resembled a shipping container with a
window punched in each side to let in light, and after three
days responding to emails and phone calls and dodging
requests from the client's representative to attend yet
another meeting to discuss progress, he was glad to escape.

He glanced at his watch.

The drilling crew were late – again.

He swore under his breath.

The project was already three months behind schedule
due to a winter that had got its dates wrong and had piled
snow on the Northumberland hills through to the beginning
of April.

The project team had descended on the area within a
single week from various parts of the world.

He'd received the call as he was finishing a project in Saudi Arabia, and the opportunity to see the green rolling fields of England once more, not to mention pints of real ale, was too good to pass up.

The company simply moved each of them around as projects were won and completed, and it was a lifestyle he enjoyed.

He turned at a shout from one of the other buildings.

'What time do you call this?' he grumbled as two men strode towards him.

'Sorry, Jack.' The taller of the two shook his hand. 'Phone call from Brazil. Had to take it. Problem with a rig over there, and they wanted my advice.'

'Nice to be wanted, eh, Greg?'

The man shrugged. 'Might as well make the most of it while the work's there.' He turned to his slightly shorter companion. 'Jack, this is Mark. He's going to be joining us today.'

Mark frowned as he shook Jack's hand. 'Is it normal for a project manager to ride out with the drilling team?'

Jack raised an eyebrow at the remark and turned to Greg, who coughed and forced a chuckle.

'Jack's very hands-on,' he explained. 'And when the drilling is behind schedule, I think he's got a right to ride out with us, don't you?'

Mark grunted a response and pointed to the large square-shaped silver case that Greg held between his hands, the strain on his face reflecting the weight of the box. 'Do you want me to help you with that?'

His boss shook his head. 'No. I'll see to it. You get in the truck.'

Jack watched as the younger man stalked round to the passenger seat and wrenched the door open. 'New boy?'

'Yeah – my last engineer went AWOL two weeks ago. Got this guy at short notice through an agency, but he seems to know what he's doing,' said Greg. 'He's not a bad worker when he remembers to keep his attitude in check,' he added with a wink.

'Rather you than me,' said Jack.

He waited until Greg had secured the silver box in the rear of the vehicle, then jogged round to the driver's door, leapt behind the wheel, and started the engine.

Once Greg was on board, Jack steered the vehicle towards the site gate and waited while the security team let them pass.

Minutes later, they were travelling along a hedgerow-lined lane, the hills rolling under the vehicle's wheels with ease. Mist rose from the valley below, burning away the light rainfall from the previous night.

After a couple of miles, Jack slowed as they approached a high-wire mesh fence that separated the road from a wide field. He braked and turned to the right at a small shipping container that had been converted into a temporary security office, guarding the entranceway through a padlocked metal gate set into the fence.

The first three weeks of the project had been spent using a government contractor who had used two teams of six men to encapsulate the property within a high metal fence that ran the perimeter of the land.

Four teams of two security men plus dogs now patrolled that perimeter day and night, leaving the project team in peace to do their work and run their tests in the middle of the fenced-off area, out of sight.

Two security officers approached the vehicle from the shelter of the container, and as one of them approached the vehicle, Jack buzzed down his window.

'Morning,' he said and handed over the occupants' three passes.

'You might be in for a quiet day today,' said the guard. He pointed at the black cloud hastening across the hills towards them. 'Especially if that one stays on course.'

'Cheers,' said Jack, redistributing the security passes to Mark and Greg.

'What's your ETA back here?'

'We'll probably be four to six hours.' Greg leaned over the central column. 'It'll depend on how easy it is to get the samples we need.'

The security man signalled to his colleague, who added the details to the clipboard. 'Okay, well – have a good one.'

He turned and walked over to the gate, selected a key from the bunch hanging off his belt loop, and swung open the metal barrier.

Jack buzzed his window up, put his hand up to the security team as the vehicle passed them, and then accelerated along the muddy farm track towards the first test well.

As the vehicle bumped and slid across the field, Jack steered it expertly over the terrain. Next to him, Greg checked his mobile phone.

'You'd think in this day and age, you'd get a bloody signal out here,' he grumbled.

'What's the problem?'

'It's my little girl's birthday,' said Greg. 'I wanted to speak to her before she goes to school.' He put down the phone and stared sightlessly at the passing landscape. 'These days, she's usually in bed and fast asleep by the time I get home.'

Jack held his tongue. All the men had complained when the accelerated delivery schedule had been revealed. Sure, they knew the company was under pressure to perform and would lose millions if it failed to bring the drilling programme back on track, but their bosses either chose to ignore or didn't understand the effect it had on the team's morale.

He checked in the rear view mirror. Mark was staring out the back window, the security hut disappearing from view as they rounded the base of a small hill and followed the track to the rig.

Jack turned his attention to the towering structure that could now be seen through the windscreen.

At nearly forty metres tall, the steel derrick of the rig dwarfed the four-wheel drive vehicle, its mass casting a shadow over the ground that had been shorn of grass and cleared for the construction crew, engineers, and geologists to work.

At the base of the rig, an assortment of machinery and equipment had been set out, ready for the testing to be undertaken.

Today, however, only the three engineers were present, their remit to obtain more samples for analysis to ensure the bore remained a valid prospect for the project.

Jack steered the four-wheel drive to within a few metres of the well, rubbed his eyes, and killed the engine.

'Right, let's get on with it,' he said, climbing out. 'I'd like to be back at the project office before dark.'

'Scared a sheep might get you?' asked Greg.

'It's not the sheep I worry about,' replied Jack. 'It's the locals.'

Both men laughed as they joined Mark at the back of the vehicle. Jack pulled open the doors and helped Greg slide the silver box towards them.

He nodded at Greg and, taking the weight between them, they lifted it out of the vehicle and carried it across the uneven ground towards the test well.

Mark followed in their wake, carrying an armful of measuring devices and a laptop bag.

Once they were at the well, the two men set down the silver box, and Jack stepped away, his gaze catching the radioactive warning symbols emblazoned in yellow and black across the locking mechanism.

'Okay, Greg. Do your magic.'

'Very funny.' The engineer crouched down and placed his hands each side of a combination lock inserted on the side of the box. 'No looking now, okay?'

Mark joined Jack and placed the bags of equipment by his feet. Both men averted their gaze as Greg rolled his thumb across the four combination numbers.

With a soft *click*, the locking mechanism released, and Greg pushed open the lid.

Jack moved until he could see the contents.

Inside the box, in individual chambers, sat six tubes, each bearing a further radioactive warning.

'Okay, let's get a move on,' said Greg and reached forward for one of the tubes.

'I don't think so.'

Jack's head snapped round at Mark's voice, his eyes opening wide at the gun that the man held steadily between his hands. 'What the fuck?'

Mark didn't answer. Instead, he aimed the gun at Greg, and calmly shot the engineer in the chest.

'Shit!'

Jack turned and fled, heading back to the vehicle, his brain trying to process what he'd just witnessed. He needed to reach the four-wheel drive, radio for help —

A fire scorched through the soft tissue in his calf muscle a split second before he heard the gunshot, and he fell to the ground.

He cried out in pain, his insides turning to liquid as he began to crawl, not daring to look over his shoulder.

Surely the security team have heard the shots, he thought seconds before he realised they were too far away, safely ensconced in their makeshift office with the radio blasting music.

He turned his head, trying to see if any of the dog patrols were within sight, but he couldn't even see the perimeter fence from where he lay.

'Shit, shit, shit,' he hissed as he heard footsteps squelch in the mud behind him, getting closer.

What the hell was going on?

Why did Mark kill Greg?

His hands slipped on the damp grass beneath his fingers, and he tumbled to the side, landing on his wounded leg. An agonising burning sensation tore through the nerve endings, and he screamed with frustration as he tried to regain his balance.

'Stop. Don't make it harder on yourself.'

The calmness in the young engineer's voice chilled Jack to the bone, and then the man was next to him. He glared at the man's boots and then lifted his chin.

Mark lifted the gun until Jack could see down the barrel.

His mouth dry, he wondered if he would see the bullet that killed him as he raised his hands in the air.

'Please, no,' he begged.

***

Mark steadied his arm and pulled the trigger.

The project manager's head exploded with the force from the close range shot, before his body fell backwards, his legs crumpling under him.

Mark flicked the safety on, turned, and stomped back to the silver box on the ground next to Greg's prone body.

He kicked the dead man's arms out of the way and then crouched beside the case and cursed.

Greg had been holding one of the thin canisters between his fingers when he'd been shot, and when he'd fallen, the canister had tumbled into the case, clipping the lead side of the box.

Now, it lay haphazardly across the rim of the box, its radioactive warning taunting him.

He exhaled slowly and reached out, turning the canister slowly back into its compartment. As it moved, his eyes opened wide, and he pulled his hand back with a jerk.

'Fuck.'

He squinted at the small crack that had appeared in the casing and then glanced at his watch and shook his head.

There was no time left. He'd just have to explain what had happened when he got to the drop-off point with the others.

Instead, he turned his attention to the security settings on the lid of the box. The lock was based on a simple combination mechanism, which could be altered only once the case was open. Now, Mark set the new combination to the pre-determined sequence and flipped the lid closed.

As he stood, the roar of a large engine reached his ears.

He raised his eyes to the lip of the small hill above the well site, spotting a second project-designated vehicle as it began a rapid descent towards him.

He lifted his hand in greeting and waited until the four-wheel drive pulled to a standstill next to Jack's vehicle. A second man sat in the passenger seat next to the driver and appeared to be talking to him as they stopped.

The driver nodded to the other occupant and then leaned out of the window and called across to Mark, the engine still running.

'Where's the other one? I thought there were going to be two of them?'

Mark waved his hand across the meadow to where Jack's body lay. 'He tried to run.'

'Didn't work, eh?'

Mark shrugged. 'What happens next?'

'This,' said the driver. He moved in his seat, revealing a gun of his own.

Mark's eyes opened wide. 'Wait, there's a —'

His voice was cut short as two bullets entered his chest in quick succession.

As his body fell to the ground, the passenger door of the ranger's vehicle swung open and the second occupant jumped out, hurrying over towards the silver box.

'Come on – help me,' he called to the driver. 'We need to move.'

'Wait,' the driver said, pointing to the ground. 'I'll get the bullet casings.'

He retrieved the two casings from his own gun and then paced the ground until he worked out where Mark had been standing when he fired his weapon, bent down, and picked up the last casing.

He pocketed all the casings before joining his colleague and, between them, they hefted the box from the ground and hurried back to their vehicle.

Swinging the rear door shut, the men clambered back into the four-wheel drive. The driver flicked the handbrake and then floored the accelerator and steered the vehicle in the opposite direction of the site gate and security office.

A smaller, less well-advertised gate appeared in a dry stone wall, an access way for the farmer whose land they were on. A single project security vehicle had been parked next to it, its windows fogged. As they approached, an orange-coloured sleeve wiped the condensation away and a face peered out, frowning.

'Shit, he's seen us.'

'Don't worry about it. The project logo's on all the doors. Just wave.'

The driver slowed to a halt and waited until the security guard had climbed out of his vehicle, huddled against the faint drizzle that was beginning to sweep across the hills, and jogged over to the gate. He threw a mock salute at them as they passed.

'Okay, wait until we're round this corner, and then floor it.'

The driver accelerated smoothly away, putting as much distance between them and the well site as he dared.

Spotting a lay-by a couple of miles later, he swung the vehicle into it, and both men jumped out.

They worked silently, the driver fetching a large water container from the back of the four-wheel drive and used it to clear the worst of the mud from the tyres and bodywork, while his passenger pulled the magnetic logos from the vehicle.

As they clambered back into the vehicle and slammed the doors shut, the passenger glanced at his watch.

'We're right on time.'

Chapter 3

Dan opened his eyes, aware of a faint breeze across his face, and noticed the door to his room was ajar.

He pulled the headphones from his ears, the faint echo of rock music stalling as he hit the 'stop' button.

A nurse stepped out from the small bathroom off to one side of the room, the colour of her uniform bright, as if she'd only recently started her shift. She checked over her shoulder and then closed the door, smiling as she approached the bed.

'Right, Mr Taylor,' she said. 'The doctors say you're well enough to be walking around, so let's get all these monitors unplugged.'

She moved efficiently, manoeuvring the wires away from his body, pushing the monitors to one side so she could access the plug sockets next to the bed.

'Doesn't that usually mean an alarm goes off somewhere?' He sat up as she straightened and swung his legs over the side, flexing his toes and ankles, eager to escape.

'No, it's okay,' she said. 'Your notes show you as being discharged this morning.'

The dressings on his shoulder blades tugged at his skin, and he grimaced as the stitches underneath the dressings pulled at his healing wounds.

'Wait,' she said, placing a firm hand on his arm. 'Let me finish.' She gestured to the loose gown he still wore. 'You're not going anywhere until I get those last patches off you.'

Dan grimaced, turned, and grabbed the sheet, stuffing it across his lap and then pulled the gown off.

His eyes met the nurse's gaze as he handed the gown to her, all too aware of his nakedness.

She was staring at the scars that dotted his chest. A split second later, with a slight shake of her head, she raised her hands and began to gently lift the sticking plasters away from his skin.

'Sorry,' she said as he flinched at one particular tug.

'It's fine,' he replied and concentrated on the name tag pinned across her left breast.

Stacey.

He swallowed, trying to ignore the sensation that was stirring between his thighs. Instead, he tried to concentrate on his own breathing, the nine times table – anything except what was going on under the sheet.

The nurse finished her task, but her hands lingered on his skin. She pulled away, and her eyes met his, a steely gaze that bored into him, taunting him.

In a split second, his instincts were screaming at him that something was wrong.

Very wrong.

He pushed her away as her hand fell to the pocket of her white shirt, and she extracted a small syringe and wrenched the safety cap from it.

Dan's eyes opened wide at the sight of the small needle that poked out from the end as she turned it towards him.

Then she lunged.

Dan brought his hands up as she reached for him, caught hold of her wrists, and twisted her hand away from his neck.

For one with such a small frame, the woman possessed incredible strength. Not to mention the fact that she appeared to be incredibly pissed off and determined to kill him.

The needle arched upwards, and he pulled his face away from its point, sliding his body away from the bed until he was crouched over the woman, her elbows on the mattress.

'Nice try,' he said, and then swore as her heel found his instep.

As his grip slackened, she wrenched her arms out of his hold, tearing herself away from his clutches until she was facing him, waving the needle in his direction.

Dan realised if she escaped, no-one would believe him. He lurched forward, reaching out for her, trying to keep his hands away from the sharp end of the weapon she held, then cursed as the sheet fell from his hips and landed between his feet as he stepped forward.

He tripped, landing in a heap, cursing profusely.

A manic giggle escaped from the woman, and she turned back, a gleam in her eye.

He reached down, desperately pushing the material away from his ankles as she drew closer.

'Now I've got you,' she hissed and stepped forward.

Dan pulled the sheet, the end of it under her feet, sending her toppling off balance.

She cried out, her eyes wide with shock, her free hand frantically thrashing in the air as she tried to find something to hold onto to stop herself from falling before her knees buckled under her.

Dan realised too late what was going to happen.

The woman landed awkwardly on her hip, the hand that grasped the syringe trapped under her own body weight.

Dan crawled across the floor to her, hoping he was wrong, that she'd dropped the weapon.

'Shit.'

Her body began to convulse, her eyes wide with fear and pain as froth bubbled between her lips, her feet thrashing at the tiled floor.

Dan launched himself towards the emergency button next to the bed, punched the heel of his hand against the red surface and then turned and dropped to the floor next to the woman.

'Come on,' he urged. 'Don't give up. I need some answers, dammit.'

Tears rolled down the woman's face as her skin began to turn a sickly blue-grey hue, and he realised he was quickly running out of time. He knocked the syringe from her useless hand, then gripped her jaw between his fingers as he tried to prise her teeth open to clear her airway.

A choking sound passed the woman's lips, before her head slumped to one side, her eyes wide and staring blindly to where Dan crouched.

'Dammit.'

He eased himself upright and then stood on shaking legs, reached across to the small cupboard next to the bed and pulled on a pair of clean boxer shorts that had been folded and left on a shelf. He ignored the jeans and a black t-shirt and instead began to search for his mobile phone.

He turned at the sound of running feet from the corridor outside, spinning on his feet with his fists raised as the door crashed open and two security guards rushed in, weapons ready, eyes wide.

The taller of the two lowered his gaze to the dead nurse on the floor, then back to Dan. 'Are you all right, sir?'

Dan lowered his fists and glared at him.

'What the *fuck* is going on around here?'

Chapter 4

Ben Hicks slowed the four-wheel drive vehicle, killed the headlights, and cruised to a standstill.

'I can't see it.'

The industrial site appeared deserted, the flat-roofed buildings leading into the barren complex. Here and there, an estate agent's sign flapped forlornly against wire mesh fencing, the once-pristine landscaping around the buildings now overgrown with weeds and ragged shrubs.

He'd driven through the convoluted roads leading around the estate until satisfied they weren't being tailed, and then turned into a short driveway that approached one of the smaller buildings as the sun had begun to dip towards the horizon.

Joe had jumped out, pushing the steel mesh gate open to let the vehicle through.

Ben had exhaled, surprised he'd been holding his breath, worried that their contact might have double-crossed them and left the gates locked.

Now he peered through the side windows, seeking out an errant security guard – or worse, a guard dog.

Nothing moved.

'It's here. Don't worry.' He checked in the rear view mirror, then over his shoulder, paranoia gripping him despite his confident assertions to the contrary. 'Come on.'

He opened his door and climbed from the vehicle, his boots crunching the loose gravel beneath his feet. He groaned, placed his hands in the small of his back, and stretched. The bulk of the gun at his waistband was reassuring.

After he'd received his instructions last night, he'd thought briefly about arguing the case against shooting Mark, but bit his tongue instead. He'd seen what had happened to men who had disobeyed orders. He had no intention of joining them.

He inhaled the night air, stretching the kinks out of his tired muscles. Pale haloes of light pooled from streetlights on the road into the estate, casting an orange glow that reflected on the cracked asphalt of the car park.

The drive south had been uneventful, but the risk had always been there. He'd eyed the speedometer fanatically, insisting they both wear baseball caps and keep the windscreen sun visors down in an attempt to disguise their faces from the numerous cameras that lined the motorway.

He glanced sideways as Joe rounded the back of the vehicle and joined him, his hand on the gun at his hip.

'Calm down,' he said. 'There's no-one here except us.'

'Are you sure?'

'Yeah.' He reached into his pocket, pulled out a packet of cigarettes, and tapped one into his palm, the small lighter dropping into his hand a fraction quicker. He flipped the cigarette between his lips, lit it, and then tucked the lighter back into the packet and tossed it towards the other man. 'Here. Let's have a walk around.'

'I thought they would have left it somewhere easy to see,' grumbled Joe, helping himself to a cigarette before handing back the packet. 'They know we're on a tight deadline.'

Ben chuckled. 'What? And have half the neighbourhood kids steal it before we turn up?' He snorted. 'Not likely.'

He led the way past boarded-up windows, an estate agent's sign nailed to the wall faded by sunlight and strewn with graffiti.

As they rounded the corner of the building, they entered a wide alleyway created by the empty premises and the neighbouring property. Old discarded metalwork and industrial bins lined the outer wall.

Ben checked over his shoulder before pointing to a second four-wheel drive vehicle parked halfway along the alleyway in front of them.

'Bingo,' he said. He handed Joe the keys to the first four-wheel drive. 'Bring it round here. We're swapping transport.'

As Joe's footsteps receded, Ben stalked towards the new vehicle. He ran the torchlight over its bodywork, grunting appreciatively at the nondescript paintwork and age.

Anything too new would draw unwanted attention. Anything too old would run the risk of being pulled over by the police.

He crouched down and reached under the wheel arch, his fingers probing until he felt the soft surface of electrical tape, and pulled.

The key fell away easily, and he stood as the dimmed lights of their previous transportation rounded the corner behind him. He raised his hand to shield his eyes from the glare, unlocked the replacement vehicle, and slid behind the wheel.

Once it had been manoeuvred into place, the two men carried the silver case to the back of the new four-wheel drive and removed a tarpaulin, draping it over the old vehicle.

Joe leant down and unscrewed the licence plate from the front and then moved to the back and repeated the action. Once he had completed this, he straightened and held up the plates to Ben, grinning.

'That's phase one done,' he said. 'Let's go.'

Chapter 5

Dan pointed at the syringe ensconced in a transparent plastic box on the desk. 'What was in there?'

Neil Evans flung his fountain pen to one side and sighed. 'Actually, it's quite ingenious,' he said, unable to contain the note of admiration in his voice as he launched into an elaborate account of the drug and its capabilities.

'In English?'

'A very effective barbiturate. Deadly in large quantities, as you saw.'

Dan ran his hand over his face and fought down the weariness that threatened to consume him.

Rest and recovery, the doctors had told him.

So much for that idea, he thought.

'I'm going to need to visit the armoury after this,' he said. 'I want my service weapon back.'

'I can't let you do that, sorry,' said Evans. The current acting head of the Energy Protection Group shrugged apologetically and pulled a document across the desk towards him and then pulled reading glasses from his shirt pocket and slipped them on. 'It says here your psycho-

logical examination isn't due until the end of next week.'
He peered over his glasses. 'Until then, you're not entitled
to carry a weapon.'

'That's ridiculous!' Dan exclaimed. 'You and I both
know that's bullshit.'

'It is what it is,' said Evans.

He was saved from a further outburst from Dan by the
telephone ringing. He snatched it from its cradle, ignoring
the glare Dan aimed at him, before his brow creased as he
listened to the person at the other end of the line.

'Okay. We'll be ready for him,' he eventually muttered
and hung up. 'The Prime Minister's senior policy advisor
is on his way. He wants to meet with both of us,' he
explained.

'I heard a rumour there was a bit of a government
shake-up while I was out of action. Is that true?'

'You could say that.' Evans checked his watch and then
leaned back in his chair. 'Six weeks ago, the Prime
Minister was nearly ousted from office. Instead, he
managed to scrape through a 'no confidence' vote.'

'That must've been an interesting few days.'

'It was nerve-wracking for the security agencies,'
agreed Evans. 'The Minister that tried to topple the PM
was making it quite clear he was going to cut our funding
as one of his first priorities.'

'Dangerous *and* stupid.'

'Yes. And now dead.'

'What?'

'Committed suicide three days after the vote to overthrow the PM failed. His wife found him. Bloody awful, actually – he'd hanged himself in the garage of their home.'

'What did the PM do?'

'He regrouped and effected an immediate Cabinet reshuffle. I should warn you – Hugh Porchester is now one of the Prime Minister's senior policy advisors, and he's working directly with us.'

Dan grunted noncommittally. He turned his head at a knock on the office door.

'I heard a rumour you've had problems seeing eye to eye with him in the past,' said Evans, lowering his voice. 'Is that going to be an issue today?'

'None whatsoever,' Dan assured him. 'I've reported directly to him during a couple of missions since that time. I'll keep it professional.'

'Good,' said Evans, pushing his chair back and standing. 'Because there are no limits to the man's ambitions. I wouldn't want to be on the wrong side of him.'

As he passed Dan to open his door, Dan failed to hide a smirk. Evans's evaluation of Hugh Porchester had been quite accurate.

He'd had a close call with the Prime Minister's advisor a few years ago when the man had been in a junior Cabinet role, but Porchester had since embraced the Energy Protection Group, often championing the unit's cause on their behalf and attending briefing sessions when the Prime

Minister was otherwise engaged. The two men had fallen into an uneasy truce, the need to guard against potential threats to the United Kingdom's infrastructure greater than their own differences.

'Where's the PM?' he asked.

Evans's hand hovered over the door handle. 'Touring Europe,' he said. 'Trying to negotiate new legislation with some of the bigger member states in the European parliament to give us Brits a bit more control as to how laws are applied in our country.'

Dan stood and faced the door as Evans opened it and welcomed Hugh Porchester. Dan shook his hand and then waited while the man placed his briefcase on the floor and settled into a chair.

Dan took the opportunity to remain standing at ease, stretching his neck and back muscles as the other two men exchanged brief pleasantries before launching into their meeting.

'All right, Evans, what happened?' asked Porchester.

'Mr Taylor was attacked at the hospital this morning. With this.'

Evans pushed a copy of the report towards Porchester, who pulled a fountain pen from his jacket pocket and began flicking through the summary pages, writing notes in the margins as he worked through the document.

'Why wasn't Taylor in a military hospital?' he asked eventually.

'We decided it would be better if he were placed in a private hospital, sir. No-one knew who he was there, or what he's done for this country.' Evans pushed his own copy of the report out of his way and clasped his hands on the desk. 'It was deemed to be safe after a thorough investigation, I can assure you.'

Hugh Porchester flung his copy of the report to one side and tapped his pen against the surface of the table. 'You're a lucky man, Taylor. First capture in Eastern Europe and then this.'

Dan pulled out a chair and sank into it, exhaustion threatening to consume his already frayed nerves. 'Any idea what's going on, sir?'

Porchester leaned forward. 'None whatsoever, I'm afraid. Although,' he added, placing his pen back in his jacket pocket, 'I'll be doing everything I can at our end.' He turned to Evans. 'I'll pass on a copy of this report to the PM, see what his suggestions are. If he authorises it, I'll contact MI5 and find out if they've got any intelligence on this.'

'It would've been good if they could've warned us,' Evans grumbled.

'I get the impression from this report that it was a rush job,' said Porchester. 'Only a select few people knew Taylor was in that hospital.'

'Have the guards been debriefed?' said Dan. 'Why weren't they closer? No-one came running until I hit the emergency alarm.'

'It seems they were distracted,' said Porchester. 'I spoke with their team leader before I came here. There were reports of an intruder in another unit of the hospital, closer to yours.'

'Let me guess – nothing there when they arrived?'

'Correct.'

'Well,' said Evans, 'the sooner we get you back to hospital, the better.'

'Forget it.'

'What?'

'I said, forget it,' said Dan. 'It's quite obvious you can't protect me when I'm in there, so I'm better off out of it. God knows what they'll try next.'

'You must rest!' Evans turned to Porchester. 'Please – tell him. His health depends on a full recovery!'

Porchester stood, gathered the report pages together, and slipped them into his briefcase. He paused. 'Exactly what do you have in mind, Taylor?'

'First I want to find out who the hell betrayed me.'

'Evans is right. You need to rest.'

'We have a traitor, sir. Possibly endangering other lives.'

'Your concern is noted, Taylor,' said Porchester and turned towards the door. 'We'll look into the mission. I've got a copy of your report.'

'So, I'm free to go?' asked Dan as he followed.

The politician nodded. 'I can only imagine that you'll be like a caged animal if we try to insist on sending you back to finish your recovery.' He shifted the briefcase in his grip. 'Just try to stay out of trouble until your psych evaluation next week, all right?'

Dan paused, his fingers wrapped around the door handle. 'Do you know who she was?'

'Lana Portnova. Russian.'

'Russian? Why the hell do the Russians want me dead?'

Porchester shrugged and waited until Dan opened the door for him. 'We've got no idea, Taylor. You're collecting quite the list of enemies, but this is the first time we've been aware that you've managed to piss off the Russians as well.'

Chapter 6

'So, if I need to make contact in the meantime, who's my liaison officer?'

Dan turned to Evans as he was ushered out of the man's office and folded his arms across his chest. He raised an eyebrow.

Evans raised his hands in defeat. 'All right, I can see you're not going to leave this alone. But stay under the radar, okay?'

'I'll do my best.'

'Come on. I'll introduce you to Melissa.' Evans brushed past Dan. 'Hopefully you can work out what her problem is while you're at it,' he murmured.

'Problem?' Dan picked up his pace to keep up with the man. 'What problem?'

Evans ignored him and instead stalked along the corridor, pausing only to tell his secretary to hold his calls for another twenty minutes.

He slowed as they approached an open-plan office, its entry cordoned off by plate glass. As Evans lifted his access card to the swipe panel, he glanced at Dan.

'That, over there, is your new analyst.'

Dan looked over to where he pointed and saw a girl barely out of her teens sitting at a desk between two computer monitors, her gaze flashing from one to the other, fingers flying over the keyboard in front of her.

A soft woollen hat had been pulled over her hair, her eyes barely visible underneath its knitted rim. Blonde hair stuck out in clumps around the back and sides before tumbling over her shoulders, and a ring piercing shone at her bottom lip. She wore a black long-sleeved top; an old green army jacket slung over the back of her seat.

Her head dipped up and down as she worked; a pair of headphones over her ears blocked out the white noise of the other workers around her.

'I'm surprised you let her get away with the clothing and the music,' Dan grinned, his gaze taking in the smart business clothes of the other occupants in the glass pod.

'She's a genius,' explained Evans. 'We actually recruited her after MI5 arrested her for hacking into their database three months ago.' He sighed. 'We tried with the clothing thing, really we did, but we worked out pretty quickly it was much easier to simply let her get on with her job.'

'Wow. Like that, huh?'

'Yes,' said Evans with a glint in his eye. He opened the door to let Dan through, barely able to contain his mirth. 'And now, she's all yours.' He moved across to the desk and motioned to the woman to lower her headphones. 'Dan

Taylor, this is Melissa Harper, the new addition to our team of analysts.'

She stood, and Dan managed to stop his jaw hitting the floor before shaking hands. He glanced down to make sure she wasn't wearing heels and was rewarded with a pair of purple laced-up boots sticking out from the end of her ragged jeans. He raised his eyes, and met Melissa's steely gaze.

'Nice to meet you,' he said.

Melissa rolled her eyes and turned to Evans. 'What's he doing here?'

'I need your help,' said Dan, gripping her hand until he held her attention once more. 'And Evans tells me you're good at what you do.'

'Is that so?'

'Melissa,' interrupted Evans. 'Perhaps you could show Dan where the kitchen is and arrange a computer for him while he's back in the office. Maybe sort him out with a new mobile phone to start off with?'

'Whatever.'

Dan let go of her hand and watched in amusement as she moved towards a storage cupboard behind her desk, unlocked it, and selected a new smartphone.

Evans slapped him on the shoulder. 'Have fun,' he said. 'I'll talk to you later in the week if there's anything to report.'

'Yeah, cheers.'

As Evans hurried away, Melissa sauntered back across the office and held out the phone.

'Try not to lose this one.'

'Thanks. I'll do my best,' said Dan, not bothering to keep the sarcasm from his voice.

'Come on, I'll show you where the kitchen is,' she said and brushed past him. 'I'll have to sort out a computer for you another time. I'm busy.'

'Great – I'll have a coffee. White with one.'

He grinned as she almost tripped and then glared at him over her shoulder and followed her out the door and along the corridor, back towards the elevators he'd passed with Evans.

Before she reached the doors, Melissa turned right and led the way into a state-of-the-art kitchen, complete with eight-burner stove top and three microwaves. She made her way across to one of the stainless steel kettles, tested its weight, then flicked the switch and began searching through the cupboards.

'Hey, look,' said Dan, sliding onto one of the stools next to the large bench that ran the length of the kitchen. 'I think we got off to a bad start.'

Melissa finished prepping the coffee and then flipped the switch as the kettle began to boil and poured the water into the mug before turning to him. She folded her arms across her chest, her face a picture of misery. 'I didn't *ask* to be your babysitter,' she said exasperatedly and then opened the refrigerator door and pulled out a carton of milk, tipping a large splash into the contents of the cup. 'Evans seems to think you need help. Trust me, I've got

better things to do,' she added and slammed the
refrigerator door on its hinges.

'Well, looks like you're going to have to put up with me
for the time being,' said Dan, trying to keep his temper.
'Given that no-one else here wants to work with you.'

'Coming from you, that's just great.' She handed him
the steaming mug of coffee.

'What do you mean?'

'Well, no-one's tried to kill me,' she said and flounced
out of the kitchen.

Dan's mouth curled up as she disappeared. 'Yet,' he
growled, taking a sip. He spat out the coffee and glared
towards the door.

'You forgot the sugar!'

***

Dan rode the elevator to the ground floor, checking
through the messages Evans's secretary had handed him
before he'd signed out.

'Welcome back, Dan.' She'd smiled as he'd scribbled
his signature across the paperwork and took the newly-
issued security pass. 'I hear you're going to be working
with Melissa Harper.'

He'd grimaced. 'Word gets around fast, Steph.'

'You're a perfect match.'

'Very funny.' He peered at one of the messages. 'Well,
well, well.'

'Thought you might say that. Have you spoken to her recently?'

'No.'

'Maybe you should.'

Dan raised an eyebrow.

'She phoned every week,' explained the secretary. 'I gave up writing down the messages after a month.'

'Ah.'

'Does the boss know your friend used to be a journalist?'

Dan had glanced over his shoulder as Melissa passed them, her gaze deliberately ignoring him and pretending to be busy with the folders she hugged to her chest. He turned back to Evans's secretary and grinned. 'He will soon.'

He frowned at two of the messages, copied the phone numbers from one into his new mobile as the elevator descended through the building and then crunched up the papers and threw them into a secure shredding bin on his way past the security gates in the foyer.

He pushed open the glass doors and stepped out into the darkened street outside, glanced up at the full moon that bathed the city and took a deep breath.

Rest and recovery, Evans had said.

That was the last thing he wanted, especially as someone clearly wanted him dead.

As he stood on the kerb, a taxi pulled up and the driver leaned over and lowered the window.

'Were you wanting a taxi, mate?'

Dan checked his watch and then rubbed the stubble on his chin. It was too late to travel home to Oxfordshire now; he was hungry and only carried the battered kit bag at his feet.

'No, that's okay. Thanks anyway.'

'No problem.' The taxi driver pulled away, turning left at the end of the street and towards the busy west London railway station two streets away.

The sun had disappeared over the horizon an hour ago, and his stomach rumbled as he realised he hadn't eaten all day, only surviving on coffee.

He wracked his memory and recalled an Italian restaurant about a mile's walk away. An idea began to form in his head.

Dan hefted his kit bag onto his shoulder and then pulled out his mobile and flicked to the only number in its memory.

He took a deep breath and hit the 'dial' button. 'Here goes,' he muttered.

The phone rang twice before she picked up.

'Sarah Edgewater.'

'Fancy dinner?'

He heard her sharp intake of breath before she replied.

'I don't hear from you for over three months, and then you phone and ask me out to dinner?'

His mouth quirked, despite her fractious tone. 'I figured if I met you in a public place, you wouldn't be able to kill me.'

A burst of laughter filled his ear. 'You bastard. Where?'

'Remember that little place off Praed Street?'

'I do.'

'Meet you there in about an hour.'

He hung up before she could argue or ask him further questions. He'd rather savour the time with her over a decent meal and a bottle of wine than try to talk while he stood on the pavement. He tucked the phone back into his pocket and set off in the direction of Paddington, a slight spring in his step.

Chapter 7

Dan took a swig of the bottled Italian beer and then set the cold glass on the wooden surface of the bar and ran his thumb over the condensation that ran down its side.

He couldn't remember the last time a beer tasted so good. He closed his eyes and cricked his neck, and then shook his head and turned on his bar stool to face the room, his gaze catching the Premiership football game on the small television in the corner.

'Cold enough?'

He grinned at the man behind the bar who'd spoken. 'Perfect. I've missed these.'

'Yeah, well, we've managed to keep our stock up since you've been gone the past few months. They don't seem to disappear as fast.'

Dan picked the bottle up and tipped it towards the man. 'Up yours, Marco.'

His comment was met with raucous laughter and a one-fingered salute, before the door opened and a couple stepped over the threshold, making a beeline for the takeaway pizza menu pinned to the far wall.

Dan chuckled to himself, took another sip, and cast his eyes around the small restaurant as Marco welcomed the newcomers and took their order.

He always enjoyed Marco's company. The man was ex-British Army with Italian parents and had taken over the family business after his parents had passed away. They'd spent many late nights regaling each other with their escapades.

The ones Dan could talk about, at least.

The business had made some changes over the times since he'd first been here three years ago, and had introduced a takeaway pizza service to boost custom in the evenings after the commuters who provided the lunchtime trade had left the city centre for their homes.

Dan enjoyed the atmosphere and the location. It was conveniently far enough away from the office end of his work, secluded enough that he could avoid large crowds, and the people that ran the place respected his privacy.

Not to mention the fact they served the best Italian food in the city, as far as Dan was concerned.

He glanced up as the door opened once more, and his breath caught in his chest.

It had been over a year since he'd last seen Sarah, months since he'd last spoken to her, and each time she had the same effect on him.

Tall, slender, she'd had her pale brown hair cut so it fell just below her shoulders, framing her face.

As the door closed behind her, she hefted her bag up her shoulder and dropped her mobile phone into it.

After several years working as a successful journalist, she now freelanced as a media adviser, preferring to stay clear of big corporations and instead helping small charities and environmental groups. She'd admitted to Dan that the career change meant renting out her cottage in the Oxfordshire countryside while she stayed in the city, but the work was more rewarding, something for which she was grateful.

He stood as she approached, put the empty beer bottle on the bar, and enveloped her in his arms.

'Hello,' she murmured.

'You smell nice,' he mumbled into her hair.

She chuckled. 'You've been drinking.'

'Only had one.'

'Hungry?'

'Yes.'

'You always are.'

He drew away and grinned at her. 'It's good to see you.'

'You're still a complete bastard for not returning my calls.'

He dropped his hands from her arms and nodded, his face rueful. 'I am. I know.'

She frowned, leaning closer to look at the scratches and bruises on his face. 'Secret stuff?'

'Yeah.' He glanced across at Marco and then pointed to a table at the back and raised his eyebrow. Once he'd got the all-clear, he took Sarah by the hand and led her through the restaurant, pulling out a chair for her that faced a wall-to-ceiling mural of the Amalfi Coast, and then lowered himself into a seat that faced the restaurant.

Sarah smiled as she placed her bag under the table. 'Some things don't change.'

'It's for your own good,' he said. 'I'd just fidget all night if I sat with my back to the room.'

'I know.' She looked up as Marco approached with the menus, deftly selected a bottle of red for them to share, and then turned her attention back to Dan once the owner was out of earshot. 'When I couldn't get through to you, I tried to call David or Mitch. They weren't answering their phones or returning my calls either, so I figured the three of you were up to something.'

Dan shook his head. 'I wasn't with them,' he said. He held up a warning finger to her as Marco approached with the wine and then took their orders.

As Marco moved away, heading for the kitchen, Dan turned back to Sarah.

'Anyway, enough about me for now. What have you been up to?'

'Busy with a new environmental group,' she replied. 'They're enthusiastic but have no real sense of direction,' she added. 'Most of my time so far has been spent trying to get them to focus on one campaign, instead of trying to fix everything they think is wrong with the world.'

'Is it working?'

'Slowly.' Sarah took a sip of wine. 'Some of them were hard to convince, until they started to see the effects of the media campaigns we've been running.'

Sarah waited until their entrées had been set in front of them and then leaned forward, her elbows each side of her plate. 'How much do you know about the oil and gas industry?'

'A bit. Why?'

Sarah shrugged. 'It's a bit strange. A package arrived at my client's office this afternoon, addressed to me.' She paused and tucked her hair behind her ear. 'Inside were all these documents about a shale gas exploration project up in Northumberland,' she said. 'It seems to be very hush-hush in case the locals get up in arms about it. The public worries about earthquakes, as well as the health risks that might be around because of the chemicals being used in the hydraulic fracking process.'

Dan paused, a mixture of prosciutto and olives on his fork. 'But?'

'You know I don't usually get involved in this sort of thing these days,' she explained. 'But the reports are about an incident at one of the test wells.'

'What, a leak or something?'

Sarah shook her head. 'No.' She lowered her voice. 'The project manager and two engineers were shot. Dead.'

Dan frowned. 'Details?'

'Not much.' She took another mouthful before speaking again. 'All it says is that three men were killed in an industrial accident. I'm presuming all the secrecy has something to do with it being a flagship project for the government – a way to show the general public that fracking is a safe exploration method. When I found out about the murders, I phoned the project head office, and they were extremely cagey. The usual excuses about helping police with their enquiries and not being able to talk to the media.'

'Not when there's a huge insurance claim on the horizon, I'd imagine,' Dan said. He cleared his plate and picked up his glass of wine. 'What else have you got?'

Sarah gestured to her bag with her fork. 'I'll show you the file after dinner. I wouldn't mind your take on it. I know there's something there; I can feel it. I just can't see it yet.'

'Okay.' He watched as she finished her bruschetta, his eyes meeting hers as she scooped up the last of the tomato and basil.

'Stop eyeing up my food. I'm not sharing.'

'Damn. Looks good.'

She put the last of her entrée in her mouth, her eyes sparkling as she dropped her knife and fork on the plate. 'That *was* good.'

'More wine?'

'Please.'

'So, any suspects?' Dan caught Marco approaching the table and held up a warning finger again. He trusted the man implicitly, but there was the issue of an active police investigation to consider, and he didn't want to compromise Sarah's trust in him.

When the man had moved away, Sarah played with her wine glass, spinning its base on the tablecloth.

'From what I can gather, the police are interested in two people,' she said. 'The project four-wheel drive was left abandoned next to the bodies.'

'They used a second vehicle.'

She nodded. 'Exactly. There were another set of tyre marks, leading away from the murder scene and across to a secondary security gate half a mile away.'

'Manned?'

'By two men and a vehicle.'

Dan leaned back in his seat and frowned. 'And they let them through, so they must've stolen another one of the project's vehicles.'

Sarah shook her head. 'None are recorded as missing, so...'

'They had a vehicle that looked like it belonged to the project. Magnetic decals or something.'

'That's what I'm thinking.'

'No identity records at the security gate?'

'No. Apparently everyone has a pass card, so they don't keep paper records.'

'Sloppy.'

'I know. Especially given the nature of the project.'

They fell silent while Marco returned with their main courses.

While he topped up their wine, Dan leaned across the table and stabbed one of the asparagus stalks on Sarah's plate with his fork.

She sighed. 'You could've ordered your own.'

'Where's the fun in that?'

Marco laughed and turned back to the kitchen, shaking his head.

'So,' said Dan once Marco was out of earshot, 'who do you think sent you the file?'

'I don't know.' Sarah cut enthusiastically into the food on her plate, before moving her water glass so Dan couldn't reach across and steal any more of her dinner. 'Maybe one of the environmental activist groups – I get approached by them every now and again.'

'What else was in the package?'

In reply, she shook her head. 'Wait until you see the documents I've brought. Then you tell me what you think.' She leaned forward. 'So, you've heard my news. What's going on with you?'

'Nothing at the moment. I've got a new boss. Met him this morning, and now I'm kicking my heels until he calls me.'

'Isn't that a bit strange?'

He shrugged. 'Hard to tell. He seems friendly enough. They've recruited a new analyst at last.'

They both fell silent, absorbed in their thoughts and savouring the food, until Sarah broke the silence.

'That must've been hard for David.'

Dan shook his head. 'I don't think he had a lot of choice.' He cleared his plate and grasped his wine glass. 'There are too many threats out there. The last thing we can afford to be is under-staffed.'

'It must be hard to find someone with those specialist skills, though.'

Dan laughed and told her about Melissa hacking into MI5's database.

'Wow. She must be good.'

'She's a pain in the arse.'

'And you're not?'

Dan raised an eyebrow and then shrugged and conceded the point.

After Marco had cleared their plates and returned with their desserts, Sarah reached out and placed her fingers on the back of Dan's hand, carefully tracing the healing scratches.

'Where were you?'

He raised his eyes to meet her gaze. 'Eastern Europe.'

'Was it bad?'

A flash of memory, of the cold floor of the abandoned prison filled his mind, and he blinked, pushing it away. There would be time to deal with that side of things when he was alone. Not here. Not now.

'Yeah, it was.'

'What went wrong?' she whispered.

'Everything.' He turned his hand and squeezed her fingers, forcing a smile that didn't quite reach his eyes. 'Eat your dessert. Or I will.'

She acknowledged the hint and changed the subject. 'Have you spoken to David or Mitch since you've been back?'

'No-one seems to know where they are.'

'What do you mean? Are they on a secret mission, too?'

He shrugged. 'I don't know. They must be. No-one at the office will tell me anything.'

'That *does* seem strange.'

'Yeah, well on top of me being sent in alone three months ago, and now this, I've got no idea what the men at the top are thinking.'

'I'm sure they've got their reasons.'

'You'd hope so.'

Sarah leaned back and leaned her spoon on the side of her plate. 'My god, that was fabulous.'

Dan reached over and, with one swipe, stole the strawberry from her plate and put it in his mouth, feeling smug as he tried not to laugh at the expression on her face.

'You bastard, I was saving that!'

Chapter 8

Now that they were truly alone, they stood awkwardly on the pavement outside the restaurant, the occasional car passing them on the street, headlights strobing the walls of the buildings next to them.

'I'll walk you down to the taxi rank.'

'Wait.' Sarah glanced down at the kit bag at Dan's feet and then reached out and took his hand in hers. 'Where are you staying?'

He shrugged. 'I'll find a motel round here. Thought I might head back to Oxfordshire tomorrow if the office doesn't want me.'

'Seems a bit lonely.'

'Now I feel pathetic.'

She laughed, a husky tone that sent shivers up Dan's spine.

She leaned closer until she could tilt her mouth near his ear. 'I've got a better idea,' she murmured.

***

Sarah moved through the apartment ahead of him, throwing her bag onto a low table as she tugged her scarf away from her shoulders.

'You've decorated,' said Dan, running his fingers along a picture frame.

'At last,' she said. 'I know your lot decorated it a few years ago, but it was just too–'

'Military?'

'That's the word.' She smiled. 'I'm sure beige works fine on the walls in the barracks, but not in my home.'

She brushed past him, and he closed his eyes and inhaled her familiar perfume and then trailed behind her along the hallway and into the kitchen.

As she reached into the cupboard for wine glasses, he ran his hand over the bottles in the rack, turning them so he could read the labels until he found the one he was hoping to find.

'You've still got some of the Shiraz.' He grabbed the corkscrew from the kitchen bench and expertly twisted it into the bottle, the cork escaping with a soft *pop*.

Sarah turned, two glasses in her hand.

Dan noticed as sadness washed over her face, and her bottom lip trembled.

'I was saving it for when you got back,' she explained and then quickly set the glasses down on the table and wiped at her eyes. 'I didn't want to drink it without you.'

'Hey.' Dan put the bottle next to the glasses and then wrapped his arms around her, burying his face into her hair. 'I'm here now.'

She sniffed and pushed her hands against his chest before raising her head. Her eyes searched his face before she spoke.

'Was it bad?' she whispered.

He inhaled, a short sharp intake of breath as his mind flashed back to the prison, the guards and their instruments of torture, and then blinked and nodded.

'Yeah. It was.' He wound his fingers into a wisp of her hair. 'I just kept thinking of you.'

Her lips found his then, exploring, searching, and he closed his eyes as he pulled her tightly against him, his body responding quickly.

He lifted her off the floor, and her legs wrapped around his waist.

He turned for the bedroom, his mouth finding the crease at the base of her neck, and then he traced his tongue across her collarbone.

She groaned, tipping her head back, before kneading her fingers into his shoulders.

'So much for the Shiraz,' she murmured.

Dan chuckled. 'It's okay,' he said as he lowered her onto the bed and began to unbutton her blouse. 'It needs a while to breathe before we drink it.'

***

Dan let the curtain drop back into place at the sound of movement from the bed behind him, the sheets rustling before a sigh reached his ears.

'Dan? What are you doing?'

He tugged the material closely together where it met in the middle of the window and turned as the bedside light flickered on.

Sarah lay propped up on her elbows, her hair tousled and a confused look across her face.

He smiled. 'Do you know how bloody sexy you look right now?'

'Stop changing the subject,' she said, her tone serious despite the quirk at the corner of her mouth. She jerked her chin at the window. 'What were you looking at?'

He moved to the bed, climbed across the sheets to her, and then sat propped against the pillows and pulled her into his arms.

'I didn't want to scare you,' he said, kissing her hair. 'But I think I'm under surveillance.'

'David?'

He shook his head. 'I don't think so. Not his style.'

She sat up and frowned. 'Then who?'

He ran a hand down her arm. 'I don't know.'

Her expression changed, and in a fleeting moment, Dan saw her change from the woman that was his lover to the hard-nosed journalist he so respected.

'What's going on, Dan? Is this something to do with why you were in prison?'

He ran a hand over his freshly cropped hair. 'Maybe. I don't know.' He held up his hand to silence her. 'It's possible.'

Sarah glanced at her watch. 'That's it,' she said and slapped her hands on the sheets. 'It's going to be light in an hour, and I'm too fired up to go back to sleep now.' She leaned over and kissed him. 'I'm going to make coffee,' she said. 'And then you can tell me what really happened in Eastern Europe.'

***

Dan wrapped his hands around the large steaming mug of coffee and inhaled the aroma.

'I'd forgotten you'd made such great coffee.'

'Very funny. I think at this time of morning you'd drink anything that had a whiff of caffeine in it.'

He smiled and blew across the surface of the hot liquid before taking a tentative sip as Sarah joined him at the kitchen table.

Beyond the blinds, dawn began its slow crawl over the eastern horizon, shafts of light beginning to spill onto the windowsill.

'Talk to me, Dan,' said Sarah, reaching out for his hand. 'You know I'm a good listener.'

He exhaled, leaning back in his seat, keeping his fingers wrapped around hers. He knew she was right, and she knew more about him than most people. He also knew she didn't need specifics, simply enough that she'd understand. He squeezed her fingers and then let go and rested his elbows on the table.

'I knew something was wrong the moment I got there,' he said. 'Gut instinct, you know? Something didn't feel right.'

'Where were you?' asked Sarah. 'A big town or a village?'

'Somewhere in between the two. A small town, if you like. Somewhere big enough that a stranger turning up wouldn't be noticed immediately.'

'All alone? No team?'

He shook his head. 'It was meant to be simple.' He ran his fingers over the raised surface of the dressings under his t-shirt before continuing. 'All I had to do was make my way to a repair shop, pick up supplies from the owner, and then take one of his cars to the location, do the job, and head for the border.'

'When did it go wrong?'

'Almost immediately. When I got to the garage, the price of the parts had gone up – doubled – since I was given the intel in London. It was crazy – the guy's business was obviously on its last legs, but there he was haggling like he had all the money and time in the world. Eventually, we came to an agreement, but then at the last minute, he switched cars on me.'

'You mean you got a different vehicle to the one you'd agreed?'

'Yeah. I was meant to get a four-door sedan – a rust-bucket – but intel told us it'd been fitted with a decent engine so I'd make it to the border without a problem.

Instead, the bastard hands me the keys and points to a two-door fucking Russian thing. The car was hot, I'm sure.'

'Stolen?'

Dan nodded. 'Or planted there. On purpose.'

Sarah frowned but motioned for him to continue.

'So, I checked that there was a full tank of fuel – at least he got that right, the bastard.' Dan clenched his fist. 'By now, it's starting to get dark. I'm meant to be in place by oh twenty-two hundred and out of there thirty minutes later. I'm running late, and as soon as I get clear of the town, I put my foot to the floor.' He caught Sarah looking at him, her eyebrow raised. 'Hey, it's Eastern Europe – no-one takes any notice of speed limits there. They're more of a guideline, okay?'

'Okay. Go on.'

'Two miles out from the target, I pass a farm track. There's a vehicle parked in it, lights off. As soon as I pass, I ease off the speed, just in case it's a bored policeman, y'know? Sure enough, seconds later, there are headlights flashing in my rear view mirror and a siren going off.'

'You pulled over?'

'I didn't have a lot of choice.'

'What happened?'

'I stopped the car, left the engine running. Wound down the window an inch and locked the doors.' His voice shook, and he coughed to try to mask it and then caught Sarah's worried gaze and knew he'd failed. 'Four of them got out. Armed to the teeth. Like they were expecting me.'

'Oh my god, Dan.'

'I didn't stand a chance,' he murmured. 'They dragged me from the vehicle and took great pleasure in kicking me about on the asphalt for a bit and then searched the vehicle.' He raised his chin. 'Once they searched the vehicle and found the parts, I knew I was done for.'

'You were making an explosive device.'

He nodded and forced a smile. 'For all the right reasons, trust me.'

Sarah covered her mouth with her hand, her eyes wide. 'Where did they take you? Where have you been?'

He shook his head. 'It was fucking awful,' he said, closing his eyes. 'We travelled for miles. They put a hood over my head. I lost track of time, to be honest.'

He rubbed his hands over his face, then stared up at the ceiling and crossed his arms across his chest. 'Apparently, there are loads of these ex-CIA prisons dotted all over the country. No-one really knows how many there are – or who's held in them. Private contractors run them now, and basically, anyone who needs to disappear, disappears.' He shivered. 'I wasn't meant to be coming out of there alive.'

Sarah tapped her pen on the table and stared at the sunshine now streaming through the blinds.

Dan noticed how pale she'd turned but let her process what he'd told her. He knew from previous experience it was often the only way.

'So what do *you* think went wrong?' she finally asked.

Dan stood, moved across the room, and leaned against the sink. 'I think I was set up.'

The pen rattled across the table before hitting the floor.

Sarah looked at him, her mouth open. 'What?'

'Someone knew exactly where I was and what I was doing.' He leaned forward, gripping the edge of the table. 'And whoever knew where I was being held was also, somehow, involved in my rescue.'

'What makes you say that?'

'No-one else knew where I was, did they? It was all supposed to be hush-hush.'

'Set up?' she finally spluttered. 'Who? *Why*?' She held up her hands, closed her eyes, and then tried again. 'Why would someone set you up?'

'I'm not sure.'

Sarah pushed her chair back, stalked across the kitchen, and bent down to pick up the pen. When she straightened, Dan took a deep breath.

'Look – it's a gut feeling. Nothing more, okay?' He leaned against the stainless steel sink, his fingers gripping the surface.

Sarah put her hand on her hip, and her eyes narrowed. 'I don't believe you,' she said. 'If you think you've been set up, you've got more than just a gut feeling, Dan Taylor.' She frowned. 'Where *is* David, anyway?'

'I don't know that either,' said Dan. 'I asked when they finished my debrief, but all they would tell me is that our group got disbanded when I was captured. Something about the PM wanting to avoid any embarrassment.'

'What about Mitch?'

Dan shook his head.

'What, nothing?' Sarah threw up her arms in exasperation. 'You two are friends – team mates. Surely they can tell you where *he* is?'

'The thing is,' said Dan, 'I don't think it's a case of them not wanting to tell me where David and Mitch are. I don't think they *know* where they are.'

'What do you mean?'

'I think they're missing, too.'

Chapter 9

Sarah strode across the kitchen, and Dan wrapped his arms around her.

'What's going on?' she whispered. 'You've been imprisoned, you're being followed, David and Mitch are missing… What the hell is happening?'

He closed his eyes and buried his face in her hair. 'I've got no idea,' he murmured. 'But I'll find out.' He snorted. 'Let's face it, I've got nothing else to do at the moment.'

She drew back and lifted her chin, her eyes glossy with unshed tears. 'Be careful, won't you?'

'Promise.'

Sarah sniffed, gave him a last squeeze, and then moved across the room to where her bag lay on the table, discarded from the previous night, and pulled out a tissue.

Dan caught sight of a padded envelope poking out from the depths of the bag. 'Didn't you have something to show me last night?'

She raised her eyebrow. 'I did. You got distracted.'

He grinned. 'So did you. Come on. Give us a top-up and pass that over here. What did you want to show me?'

Relief flooded through his system as he watched her gather herself, before she slid the folder from her bag and across the table to him.

'I'll make more coffee. You read that first, then I'll ask you some questions.'

As Sarah busied herself with the coffee machine, Dan flipped open the envelope and pulled out its contents.

First were copies of police reports about a freak accident that had killed three men. The reports soon became thin on any new information within twenty-four hours of the first reports.

Dan skim-read through the documents and then pushed them to one side and began to thumb through a large sheaf of paper held together by a metal clip. On the front of it, a company logo had been stamped above the phrase 'Environmental Impact Statement'. The document had been downloaded from the project website, a publicly available report that had received government review and approval prior to the site work commencing.

'Have you got a highlighter pen?'

'In my bag – help yourself.'

Dan pulled the bag towards him and then shoved his hand inside, cursing as his fingers found everything except a highlighter pen.

'What the hell have you got in here, woman?' he grumbled.

'All the necessities,' Sarah replied. 'Try the inside pocket.'

Dan unzipped the inner pocket and grabbed the first highlighter he found and, relieved, pushed the bag away.

He turned his attention back to the report and began skimming through its contents.

In his former career as a geologist, he'd co-authored many reports like the one he held in his hands and figured it would follow a similar format.

He quickly dismissed the start of the document, which comprised a history of the project and the site location, and began to read through the sections that described how the client and its contractor would manage the project and any environmental impact.

He grunted a thanks as Sarah placed a refill on the table in front of him and then heard her footsteps pad away along the hallway to the bathroom. As the shower started up, he flicked another page, highlighting any phrases that caught his attention before moving on.

After ten minutes, he pushed the report to one side and began sifting through the project's processes and procedures that Sarah had been sent.

He rubbed his hand across his chin, the stubble prickling his fingers.

Why did someone send all the documents to her anonymously?

He reached across for his coffee mug and gulped half of its contents before setting it to one side and turned a page.

His heart skipped a beat.

He thumbed back a few pages, scrubbed the highlighter pen over a whole section, and then resumed reading.

Next, he picked up a copy of the early police report about the attack that Sarah had somehow wrangled from one of her contacts. As he read through the contents of their findings, one thing became clear to him. The people who had carried out the assault were professional. The ambush had been precise in nature, echoing military training rather than any rag-tag activist group.

An idea began to form in his head. He pushed the chair back from the table and began sorting the documents into two piles. Once that was complete, he pushed the bigger pile to one side, and then laid out each of the documents in the smaller pile across the surface of the table.

At some point, he was aware of movement behind him.

'You've been busy.' Sarah moved until she was standing next to him. 'What do you think?'

He wrapped his arm around her waist and gestured towards the documents in front of him. 'I think you've worked out for yourself that this was a well-planned attack.'

'It seemed too coordinated for an activist group,' Sarah nodded. 'And extreme. Almost clinical, the way it was carried out, right?'

Dan nodded. 'They'd have spent weeks, if not months monitoring that site.'

'How?'

He shrugged. 'Either in situ – having men on the ground, spying on the progress and the project team's routine, or by using a drone. They're easy to get hold of these days. All they'd have to do is stay high enough to keep out of the line of sight and rig up a camera on it. The men on the ground wouldn't hear it over the noise from the drilling equipment.'

He searched through the other paperwork. 'Were you sent a copy of the initial ballistics report?'

Sarah moved around the table until she reached out and picked up three pages, a staple in the right hand corner, and handed it across. 'This is all that was in there.'

'One of the documents says that the usual engineer that Mark Harvey replaced went missing two weeks ago,' said Dan. 'Any ideas where he is?'

'I made some enquiries before I met you for dinner,' said Sarah. 'His body was found under a railway bridge in Leeds. He'd been beaten to death.' She pointed to a newspaper clipping that she'd printed off from an internet site. 'The police are treating it as a robbery gone wrong.'

'Convenient.'

Dan skimmed through the information and cocked an eyebrow. 'Two different weapons.'

'I figured two men in the other vehicle, both shooting?'

He shook his head. 'Not the way the bodies were found. Got a pen?'

'In my bag.'

'I'm not going in there again.'

Sarah sighed, pulled open her bag, and handed him a blue ballpoint pen.

'Thanks.' Dan flipped over a page and sketched out the murder scene. 'This is what I mean.' He pointed to the first body. 'This guy was shot at point blank range, his body found right next to the drilling equipment, yes?'

'Correct.'

'Then the second man tries to run away, and his body is found over here,' he added, circling the stick figure he'd drawn.

'Okay.'

'This guy, the third man. He's closer to the project vehicle – the original one – than the guy next to the drilling rig.' Dan glanced up at Sarah. 'Do you see?'

She shook her head. 'Show me.'

'If he'd just seen one of his mates killed, and the other one running away, why isn't he running as well?'

Sarah's mouth opened in a gasp. 'He was the *killer*?'

Dan nodded. 'And then he was killed. Presumably by the people that turned up next.'

'Why?'

Dan shrugged. 'Maybe that was their plan all along. Use him to get close to the project team and then eliminate him as well.'

'Yes, but *why*?' She frowned. 'Why kill three men in cold blood next to a drilling rig? If it's to stop the project, it's incredibly extreme, isn't it?'

'We've agreed this wasn't done by activists,' said Dan. He pulled one of the documents towards him and tapped the logo at the top of the page. 'This is a government-funded project, right?'

'Yes. They're using it to demonstrate the viability of coal-seam gas as an energy source. If it works, they're hoping to attract private investors and win over public opinion about fracking.'

'And ease the UK's dependence on imported oil and gas,' added Dan. 'So the government would have a vested interest in approving the project to go ahead.'

'What do you mean?'

Dan slid the Environmental Impact Statement towards her. 'This EIS is a bit thin for the sort of project they're doing, to be honest. It skims over some of the techniques they're going to employ to test the viability of the test wells.' He flipped through the pages until he was halfway through and pulled one of the other documents towards him. 'This is the project's Materials Statements and Data Sheets – they have to have one of these for every single liquid, gas, or other product that could cause harm to their workers or the environment, do you follow me?'

'Got it.'

'Okay. Usually, I'd expect the MSDS to reflect every item listed in the EIS. It's a logical progression from one document to the other – if you list something in the EIS that could harm the environment in any way, then you *should* have an equivalent MSDS to explain what you're going to do in the event of the unthinkable happening.'

'Go on.'

Dan tapped his finger on the paragraph he'd highlighted in the EIS. 'This doesn't have an MSDS entry.'

Sarah leaned across and read the text above his finger. 'What is it?'

'I think it's what those three men were killed for,' said Dan. 'It's why the police don't want the press involved. It's why you were sent all this information anonymously. This attack has nothing to do with the drilling project.'

Sarah frowned, her expression perplexed. 'What do you mean?'

Dan held up the EIS and tapped the highlighted section. 'Those men were killed because they had access to this item listed here.'

'What is it?'

'It's a radioactive isotope.'

Chapter 10

Vasili Malikov stared sightlessly through the tinted glass of his office, his hand turning a solid gold cigarette lighter, a soft *tap* the only sound in the room as it met the teak surface of his desk.

The lighter had been a twenty-first birthday present from his father, taken from a German officer in the barren wastelands of the Eastern Front as the Second World War entered its final throes.

Malikov had queried how a German officer had come by such a prized possession; his father's answer had simply been to turn the glinting object in his son's hand, revealing the embossed Jewish script on the reverse.

No other explanation was needed. The Malikovs were adept at finding treasure though other people's misfortune.

Vasili's father had foreseen the end of the vast Communist empire, using the wiles that had seen him survive the war and provide a comfortable existence for his family under years of repression to ensure a sizeable fortune was realised as soon as Yeltsin came to power.

However, the last ten years had seen an unfortunate turn of events, and the younger Malikov was silently grateful his father had not lived to see his business flounder under the new leader's rule.

Vasili had found himself in a situation where he had to be both businessman and politician, ruthless and merciless.

Now, the muscles in his jaw tightened, his teeth clenched as his mind worked through his options, which were diminishing at an alarming rate.

He cast aside the cigarette lighter with a snarl and pushed himself from his leather chair. There was no time for pity or remorse.

His eyes fell to the photograph on his desk.

His wife had divorced him fourteen years ago upon their arrival in London, and he had let her go willingly rather than have her expensive lawyer enquire too closely about the fading bruises on her face.

Within seven months of leaving him, she had been the subject of London society gossip, marrying a titled Englishman and bearing him a daughter two years later.

He'd never met her, severing his former wife from his own life completely.

And yet –

He reached out and ran his finger down the cold protective glass, tracing the line of her cheek.

He snatched the photo frame from the desk and hurled it at the wall, turning his back as the glass shattered against the surface, and walked towards the door.

He wrenched it open.

The thug of a bodyguard faced him, his thick eyebrows knitted together in consternation.

'Get someone in there to clean up that mess,' growled Malikov.

'At once,' the thug said and moved aside.

Malikov's eyes swept the room.

The penthouse apartment boasted vaulted ceilings, a polished steel staircase winding up through the space to his private quarters. To his right, a wall of glass provided a panoramic view of the capital's skyline, the early morning sky a hue of blues, yellows, and pinks above the metropolis.

About the room, three more men draped themselves over black leather sofas, their attention drawn towards the football match on a widescreen television that hung on the wall to his right. One of the men caught Malikov's stare and heaved himself from his seat before making his way to a corner bar.

'You look like you could do with a coffee, Vasili,' he said over his shoulder. 'It's the wedding anniversary today, isn't it?'

Malikov shrugged.

There were no secrets between him and Alexsei Krupin. They'd grown up together, coming to each other's defence in the concrete apartment blocks north of Moscow where they'd bullied and fought over territory with the other kids.

Krupin was a natural choice for Malikov's head of security.

Others would look at the large man with his neck bulging out of his collar and his lumbering gait and made the mistake of assuming he was simply a hired thug.

Behind the façade, however, Malikov knew there was a shrewd man. Competent, resourceful, and loyal.

Malikov ignored the two men that continued to watch the football game; Krupin ran the security detail on a twenty-four hour shift rotation. If these men were relaxing, it meant their work was done for the day. Proper rest meant they could be depended upon to protect him.

His eyes flickered to the security monitors set below the television, the black and white images showing the two guards stationed outside the apartment elevator doors, two more patrolling the underground car park below the high rise building.

'Here.'

He turned at the sound of Krupin's voice and took the bone china cup and saucer from him, noting from the aroma that a generous measure of brandy had been added.

He took a sip and jerked his head towards the floor-to-ceiling windows and then moved across the room, the soles of his shoes silent on the plush carpet.

He turned, his back to the glass as Krupin joined him.

'You look troubled, Alexsei. What is it?'

A sigh escaped the big man. 'Vasili, it's not too late to back away,' he said, keeping his voice low under the bland television commentary that filled the room. 'No-one will think any less of you.'

Malikov placed his coffee on a glass table next to them and held up his hand. 'Enough. We proceed as planned. You've made the necessary arrangements?'

'The house has been swept for any listening devices, and they've finished a full inspection of all the perimeter fences,' replied Krupin. 'I've been informed that your nearest neighbours are away, visiting the south of France for the summer. There are some maintenance issues with the security camera system that should be fixed by this evening.'

Malikov reached out and squeezed the other man's shoulder. 'We'll leave as soon as it's ready.'

Chapter 11

The large steel doors began to slide back into place with a loud squeal, and Ben stalked across the concrete floor towards Joe.

'I thought you were going to make sure this place was ready?' he grumbled.

Joe shrugged. 'It's only meant to be temporary.'

'It bloody will be, if anyone heard those doors closing.'

'Don't worry. This estate has been deserted for over a year.'

Ben shoved his hands in his pockets and turned away, his eyes adjusting to the gloom.

His head snapped up at the sound of loud fluttering above, his heart missing a beat until he spotted the small group of pigeons that congregated amongst the roof trusses.

A crack of sunlight in the corrugated iron roof revealed their way into the warehouse.

Beyond the thin walls of the building, the sound of traffic from the main road reached his ears, the gentle breeze outside wafting the noise towards the industrial estate.

A long, wide crack had split the floor under his feet, and he followed it to its source, a steel beam that towered above him, disappearing into the gloom of the roof trusses.

'Why's it deserted?' he called over his shoulder.

'Subsidence,' said Joe. 'Blame it on the Council trying to do a job on the cheap. By the time anyone realised, it was too late.'

Ben grunted. He'd worked on building sites in the past, seen first-hand the shortcuts impatient site owners would force construction teams to take.

He hawked onto the floor and then continued to walk the perimeter. Towards the back of the vast space, he found a staircase. A chain draped between the steel bannisters, a bright red warning sign attached to it.

'What's up here?'

'Mezzanine level. It opens up at this end. Rotten as hell, according to my contact. Nothing up there except rats.'

Ben reached out, grasped one of the bannisters, and gave it a firm shake.

The whole structure seemed to sway with the movement, and he stepped away.

'Shit,' he murmured and raised his gaze to the top of the stairs. 'The whole bloody place could fall down on us.'

He shook his head and made his way back to the vehicle, where Joe was opening the rear door.

The case could be lifted by one person, but it was easier with two. The container was bulky, rather than heavy, so between them they carried it across the floor to a large misshapen bulk hidden under a tarpaulin.

Placing the case on the floor, they each grabbed an end of the dark plastic and pulled.

A four-door sedan was revealed, its paintwork dirty and rusted in places.

'Red?'

Joe shrugged. 'More chance of it being stolen by the local kids once we've finished with it,' he said. 'More effective than torching it. Police are always suspicious of burnt-out cars. It'll be months before this thing's discovered.'

Ben grunted. It made sense, but in the meantime, he couldn't help thinking they'd stick out like a sore thumb.

Joe noticed his discomfort. 'Listen, we're only going to be driving this at night. And only for a short time,' he said. 'Don't worry about it.'

Ben exhaled and held up his hands. 'Okay, as long as you're sure.'

'I'm sure. Now help me get this in the back of the car so we can eat. I'm fucking starving.'

Half an hour later, they'd taped cardboard over the few windows set high up in the walls of the warehouse and had set about heating up their meagre food supplies on a small camp stove that had been left with the car.

Ben placed his empty container on the floor next to his feet, rubbed his hands on his jeans, and then twisted on the crate he sat on.

'Did you hear that?' he frowned.

Joe looked up, a spoonful of food held midway to his mouth. 'What?'

'Listen.'

They fell silent until Joe lost patience and started eating again.

'I told you,' he said through a mouthful of pasta. 'Rats.'

Ben glanced over at the sleeping bags and bed rolls they'd set up next to the larger vehicle and shivered. 'As long as they stay up there,' he growled.

Joe chuckled, before pointing with his spoon to the exposed part of the mezzanine level that acted as a balcony above their heads. 'We'll throw the food containers up there,' he said. 'That'll keep the little bastards busy.'

'How long do we have to stay here for?'

Joe belched and put his bowl on the floor. 'Until tomorrow. Then we'll go to a safe house. We wait there until he calls.'

'When do we get the rest of our money?'

'He'll give us a location. We drop the case off, and the money is transferred. We'll get a notification two minutes after the drop-off.'

Ben grunted and then fell silent.

The two men had worked together before, successfully too. Not too often, though. A couple of jobs before this. For pocket change, compared to the payout they'd negotiated for this one.

It'd taken months of research – that was his forte – and then the planning phase.

Now he was within forty-eight hours of retirement.

He raised his gaze to the cobwebs that glinted in the light of the two camping lanterns they'd placed on the floor to alleviate the gloom and then smiled.

'What are you thinking about?' asked Joe.

'The Caribbean,' replied Ben. 'And women with big tits.'

Chapter 12

'What are you going to do?'

Sarah hurried through the apartment, following Dan as he pushed his belongings back into his kit bag.

'I have to get back to the office. Let them know we've got a problem on our hands.' Dan shoved an errant sock into the bag and then swung it over his shoulder. He turned, to see Sarah standing in the doorway, crestfallen. 'Hey, come here.'

She cleared the space between them and wrapped her arms around his waist, burying her face into his shoulder. 'You've only just got back,' she whispered.

'I know.' He rubbed her shoulders and kissed her hair. 'Can you work from home today?'

'Yes. Why?'

'I'd feel better if I knew where you were.'

'You said you think your life's in danger.'

'I did.'

She drew back and peered up at him, tears threatening to fall. 'Then, *why*? Why do you have to go? Why can't you phone them and tell them what you've found out?'

Her fingers clutched at his t-shirt, her nails scratching lightly at his skin underneath.

'You know why,' he said softly. 'It's what I do. And until I find out what's happened to David and Mitch, I don't know who I can trust.' He shrugged. 'I'm not going to convince Porchester how urgent this is unless I can tell him to his face.'

He wrapped his fingers in her hair, closed his eyes and inhaled her scent before gently pushing her away. 'Come on, walk me out.'

A sigh shuddered through her body as he clasped her hand in his and led the way through the hallway, and he wondered if they'd ever get the chance to spend some real time together.

'I've got to go,' he said and pulled the door open. 'Keep this locked, okay?'

'Dan?' Sarah rushed to the threshold and clung to the door frame. 'Be careful.'

He winked. 'Keep your head down. I'll call you later.'

***

'Dan? I didn't expect to see you back here so soon.' Evans steered Dan towards his office. 'What's the matter?'

'Is Hugh Porchester joining us?'

'Yes, why?'

'I'd rather not repeat myself, if that's okay with you, sir.' Dan took the seat Evans directed him to, placed the folder that held collated copies of Sarah's evidence onto the table in front of him, and clasped his hands over it.

'Ah, I — all right, well,' blustered Evans and checked his watch. 'He should be here in the next ten minutes or so.'

'Great.'

Dan leaned back in his chair, keeping eye contact with the man. 'You don't mind if we wait then?'

'Um, no, okay. Shall I order coffee?'

Dan shrugged. 'Fine by me.'

'Okay, good — back in a minute then.'

Dan allowed a smirk to cross his mouth as the door closed and then flicked absently through the contents of the documents while he waited. After five minutes, he was bored and began to pace the room.

Eventually, Evans returned, a harried expression etched across his face, with Porchester in tow.

Dan waited until the two men had helped themselves to coffee and settled into their seats and then cleared his throat. 'First of all, could you tell me why the government is funding a shale gas drilling study in Northumberland?'

Porchester spluttered, lowered his cup and saucer onto the table with a clatter, and stared at Dan. 'How could you possibly know about that?' he demanded.

'It was brought to my attention,' said Dan. 'I thought all fracking had been stopped by the government pending a further environmental enquiry?'

Neither of the men replied for a moment, until Porchester broke the spell.

'Dan, this is highly confidential. The public can't find out about it,' he began and held up his hand to stop Dan from interrupting. 'The government has to have a number of options available to it for the country's energy needs.' He sighed. 'Nuclear is turning out to be one of the biggest tits-ups of the 1950s – trying to maintain and close the old power stations is a major headache – and wind power simply can't generate the sort of power required. If OPEC doesn't sort its house out soon and oil prices suddenly skyrocket, we're left with imported gas. You can imagine how the average household energy costs will spin out of control if that happens.'

'So you're secretly continuing the fracking programme, is that it?'

'Yes.' Evans leaned forward. 'Why are you so suddenly interested?'

Dan opened the padded envelope and pushed the copied local newspaper cuttings across the table. 'I'm presuming you're aware three men were killed on site last week?'

Porchester glanced sideways at Evans and then nodded. 'It was brought to our attention, yes.'

'Have all the project team been required to sign confidentiality agreements when they're employed?'

'Yes.'

'And I'm presuming you or someone else silenced the media?'

'We're under strict instructions from the top.'

'Right.' Dan flipped open the Environmental Impact Statement, the highlighted section even brighter in the sunlight that broke through the window blinds. 'Have either of you seen this before?'

Porchester reached out and took the document from Dan, flicked open his reading glasses, and peered at the page. 'I believe I was sent a copy of this after it was approved, yes.' He handed the document to Evans, glanced at his watch, and frowned. 'Dan, I'm sorry, but I have another meeting to go to in less than thirty minutes. What is it you wanted to see me so urgently about?'

'There's a case of caesium-137 missing.'

'What?'

Dan pointed at the open page. 'This. It's gone.'

'How do you know?'

'There's no mention of it in the police inventory report relating to the crime scene.'

'What is it?'

Dan leaned across the table and picked up the glass of water in front of him, turning the tumbler in his fingers before speaking. 'It's a radioactive isotope.'

He took a sip and peered over the rim of the glass at the men in front of him as their expressions changed from one of disbelief to fear.

Porchester paled. 'How much?'

'Enough to build a dirty bomb.' Dan pushed the glass away.

'What the hell is a drilling crew doing with radioactive material?' asked Evans, his brow furrowed.

'Calm down,' said Porchester. 'I'm sure there's a perfectly reasonable explanation – right, Taylor?'

Dan turned to him. 'They only use a small amount at a time. It's a common fracking method,' he explained. 'It's used to calculate the composition of gas and water underground. The gamma rays from the isotope act like an X-ray and show the drillers what composition the soil and rock they're working with has.'

'And we let them do this?'

Dan shrugged and pointed at the report. 'It's on all the Environmental Impact Statement issued for approval by Government.'

'Jesus Christ.' Evans slumped back into his chair and ran his hand over his receding hair line. 'How were they able to steal it? I mean, they couldn't simply walk out with it, could they?' He turned to Porchester for assurance, but the other man shook his head.

'The isotope is signed out to a single member of the drilling team, not the contracted company,' explained Dan. 'It's kept in a concrete and lead-lined container.' He flicked through the copy investigation notes. 'Needless to say, the container was missing when the bodies of the drilling team were found.'

'What I don't understand is why the drilling team took the whole consignment with them that day,' said Evans. 'Surely they wouldn't normally do that.'

'That's correct, sir. I'd have to suggest that they were cutting corners, trying to save time instead of going back to base before each test drill that day – according to the report I have, they were already three months behind schedule due to bad weather,' said Dan. 'The other possibility is that someone on that drill team was involved in the theft.'

'But all the members of the team were killed,' argued Porchester.

Dan pushed across his sketch from that morning and explained his findings against the preliminary ballistics report. 'I think the third man was the initial shooter. He killed the project manager and the lead engineer. Then he was shot by whoever turned up in the rogue vehicle.'

Porchester's eyes widened. 'You mean to say he was killed by his own people?'

Dan shrugged. 'No honour amongst thieves, sir.'

Evans leaned back in his chair and exhaled. 'Any idea where this bomb might go off?'

'There's nothing in the documentation I've seen. I'll leave that part of the investigation to you,' said Dan pointedly.

Porchester pushed his chair away from the desk and began to pace. 'All right, Dan. This is what I want you to do. Get yourself up to Northumberland and speak to the client representative there. We'll phone ahead to arrange access to all their files.' He tugged at his tie. 'Jesus H. We were assuming the men were shot by environmental extremists or something.' He pointed at the EIS. 'Find out how much is missing and why this is the first time we're hearing about it.' He glanced at the open diary in front of him. 'You've got forty-eight hours.'

'Onto it, sir.'

Chapter 13

Dan drummed his fingers on the steering wheel and glared through the windscreen at the traffic jam in front of him.

The motorway was in a constant state of disrepair, with one section being completed only for another road works project to start five miles further north, and he was fed up with the stop-go rhythm of the journey.

He glanced at his watch. Four hours had passed since he'd left London, enjoying the freedom of driving a powerful sedan as he'd sped past Northampton, the stereo system blaring out a mix of classic 1970s and '80s rock music.

The novelty had worn off forty miles north of Leeds.

As the traffic crawled towards the next intersection, he swung left out of his lane and steered the sedan up the slip road, leaving the bedlam behind him.

After the concrete spaghetti loops of the motorway junction disappeared in the rear view mirror and the car picked up speed once more, he'd relaxed and concentrated on powering through the twisting curves that led across the Yorkshire moors towards the north-east.

He glanced down as his phone began to ring in its cradle, Sarah's apartment number splayed across the front of it.

'Hey.'

'Hi,' she said. 'Where are you?'

Dan caught a fleeting glimpse of a sign as it flashed by. 'Almost at Durham.'

'Traffic bad, huh?'

'Yeah. I'm not going to make it to Northumberland tonight,' he said. 'I'll find a motel or something within the hour. Drive straight to the project office in the morning. What's happening there?'

'Your friends were still parked outside until a couple of hours ago. Haven't seen them since.'

'Is that so? Huh.' Dan scratched his chin. 'You've locked the door, right?'

'Yes. I'll keep the answering machine on when I pick up the phone too. Just in case.'

'Good.'

'What did they say when you went to the office? Did they know about the theft?'

'No – I don't think so. They looked shocked, that's for sure.' He smiled. 'They weren't too pleased that news of their secret project got out either.'

Sarah chuckled. 'I'll bet.'

Dan grew serious. 'That's why you have to stay there until I get back, okay? No going to work or even to the shops.' He frowned when the silence stretched out between them. 'Sarah?'

She sighed. 'Yes. I hear you.'

'I mean it. Stay out of sight until I get back. I'll be back Friday night, okay?'

'If I'm going to stay cooped up here until then, you'd better bring Chinese takeaway when you turn up,' she grumbled.

***

Early the next morning, Dan left the motel and pointed the car in the direction of the project office.

A bulky man wearing a navy blue uniform of trousers and polo shirt with the company's insignia emblazoned across the left pocket emerged from a temporary office to the right of the security gate, his colleague peering out through the window, a clipboard in his hand.

Dan buzzed down the window and held up his EPG security pass. 'Morning. I believe you're expecting me. Dan Taylor.'

'Thanks, Mr Taylor,' said the man. He peered at the pass before handing it back and pointing towards the project office on the other side of the gate. 'Park your car to the left of the office, and then go through the main entrance there. There'll be a quick induction for you to complete before our site manager will collect you.'

'Cheers.'

The project team moved efficiently, and within the hour, Dan was sitting in the office of Bill Dawson, the site manager.

'So, how did the local community feel about there being a stock of isotope being kept on site?' he asked. 'I can't imagine all those people with placards outside were too keen.'

Dawson shuffled in his seat. 'They don't know,' he said.

'How did you manage that?'

'Listen, we only have to set out in our Environmental Impact Statement that we'll use industry standard techniques to do the drilling,' Dawson said. 'There's no legislative requirement for us to have Material Data Sheets for the stuff on record.' He shrugged. 'It's the same worldwide – they've been doing fracking like this in the United States and Australia for years.'

'Is that legal?'

'Of course. What you've got to realise though is that it's normal to omit it from the data sheets provided to the public, so they don't freak out about radioactive materials. Fracking's already controversial.' He leaned back in his chair.

'You're joking.'

'Not at all. As long as we agree to follow the manufacturer's product guidelines to the letter, we're covered.'

'Except that someone didn't follow the guidelines, did they? One of your engineers decided to take the whole stock of isotope out to the drill site, instead of the required amount for testing.'

Dawson cleared his throat. 'That's correct.'

'How much is missing?'

'All of it.'

'Volume?'

Dawson sighed. 'There were six refills in the case that was stolen.'

Dan ran through some rough calculations in his head, his heart lurching in his chest as the implications of what he was hearing began to surface.

He stood and jerked his head towards the door.

'Come on,' he said. 'You'd better show me the drill rig and where those men were murdered.'

Chapter 14

Malikov gripped the hand rest set into the leather interior of the car door as Krupin swung the vehicle in a sharp right turn off the main road.

They'd left before dawn, after Krupin confirmed with the security detail that the street outside the apartment had been checked for any unwanted witnesses.

The UK's security services were spending more and more time and effort chasing extremists rather than keeping an eye on other threats to national security of late, but it paid to be cautious.

Upon reaching Hendon, Krupin had pulled the car behind a row of houses, the separate garage block for the properties creating a concrete screen from prying eyes in the early morning light as he'd removed the licence plates and replaced them with a different set.

He would repeat the exercise before they returned to the city.

If they returned.

Malikov set his jaw as the vehicle's suspension bounced and jolted over the potholed asphalt that led away from the main road.

It had been months since he'd travelled to the property.

Krupin had phoned ahead the night before to ensure the necessary arrangements were taken care of; a full investigation to check on unwanted activity near the perimeter of the surrounding land proved fruitless, as had a sweep of their communication systems. The security cameras only alerted the guards to the wildlife, nothing more.

They were ready for Malikov and his guests.

The Georgian house provided perfect seclusion for Malikov's needs, and it gave him great satisfaction to thumb his nose at the landed gentry who had bankrupted themselves trying to stop the old building from going to wrack and ruin.

It had been the same all over the country for the past ten years or more; English aristocrats suddenly finding their old ways of life were well and truly extinct following the global financial crisis, and their only option to save face was to sell to Russian oligarchs and Saudi investors who then used the properties only sparingly, because they could afford to.

Malikov had seized upon the chance to purchase the house, especially after his ex-wife had taken up with the very class of people he despised so much.

Whatever the new Russian regime thought of him, he was still a Communist at heart.

He was simply a very opportunistic one, and ruthless at that.

After a couple of miles, Krupin braked and turned the car to the left, through wrought iron gates that swung shut automatically in the vehicle's wake, the car's tyres crunching over speckled gravel that covered the driveway.

Unknown to his neighbours, Malikov had installed a state-of-the-art camera system upon moving in. The cameras were positioned along the length of the lane from the main road to the front gates of the house, which was manned on a twenty-four-hour basis from the security hub in the old servants' quarters.

His men patrolled the perimeter of the property from the small woodland that swept along the boundary with the farm to the north of his land, all the way to the front gates and the two paddocks that the car now drove past.

It was more secure than his apartment in the city could ever be, and perfect for his current requirements.

As the driveway levelled out, the house came into view, its roof dominated by four large chimneys, while the old turning circle for a horse and carriage at the front was bordered by mature magnolia and rhododendron bushes.

The house was three storeys high. A visitor would assume the front rooms were bedrooms, given the net curtains and soft drapes visible from the ground, however Krupin had insisted that the front rooms be given over to Malikov's security detail, and the oligarch had acquiesced.

The angle of the windows from the rooms gave the guards a broad vista across Malikov's land and more than adequate coverage of the surrounding countryside.

The car swept into the turning circle, and Krupin brought it to a smooth standstill at the front door.

Malikov waited until Krupin climbed from the driver's seat and opened the back door for him and then climbed from the car and stretched, inhaling the fresh air as he gazed out across the landscape.

A light breeze caught his hair, lifting it from his collar, and he noted the first hint of autumn in the wind.

Krupin squinted into the distance, shielding his eyes from the morning sun. 'It's a perfect day, Vasili,' he said and then dropped his hand and walked to the back of the car. He lifted two suitcases from it with ease and locked the vehicle before leading the way to the front door. 'You should go for a walk. It's been a stressful few days for you.'

Malikov shrugged, brushed past Krupin, and pushed the front door open. 'There will be time to rest when we are finished,' he said. 'Don't worry about me.'

'Easier said than done,' muttered Krupin as he set the cases in the hallway.

Both men turned at footsteps that drew closer from the direction of the kitchen.

'It is good to see you, Vasili,' boomed a voice, before a broad man in jeans and t-shirt appeared, his thin black hair slicked back over a wide forehead. 'You're looking too pale,' he said as he reached them. 'I'll soon put that right.'

Malikov shook the man's hand. 'It's good to see you, too, Andrei. I'm looking forward to some proper food. Are the guards treating you well?'

'As can be expected,' said Andrei. A scowl crossed his face. 'Although I wish they'd stay out of my kitchen.'

'It cannot be avoided,' said Krupin.

Andrei shrugged and changed the subject. 'I presumed you'd both be hungry after your drive, so if you'd like to freshen up, I've prepared a lunch for you.'

'Good,' said Malikov. 'I'll be back down in half an hour.'

'Understood,' said Andrei and then nodded at Krupin and retreated back down the hallway.

Krupin followed up the staircase carrying both suitcases, wielding them as if they were lightweight shopping bags instead of two weeks' worth of clothing and other paraphernalia.

As they approached an open door leading to a master suite, Krupin placed the larger case on the floor.

'I'll check in with the guards before joining you for lunch,' he said.

Malikov nodded. 'As you wish,' he said and wheeled his case across the carpeted threshold, closing and locking the door behind him.

He left the case next to the door and made his way across the expansive master suite to the large window that took up a third of the wall. Facing out over the rear of the property, the room overlooked a large landscaped entertaining area comprising a pool, barbeque area, and a terrace that led to manicured gardens.

Malikov put his hands on his hips and fought down the rising pressure in his chest.

He wouldn't – couldn't – go back to Russia.

He'd burned his bridges with his home country too long ago, disobeying orders from the Kremlin.

If he failed now, the embarrassment to them would be his death sentence.

He shivered, despite the warmth of the air.

All the UK-based oligarchs knew what happened to people the Kremlin deemed a threat to its leadership.

Chapter 15

Dan ignored the cool breeze that whipped across the barren landscape and glared at a lone sheep that had appeared at the top of the hill above the drill rig site, its forlorn bleat carrying across the moor.

Instead, he reached into the vehicle and pulled a handheld Geiger counter from the back seat. He zipped up his jacket, slammed the door shut, and stalked after Dawson, who was hurrying towards the drilling equipment.

His desert boots sank into the thick vegetation under his feet, and he wondered if the farmer that owned the land was making enough from sheep farming or whether he was hoping the potential fracking operation would sustain his agricultural business.

He inhaled deep breaths of the fresh air, glad to be out of the city and back in the countryside.

'How long was it before the bodies were discovered?' he asked as he caught up with Dawson.

'A few hours. They were due to come off shift at six o'clock. When they didn't show up, our project administrator phoned through to the security office here.'

'And the security men were the ones to find them?'

'Yes. They radioed the police from here before phoning the project office and reporting it to us.'

Dan turned and surveyed the field behind the vehicle.

The security gate was at least half a mile away. A rough track had been etched through the meadow by the wheels of the project vehicles, their regular route taking them around a curve at the base of the hill. It meant the team were out of sight of the security office as they worked.

Dan frowned. 'I'm surprised the guys in the security office didn't hear the gunshots.'

'Easy,' explained Dawson. 'They were inside with the radio on.'

'I suppose that makes sense. Must be pretty monotonous for them, being posted out here.'

'They gave full statements to the police.'

'I'm sure they did. Do they still work here?'

Dawson shook his head. 'They were demobilised the day after the incident.' He paused and stared off into the distance. 'Had to sign confidentiality agreements, of course, given the nature of the project.'

Dan cursed under his breath. If the men had disbanded and signed confidentiality agreements, it'd be highly unlikely he'd be able to talk to them within the timeframe Hugh Porchester had given him.

'Were you here that day?'

'Yeah. I drove up here as soon as they phoned it in. When I got to the main gate, there were already two police cars blocking the way.' He blinked and looked towards the drilling rig. 'They asked me to go with them, to see what had happened.'

'Okay. Walk me over to the scene and show me where the bodies were found.'

'Over here.'

Dan switched on the Geiger counter and followed a few paces behind Dawson, pointing the meter left and right as he progressed towards the drill rig.

The steady tick of the instrument accompanied his footsteps. His brow creased as the needle began to rise immediately, indicating a residual trace of radiation.

He glanced up to check their progress, but they were still a hundred metres from the rig itself, and shook his head.

It didn't make sense.

He stopped, the breeze ruffling his hair, and gave the Geiger counter a slap with the heel of his hand before continuing to follow after Dawson.

The man had reached the drill rig and had turned, a frown on his face.

'Everything okay?'

Dan held up his hand in reply, his eyes flickering over the meter.

As he paced forward, the instrument began to click with a greater urgency, the meter continuing its steady rise.

Dan's heartbeat began to increase, an idea forming in his head.

He thumbed over the on/off button and silenced the machine before he reached Dawson and then spoke before the man had a chance to question him.

'So, tell me what happened when you got here,' he said. 'What did you see?'

Dawson swallowed and then raised his hand and pointed at the drill rig. 'Greg was lying here,' he said, his voice quavering. 'I could see straight away why the security guards had called the police rather than an ambulance.' He stopped talking and shook his head. 'Sorry – I can't get it out of my head.'

'That's natural,' soothed Dan. 'Take your time.'

Dawson cleared his throat. 'There was so much blood – I overheard the police say that he'd taken a shot directly to his lungs, that he'd have been killed straight away. I don't think he even knew what was going to happen. His eyes…' He stopped and shook his head. 'His eyes were open, and he looked *surprised*. Does that make sense?'

Dan nodded and waited for Dawson to continue.

'Mark Harvey was found here,' the project manager said and pointed at an area only a metre away from where they stood. 'Again, he didn't stand a chance. I'm not an expert, but it looked like he was shot at close range. Jack was found over there, about eight metres from the drill rig. He was facing away from the rig.'

'Shot in the back as he was running away,' Dan murmured.

'Yes, that's what the police said.'

'Poor bastard.' Dan shook his head. 'Listen, I've got to run some tests and take some notes. Are you okay to wait over by the vehicle? I need to be careful I don't disturb too much, in case the police want to come back here.'

'Sure, no problem.'

Dan waited until Dawson had turned and started walking away and then switched on the Geiger counter once more.

His eyebrows shot up as the meter flew across the display.

'Fuck.'

He frowned and then walked around the drill rig and towards the area where Jack had been found face down. He glanced at the meter. It had dropped slightly from the reading it had given off next to the drill rig.

'That doesn't make sense,' Dan murmured. 'Unless…'

He spun on his heel, switched off the Geiger counter, and took an arching route back towards the project vehicle, avoiding going too close to the drill rig.

Dawson was already sitting in the driver's seat, staring out over the open fields, lost in thought, and jumped when Dan ripped the passenger door open and climbed in.

'You're going to catch whoever did this, won't you?'

Dan looked the man in the eye. 'I'm going to do my best.'

'Good.' Dawson sighed. 'Do you need anything else?'

'No, that's okay,' said Dan. 'Thanks – I've seen everything I need to here.'

They travelled in relative silence back to the project office, and then once Dan had signed out and thanked Dawson for his time, he hurried across to his vehicle and drove it through the gates.

As he pointed the car towards the motorway, he scrolled through the short contact list in his phone, selected a number, and hit the 'call' button on the steering wheel.

'Evans, it's Dan. We've got a problem,' he said.

'What's wrong? Did you visit the site?'

'Yeah. Just left.'

'Any indication where the stolen isotope is?'

'No, but that's the least of our worries.'

A moment's silence filled the interior of the car before Evans spoke. 'Go on.'

'I took a Geiger counter with me, to see if it'd give me any clues.'

'And?'

'The meter reading shot through the roof right next to the drill rig.'

'Residual from the density measuring device they were using?'

'No. Too high for that.'

'Then what are you thinking?'

'It's not a simple case of looking for a stolen isotope any more,' said Dan. 'We've got a radioactive leak on our hands.'

Chapter 16

Dan stalked into the secure open office and hurried towards Melissa's desk.

The woman was engrossed in the data scrolling across the three computer screens in front of her. Her head bobbed up and down to the music that played through headphones, the treble bleeding into the air around her.

She ignored Dan as he approached, turning her attention to the report next to her mouse mat and then back to the computer screen.

He didn't wait for her to acknowledge him. Instead, he reached out and flipped the headphones from her head.

'Oi.' Melissa caught the headphones before they tumbled to the desk. 'Careful – they cost two hundred quid.'

'Two hundred *pounds*,' said Dan. 'Come on. We've got work to do.' He folded his arms across his chest. 'Now.'

She sighed, locked her computer, and pushed her chair back. 'Where?'

'What's the most secure meeting room in the building?'

'Conference room.' She jutted her chin in the direction of the corridor. 'Along there.'

'Lead the way.'

***

'Don't you usually get involved in work like this?'

Melissa shook her head. 'No. They normally leave me to do the computer stuff.' She leaned forward and began to flick through the pages of the documents that had been sent to Sarah, her eyes widening as one of the crime scene photographs caught her attention. 'This is *way* more interesting, though.'

'Right. Here's the deal,' said Dan and pulled his chair closer to the table. 'You cut the attitude with me, and I'll include you in my investigation. Sound good?'

Melissa's eyes lit up. 'Really?'

'Really.' His mouth quirked. 'I think despite the fact you've got a clear disregard for authority, you're brighter than half the analysts sitting out there. David gave you this job, didn't he?'

She nodded and then quickly looked down at her hands. 'I was in trouble.' She cleared her throat and then frowned. 'A lot of trouble.'

'Yeah. I heard.' He smiled. 'That's probably why we're going to get on like a house on fire.'

Her head shot up, her mouth open in surprise, and then a faint smile crossed her lips. 'Okay.'

'Good. Let's get started.' He leaned back in his chair. 'There are going to be three rules. First, nothing you and I talk about in this room, none of the work I give to you, gets broadcast outside this room, understood?'

'Got it.'

'Second, if anyone asks you what you're helping with, lie. All right?'

'Yes.'

'Great.' He picked up one of the reports.

'Hang on,' said Melissa. 'You said there were three rules. What's the third?'

Dan flicked the page and kept reading. 'Don't forget the sugar in my coffee.'

***

Dan ended the call to the project office and cursed.

The rest of the team had gone home for the night, and he and the analyst had the office to themselves. The automatic lighting had flickered off around the edges of the room from the lack of activity, the remaining spotlights pooling over Melissa's desk.

Dan squinted into the gloom and tapped the mobile against his chin.

'What did they say?'

'Nothing that's going to help us,' he murmured. 'Apparently someone from the team ordered an extra set of storage equipment four weeks ago, which seemed unusual but not enough to raise any flags.'

'Mark Harvey?'

'Yeah. Signed for them at the gate when the delivery van got there.'

'So he hoarded the supplies without the team finding out?'

Dan shrugged. 'He'd have easily been able to put the gear into his car without anyone questioning him.'

Melissa spun her chair left and right, her hands gripping the sides, a frown on her face. 'Surely they would have queried the extra costs when the invoice turned up, though. They'd have to account for it.'

Dan tucked his phone into his back pocket. 'Apparently their contract stipulates they can't raise an invoice until the end of the month.'

'Giving Mark a clear four weeks before the extra equipment was queried.'

'By which time, he'd be out of the way.'

Melissa turned back to her computer. 'Clever.'

'Yeah.' Dan pulled a chair across to her desk and sat next to her. 'They were planning this for a long time.'

'Surely there have to be easier ways to get hold of a radioactive isotope,' she said, wiggling her mouse so the screens flickered to life once more. 'What about all the stuff used in hospitals – X-ray and MRI machines?'

'There're strict disposal controls in the health service because of that risk,' said Dan. 'Not to mention they'd be trying to steal it from a very crowded environment. More chance of being caught.'

'How would it leak?' asked Melissa. 'I thought the case was concrete and lead-lined.'

'Either a stray bullet clipped the case or one of the canisters inside was damaged.'

'Bullet casings?'

Dan shook his head. 'They were too clever for that. The police forensics report confirms no bullet casings were found on the scene.'

'But the security men at the site gate let them back through.' Melissa frowned. 'If they were wearing radiation suits, they'd be stopped.'

'Or the security guards would be dead, too.' Dan drummed his fingers on the desk and then stopped. 'Unless they didn't know they had a leak.'

'So the box wasn't damaged by gunfire,' said Melissa.

'Here's a thought,' said Dan. He pushed his chair back and began to pace the room. 'We know the two legitimate project men were killed by the rogue engineer,' he said. 'What if it's not the box that's leaking, but what's inside?'

'One of the vials?'

'Yeah. What if Mark Harvey pulled out a gun and Greg dropped a vial – in shock?'

Melissa nodded. 'That would work.'

Dan held up his hand, a thought forming. 'The two unidentified thieves wouldn't know about the leaking vial. Mark would've put it back in the case before they showed up – they'd have been in a hurry to leave the area in case someone heard the two gunshots.'

Melissa leaned forward. 'And they shot him before he had a chance to tell them.'

'Right, here's what we'll do. You start with all the hospitals within a fifty-mile radius of the project site. Phone and ask if anyone's checked into accident and emergency in the last week showing signs of radiation sickness – vomiting, the lot.'

'Won't the hospital have reported it to the police if someone turned up with radiation sickness?'

'They will.' Dan's eyes flickered to the closed door and the frosted glass that obscured them from view. 'But I have a feeling we're not being told everything about this case. Probably on purpose.'

'Oh.'

'Sign out a mobile phone for yourself. When you phone the hospitals, give them your number and mine. If anyone checks in that raises suspicions, I want us to know about it first.'

'I've got a better idea.'

'What?'

'Wait here. Don't move. I'll be back in a minute.'

Dan frowned but held his tongue as Mel scooted from her seat, ripped open the door to the meeting room, and headed back in the direction of the open plan office.

He leaned back against the windowsill, forcing himself not to rush after her to demand what she was doing. The paranoia of not knowing who he could trust was beginning to wear him down. He rubbed his hand over his eyes, exhausted.

He heard footsteps on the carpet outside approaching at a fast pace, and then Mel reappeared, her hands holding something wrapped up under her sweater. She peered over her shoulder before she kicked the door shut with her foot and hurried towards him.

'Here. Take one of these.'

Dan held out his hand and then laughed when she dropped the item into it.

'Jesus, where did you find these? I haven't seen a mobile phone like this for at least ten years.'

'Exactly,' said Mel, pulling a second, identical phone from her sweater and tucking it under one of the reports on the desk. 'That's the point.'

'What is?'

Mel took the phone from him and switched it on. A melody played out across the room, its cheerful tone out of place within the sombre surroundings.

'What's the biggest problem with mobile phones these days?'

Dan's mouth quirked. 'No matter how much your provider charges you, your signal still drops out anywhere near Shepherds Bush?'

'No, and stop being obtuse,' said Mel. She passed the phone back to him. 'Every mobile phone these days is *traceable*. You can't hide anywhere.' She gestured outside. 'Think how many people the security services have caught, simply based on tracking their location via GPS or hacking into phone records. All because we want smarter, faster technology to stay connected.'

'So, no location emitter, no email, no GPS, no Wi-Fi connection – *nothing*.' Dan turned the phone in his hand.

'Right,' said Mel. She leaned over to the table and picked up her identical phone. 'They just make calls and send texts. If you want added security, you can remove the battery and SIM card, but at least if you forget, the police aren't going to turn up at your door immediately.'

'And we need these because?'

'Because someone wants you dead. That's why.'

Dan waved the phone in front of her face. 'How good are these? How sure can you be?'

Mel crossed her arms. 'I'm sure,' she said. 'You wouldn't believe what the street value of these old phones are. All the drug dealers are buying them these days.'

Dan's eyebrows shot up. 'Really?'

'Really.' She turned back to the table and started collating the papers. 'I'll put these in a secure place, one only I have access to,' she said. 'What are you going to do?'

'I'll make some discreet enquiries. See if I can find out how sick these people are going to be based on the number of vials we know are missing.'

Melissa nodded. 'Let's get on with it.'

Chapter 17

Alan Wright groaned and rolled over, sweat bubbling on his forehead.

The flattened cardboard that served as his bed reeked. He'd been violently ill, the convulsions so sudden that he hadn't been able to make it across the room to the bucket that he'd set up as a crude toilet.

Spasms had shaken his body, and he'd spent most of the time cursing the cheap meal he'd bought with loose change from the run-down cafe at the end of the road two days before. He knew he'd end up with food poisoning sooner or later eating there, but they were the cheapest in the area and meant the change he'd begged from strangers during the day would last a bit longer.

He wiped his face with the flap of his shirt and shivered, his skin covering with goose bumps, and stared at the ceiling.

Pipes criss-crossed above his head, their route dictated by old air conditioning ducts, toilets that no longer worked, and power-starved electrical conduits.

To the far side of the mezzanine level, a large window allowed light to filter through its dirty panes, the edges of the framework rusty and covered in pigeon shit.

The building was silent, save for his ragged breathing.

He blinked, tears threatening his resolve.

He'd been ill before, sure, but not like this. He pushed back the sleeve of his shirt and squinted in the faint light at the blisters on his skin, its surface red and raw.

He swallowed, more of the blisters scratching at his throat.

He lowered his arm across his eyes and wracked his memory. Had he had chicken pox as a kid? Wasn't it dangerous if contracted as an adult?

He wiped his face with his sleeve once more.

He'd leave it a few more hours. If he didn't feel better, he'd walk to the hospital. It was only a mile away, and the fresh air would probably do him good.

'You've been cooped up too long, Al,' he reasoned.

A sudden urge to pee took him by surprise, his eyes flickering open as he tried to fight the exhaustion.

He raised his head, eased himself up until he was sitting, his hands propping up his body weight, and fought the wave of dizziness that gripped him.

He grimaced at the pool of vomit on the floor.

As he shuffled on the cardboard to try to stand, his gaze fell to the jacket he'd bunched up to use as a pillow.

He frowned, and then leaned forward and reached across, pulling it towards him.

'What the hell?' he muttered.

A small clump of hair lay within the folds of the material.

He raised his hand to the back of his head, his fingers working across his skull, and then stopped.

A smooth exposed piece of skin appeared under his touch. He removed his hand and looked at his fingers.

More hair.

He swallowed, and then raised his eyes across the mezzanine floor.

A wire fence enclosed the space, preventing anyone from falling to the abandoned warehouse below. He'd heard the double doors to the warehouse slide open on a squeaky mechanism yesterday, before a four-wheel drive vehicle had roared into the space.

He'd crawled closer to the edge, keeping his head low, in time to see a man clamber from the driver's seat.

A second man had closed the warehouse doors and then joined the driver, before they'd moved to the back of the vehicle and opened the back door.

They'd carried a metal box between them, and by the way they'd shuffled across the floor towards a second car that had been concealed beneath a tarpaulin, he'd assumed the contents were heavy.

The men had left that morning, taking the car and leaving the four-wheel drive vehicle, stripped of its licence plates.

Alan had waited until he felt safe they wouldn't return and had made his way down the rickety staircase to investigate.

He'd been lucky when the two men had turned up; he'd bundled up his collection of cardboard he used for a sleeping mat and had folded it up, shoving it up against the wall in a darkened corner before retreating to the shadows as their vehicle had entered the warehouse.

He'd held his breath as one of them had shaken the stair bannister, praying the man wouldn't find him, and had sighed with relief when the man's companion had mentioned the rats.

He'd strained his ears to hear what they'd said while they were cooking their food, his stomach rumbling so loud that he'd thought they'd discover him for sure.

When they hadn't, he'd resolved to find out what they were up to, more as a way to break up the monotony of his day rather than any inclination to be nosey.

They'd been clever though, taking turns to sleep and guard whatever it was they had carried to their car, and so Alan had waited until they'd gone.

When he'd reached the abandoned four-wheel drive vehicle, he reached out to open the driver's door and then snatched his hand back.

He had no idea what he'd find, and he didn't want his fingerprints found.

He'd pulled his sleeve down to cover his hand and had then opened the door, holding his breath.

The vehicle was empty, cleaned of any sign of its previous occupants. He'd checked all the seats thoroughly, looking for loose change or anything else that could prove useful, and had given up after half an hour with a huff of disgust.

He'd climbed out and made his way round to the rear of the vehicle, the back door swinging easily on its hinges.

He'd sought out a clue as to what the men had been transporting. It had looked reasonably heavy, the way both of them had carried it across the floor to their replacement car, and sure enough, the upholstery showed signs of a heavy object, indentations still clear in the fabric.

Frustrated, he'd slammed the door shut and returned to his bed, none the wiser for his investigations.

Now, Alan stared at the clump of hair in his palm and wondered what the two men had really been up to.

And what the hell was making him so sick.

Chapter 18

'What's wrong?'

Malikov peered over the reading glasses he hated to wear and then pulled them from his face as Krupin closed the door to the office and hurried towards him.

'I've been trying to contact you,' he said accusingly and pointed at the mobile phone on the desk. He picked it up and frowned. 'It's switched off.'

'You know I hate those things,' snapped Malikov. 'What's the problem?'

'I've just found out our assassin failed,' said Krupin. 'The government somehow managed to keep it secret. It's taken until now for my contact to get confirmation.'

'So, Taylor is still alive, is he?' Malikov leaned back in his chair and rubbed his chin. 'That's unfortunate.'

Krupin perched on the end of the desk. 'I've also received word that he visited the project site yesterday.'

Malikov unleashed a torrent of curses in his mother tongue and then exhaled. 'He's onto us.'

'I spoke with Paval. He arranged for the documents relating to the isotope theft to be given to Taylor's girlfriend.'

Malikov beat his fist against the arm of the chair, the beginning of a headache pulsing behind his eyes. He reached out for the small bottle of pills on the desk, unscrewed the cap, and threw two down his throat.

'Was that wise?' he gasped, beating his chest with his fist to force the pills down. He reached out for a glass of water, fighting down the urge to cough.

Krupin ignored his discomfort. 'It will divert attention away from us. Don't worry.'

'This changes everything,' Malikov said, turning the bottle in his hand. He set it on the desk and raised his eyes to Krupin. 'Doesn't it?'

'We could still take delivery,' said Krupin. He checked his watch. 'He still hasn't located the isotope.'

'No, but he will,' replied Malikov. 'He will.' He stood, crossed his arms over his chest, and stared out the window at the terraced garden. 'What happens if we don't take delivery?'

Krupin shrugged. 'It can't be traced back to us. The first instalment was paid in cash using a secure drop-off location. Used notes.' He stood and joined Malikov at the window. 'It would only take a phone call to have them arrested.'

'Or,' said Malikov, wagging a finger at Krupin, 'we simply walk away. If we continue to try and control this situation, it could expose us further.'

'If you do that, they're likely to panic, and there's no guarantee who will buy the material,' said Krupin. 'Given what you're trying to achieve here, is that wise?'

Malikov sighed. 'Probably not,' he conceded. 'Any news from the negotiations?'

'Apparently the Prime Minister is still pushing his agenda of keeping this country in the European Union, but trying to do so with concessions.'

Malikov grunted. 'I would have hoped that we would have been more persuasive.'

'We have to be careful, Vasili,' said Krupin. 'If we push too hard, the Prime Minister will become suspicious. We knew this could take time.'

Malikov's eyes fell to the bottle of pills on the desk, before he snapped his attention back to the view from the window.

'What's the news from Moscow?'

Krupin frowned. 'The sanctions are weighing heavily on business. The leader is sabre-rattling, picking fights he knows he can't win simply to divert the country's attention from the state of the economy.' He cracked his knuckles. 'There was another demonstration two days ago.'

'Really?' Malikov pondered the point for a moment. 'Nothing in the news?'

'Six protestors killed. Not the sort of thing that's good for public relations.'

Malikov returned to his desk and sank back into his chair. 'Something's going to give, Krupin. I can sense it.' He tapped his fingers on the desk, momentarily lost in thought.

'You think he'll make a mistake?'

'It's a worry,' agreed Malikov. He rubbed a hand over tired eyes. 'That's why what we're doing here is so important.' He thought for a moment and then sighed. 'All right. Let's see what happens while the Prime Minister is in France. If there's no progress by the time he arrives in Germany, we'll have to consider our options.'

'In the meantime,' said Krupin, pointing at the display on his smart phone, 'how are we going to deal with him?'

Malikov picked up a photograph from the desk and handed it to Krupin.

'Use her. Maybe that will convince him we mean business.'

Chapter 19

Sarah tapped the button for the pedestrian crossing and checked her watch.

She bit her lip. She knew she shouldn't have left the apartment, but the property had CCTV cameras installed in its hallways and on the outer perimeter to protect its inhabitants. All her work had been locked away in a safe she'd had installed in her bedroom wardrobe, so she didn't feel that the men who had been parked outside her home for the past twenty-four hours would attempt to break in while she was out.

She hadn't told Dan when they'd last spoken, but the frustration of being cooped up with nothing to do until he returned had begun to grate on her nerves.

Surely a quick trip to the supermarket is okay, she'd reasoned. Besides, knowing Dan, he'd return to the apartment empty-handed so she needed to get food supplies.

She reached into her bag and pulled out her phone. Still no missed calls from him.

She sighed, dropped the phone back into the bag, and then tapped her fingers on the leather strap that hung over her shoulder.

The afternoon was drawing to a close, the commuter rush to leave the city already an hour old, and the crowd of people next to her grew as offices emptied and people made their way towards the entrance to the Underground station on the opposite side.

The illuminated icon of a walking man on the opposite display flashed from red to green, and she joined the throng of pedestrians that surged over the demarcated crossing.

Halfway across, her elbow was grabbed, something pointed into her spine, and a voice hissed in her ear.

'Keep walking. Don't scream.'

Sarah's heart leapt painfully, and she gasped as the grip on her arm increased.

'Move. Over there.'

She was steered away from the small crowd that converged on the pavement and led towards the entranceway to an alleyway that ran behind a row of shops.

She swore under her breath, her mind working through all the self-defence moves Dan had taught her when they'd had time. None of them were of any use to her with a gun against her back.

'Smile. People are staring.'

She forced a smile on her lips, her eyes darting to the left and right as they neared the alleyway.

What's going to happen to me?

The man stopped, pulling her to a halt at the entranceway, then shoved her forward and kept pushing until they'd passed a large industrial waste bin.

She bit her tongue as he let go of her elbow and then jerked her forward until she was facing the wall.

'Hands against the wall.'

She stretched until her fingers touched the brickwork of the building in front of her and closed her eyes. She gagged as her assailant's hand began to search her clothing, his fingers lingering too long over her breasts.

'I'm not carrying a gun,' she said, her voice shaking.

'You're a journalist. I'm more concerned with a wiretap,' the man said and then straightened. 'Lower your hands. Move towards the wall until I tell you to stop.'

Sarah followed his instructions. 'Now what?'

'Now you're going to listen,' said the man, his mouth close to her ear.

***

Dan handed over a couple of twenty pound notes and waited for his change, before he slid onto one of the stools next to the counter and turned his attention to the European football match being played on the television above the kitchen door.

His phone began to vibrate in his jeans pocket, and he fished it out, smiling as he recognised the number.

'I've just ordered the food. I'll be there in twenty minutes.'

'Dan?'

He frowned. Sarah's voice was shaking, panicked.

'What's wrong?' He turned away from the television, his heartbeat increasing.

'I-I was really stupid,' said Sarah. 'I was going crazy cooped up here, so I thought I'd go and get some groceries for the weekend.'

Dan stood, already heading towards the door. 'What happened?'

'There was a man – he grabbed me when I was crossing the road. I think he had a gun.'

'Sir – sir! You forgot your food!'

Dan shook his head and waved his hand at the Chinese owner, before launching himself out the front door of the restaurant towards his car. He checked over his shoulder when he reached the vehicle but saw no-one watching him. 'Where are you now?'

'At home.'

'Door locked?' He aimed his key fob at the car and leapt in as soon as the indicator lights blinked.

'Yes.'

'Buzz me in when I get to the apartment,' he said. 'Then I'll knock five times when I get to your front door.'

'Okay.'

He hung up, turned the key in the ignition, and tossed the phone into the coffee cup holder next to the handbrake. Sliding his seatbelt across his chest, he swung out of the parking space in front of the takeaway shop and accelerated into the traffic.

'Shit.' He drew up at the first red light and tapped his hands on the steering wheel as traffic crossed the intersection in front of him. 'Come on,' he urged, and then as the lights turned green, he shifted up the gears as he sped towards the apartment.

He drove a zig-zag course through back streets, the tyres squealing in protest as he cut corners and broke the speed limit in several places, grateful the route took him in the opposite direction to the commuters streaming out of the city towards their homes in the suburbs and beyond.

As he approached the apartment, he slowed and drove past the building, his gaze roaming the vehicles parked on each side of the street.

The sun was now well below the horizon, and the street lamps had begun to pop to life along the road, their orange glow pooling over the pavements and facades of the buildings that cloaked the road. Subdued light shone through windows, muted by blinds and curtains as families and flatmates settled in for the evening.

The mysterious sedan and its occupants were nowhere to be seen.

Satisfied, Dan completed a circuit of the block and then parked in a space a few metres down the road, grabbed his mobile phone, and jogged back to the apartment block.

The entranceway comprised two double doors, only accessible with a resident's key code or by pressing a doorbell next to the apartment number.

Dan stabbed the button for Sarah's apartment and didn't wait for her to speak when the connection was made.

'It's me.'

A loud *buzz* emanated from the lock, and Dan pushed open the door, closed it, and then tore across the wide hallway and up the winding staircase two steps at a time, his long legs closing the distance towards Sarah's apartment in under thirty seconds. He wiped sweat from his brow as he jogged towards her apartment and then knocked five times.

Sarah ripped open the door before his knuckles had left its surface, her face pale.

He pushed her back, slammed the door, and hugged her hard.

When their breathing had calmed, he ran his hands down her arms.

'Pack whatever you can into a small suitcase,' he said. 'We're leaving. Now.'

Chapter 20

Hugh Porchester exhaled as his driver turned into the familiar tree-lined cul-de-sac and eased the car to a standstill under a streetlight outside a modern four-bedroom house.

He preferred the trappings of his parents' home in Gloucestershire, but he had to keep up appearances of a different sort when working his way up through the government ranks. It wouldn't do well to alienate himself from the very people he sought to serve. And prestige meant the occasional sacrifice.

'You've got your next meeting in an hour, sir,' said the driver. 'I'll leave the engine running, shall I?'

'No,' said Porchester. 'Don't, Josh. You'll only get the snide bitch at number fifteen moaning about noise pollution again.'

The driver chuckled and killed the engine. 'Right you are, sir.'

He stepped from the car, walked round to Porchester's door, and opened it, his back to him.

As the politician stepped out, he noticed how Josh kept his eyes on the surrounding properties, his head turning as he conducted constant surveillance. He automatically followed the man's gaze.

'Anything?'

'No. All good.'

'Come on then.'

Porchester led the way from the tree-lined pavement through a small gate, past carefully manicured flowerbeds, and up to the front door. He punched in a six-digit security code and pushed it open.

'I'm home,' he called.

The house remained silent in answer, despite lights coming from the kitchen and living room.

Porchester checked his watch and then cursed.

'Everything all right, sir?'

'It's Emily's ballet. Her class is putting on a show tonight. I forgot. I was meant to be there.'

'Flowers, sir.'

'Eh?' Porchester turned and frowned.

'Buy your wife some flowers, sir.' Josh's mouth quirked. 'They've gotten me out of the shit on a number of occasions. Sir.'

Porchester smiled. 'Good thinking.' He shut the door and made sure the locking mechanism clicked into place. 'Right, I'm going to freshen up. Back in a minute.'

He left Josh standing in the hallway and climbed the stairs to the master bedroom.

Dan Taylor's investigation into the stolen isotope worried him. No doubt there were some long days and nights ahead until the thieves could be located and apprehended, all without alerting the general public to the fact that there was a very real danger someone in the country was intent on building a dirty bomb with the stuff.

He groaned as he removed his jacket and tie. Lily would kill him. She was already having trouble adjusting to the increased workload.

What with some of the extracurricular activities he'd been involved in of late, there'd be no telling what would be left of his marriage if his current situation didn't change – and soon.

He stripped down to his boxers, threw the bundle of clothes into the laundry basket, and flipped the taps in the en suite shower. While he waited for the water to warm up, he selected fresh trousers, matching jacket, pale shirt, and a tie in the Party's colours and laid them out on the bed. For good measure, he added an extra shirt and a more sombre-coloured tie.

Just in case things didn't go to plan.

He shook his head to clear the thought, unclasped his watch and placed it next to the washbasin, and then climbed out of his boxer shorts and stepped into the shower.

Porchester closed his eyes as the jets of water pummelled his aching shoulders. He was tense, something that seemed a permanent problem of late. He'd woken up almost hourly in the night for the past three months, and the strain was beginning to have a lasting effect on his body.

He opened his eyes and reached out for the shaving foam and razor, rubbed the steam off the wall-mounted mirror and began to methodically scrape at the stubble on his face.

Somehow he'd make it up to Lily.

When she found out what he'd really been up to, what he'd been trying to achieve all this time, she'd forgive him for neglecting her and their daughter so much.

He hoped.

He rinsed the last of the soap from his body, switched off the taps, and stepped out from the shower, grabbing one of the fresh towels that hung from a rail set into the tiled wall next to him.

He wrapped the towel around his waist and padded back to the bedroom. Once dressed, he grabbed the spare shirt and tie and hurried back downstairs.

Josh held out his hand to take the clothing from him.

'Thanks,' said Porchester and turned towards the kitchen.

The driver was right; he'd ask his secretary to order a bouquet of flowers for Lily, maybe a teddy bear for Emily, too. In the meantime, he'd leave a note to let her know he'd be out of touch for a while, dealing with a crisis.

He glanced across at the refrigerator door as he made his way across the room to the kitchen bench; Emily's drawings covered its surface, and he wondered how he'd missed the fact that her artistic skills had improved dramatically over the past six months. Then he frowned, as he realised the most recent two only depicted Lily, not him.

He exhaled and, turning his head, reached out for the notepad and pen that lay on the kitchen bench.

His hand froze in mid-air.

Lily's usually neat handwriting covered the open page, except it was a scrawl, the message written hurriedly and to the point.

Porchester read it twice, his heart beating painfully.

His throat dry, he checked over his shoulder.

Josh was still in the hallway out of sight, whistling under his breath.

Porchester ripped the page from the notebook, folded it into a small square, and put it in the pocket of his trousers and then grabbed the notebook and threw it into the rubbish bin, making sure the lid closed properly.

He took a deep breath, smoothed back his damp hair, and walked back towards the front door.

'Ready, sir?'

Porchester nodded. 'Let's go,' he said. 'I've got a busy schedule.'

Chapter 21

Sarah dropped her suitcase at the door and stood, open-mouthed, as the lights flickered on.

'How long have you known about this place?' she managed.

'A while,' Dan replied. 'It's an old safe house David organised for me and Mitch.'

'Does anyone else know about it?'

'No,' he said. 'Just them, and now you.'

He bent down, picked up her suitcase, and moved it to the foot of the stairs alongside his kit bag. 'We'll sort those out later. Let's set ourselves up downstairs first.'

He led the way through the hallway and into a large kitchen that took up the whole back of the house.

To the left, the kitchen opened into a formal dining room, its window facing the street outside. A window along the back wall of the kitchen allowed a view of the back yard, its perimeter protected by a high stone wall.

Dan leaned over and pulled the blinds shut, checked the locks on the back door were secure, and then walked past the kitchen bench and gas hob towards another door set into the wall. He glanced over his shoulder.

'Remember you've signed the Official Secrets Act, okay?'

Sarah nodded, her eyes wide.

He winked, pulled open the door, and punched a password into a security panel set into the steel surface of a second door.

The soft *click* of the mechanism filled the space, and Dan pushed the door open, reaching round the frame until he found a cord, and pulled it.

Lights flickered to life, illuminating a staircase that disappeared under the house.

Sarah peered round his shoulder. 'What's down there?'

'Come on,' he said. 'I'll show you.'

The air cooled as they descended, all the heat from the day trapped above ground due to the bunker-like qualities of the basement.

It was why the house had been chosen in the first place. Rather than for its grand layout upstairs, the basement offered the team a secure bunker for their activities – especially when they had to operate outside of the auspices of formal orders to get the job done.

Once at the foot of the stairs, Sarah walked towards a set of thin silver-coloured drawers set into the wall and ran her hand over the surface.

She jumped back as one slid open under her touch and then moved closer and peered inside.

Dan joined her, removed one of the guns from its cushioned housing, and then swept his hand over another drawer and picked out two full clips of ammunition.

He tucked the gun into his waistband, his eyes meeting Sarah's.

'I can't do this without a weapon,' he said.

'Where's yours?'

'They won't let me carry until I pass a psych evaluation next week.'

Sarah frowned. 'Psych evaluation?'

'More bullshit. Don't worry about it.'

Dan moved round the room, switching on computers as a series of screens flickered to life, displaying eight different views of the street outside.

'You've got your own CCTV network?' Sarah moved closer to the screens, her arms across her chest as her gaze followed a taxi from the end of the street to a house beyond Dan's.

He turned to her and grinned. 'When we started, we had the basics. This is something I've been adding to each time I've been back,' he explained. 'For emergencies.'

'Does David know about this?'

'Sort of. Like I said, I wanted this for emergencies,' he said. 'Everyone needs a back-up plan, right?'

Sarah peered around his shoulder as he keyed through the commands.

'How the hell did you get this set up?' she demanded. 'There must be thousands of pounds worth of equipment here.'

'Someone in the IT industry owed me a favour,' he said. He finished checking a screen that displayed a list of licence plates and facial recognition triggers, running his finger down the list of names. 'Okay, well nothing to report, so we haven't been followed.' He sighed, almost letting the tension ease from his body but not yet able to relax. 'Not much else we can do tonight.'

'Right,' said Sarah and ran a hand through her hair. She pointed up the stairs. 'Let's have a drink and eat.'

***

Dan flicked through the pages of research Sarah had brought from her apartment and twisted his fork into the plate of spaghetti in front of him.

They'd debated using the dining room before dismissing the large area as too formal. Instead, they sat companionably at the kitchen bench, perched on stools either side, a bottle of wine between them.

Sarah leaned forward and topped up their glasses. 'Are you any closer to finding out who betrayed you?'

Dan put his fork down and sipped the red before speaking. 'Mel made some low-key enquiries through some formal channels to see if anything came up, but the place is silent.' He sighed. 'I can't push her harder than that, or whoever set me up will know I'm onto them before I've had a chance to work out what's going on – and why.'

'What's the next step?'

'It's kind of hard to think about that, what with this stolen isotope to find,' he said. 'But Mel reckons she'll run some checks through other channels.' He rolled his eyes.

'God knows what that means, given her background. We'll all probably end up in prison.'

'I can't understand why someone would do this to you.' Sarah sat back and pulled her wine glass towards her, staring at the dark liquid as she swirled it around. 'Like you said, all the people you've dealt with are either behind bars or—'

'Dead. I know.'

***

Dan hissed through his teeth as Sarah applied an antiseptic lotion to the stitches that laced across his shoulders and tried not to swear.

'Stay still,' she murmured. 'Nearly done.'

'Sorry.'

'It's okay. You make me nervous when you do that.'

'You make *me* nervous when you do that.' Dan clenched his teeth.

She chuckled under her breath, but there was little humour in her voice.

He knew his scars scared her – they represented a past he fought to put behind him and a future that, at best, seemed uncertain.

After a few years apart, they'd slowly drifted towards each other again, but neither of them was prepared to commit to anything more serious than the occasional dinner or overnight stay – if Dan was honest, it scared him that people could harm Sarah or use her to get to him. And he knew Sarah was scared she'd lose him because of his work. It was why they tried their best to keep their on-again, off-again relationship low-key.

The fact that someone had found out he'd gone to Sarah's apartment after returning from Eastern Europe and had then accosted her in broad daylight only a short distance from her home had rattled him.

Much more than he was willing to admit to her.

Somehow, he had to work out who was trying to kill him – and why.

'Done.'

Her voice broke through his thoughts, and he looked over his shoulder at her as she tidied away the bottle of antiseptic and dirty dressings.

He slipped under the cool cotton sheets as she padded into the en suite bathroom and dropped the dressings in a small waste bin under the basin, and propped himself up on the pillows, wincing as one of the dressings caught on the material.

By the time Sarah joined him, he'd done his best to hide his discomfort – he'd suffered worse, in the past, and he reminded himself he was at least at home, not in the guts of a far-flung prison knowing he'd been betrayed, believing he'd been forgotten.

She sighed as her cheek touched the pillow beside his, as if all the tension was leaving her body, for a while.

'What's happening, Dan? Why are these people trying to kill you?'

Dan lifted his arm so she could snuggle up next to him, her breath caressing his chest. 'I don't know. I've been thinking about the jobs I've done over the past few years, and I can't think of anyone that could get this close to me.'

'Is there anything I can do?'

'Stay out of trouble,' he said.

In reply, she smiled up at him.

'I'm serious,' he said. 'No poking around asking questions, not until I've got a better idea of what's going on around here.'

'Okay.'

She stretched, her warm lips finding the skin of his neck before travelling slowly down his arm, and he closed his eyes, unable to stop the groan that escaped him.

'Why couldn't you have done that instead of using the antiseptic?'

Chapter 22

Ben wrenched the steering wheel, executing a sharp right hand turn before pulling the vehicle up to the kerb.

He squinted through the windscreen at the towering apartment blocks that boxed in the street, the concrete fascia covered in grime and graffiti.

Here and there, a splash of colour broke up the grey monotony; laundry hung over lines beside front doors.

The arrangement had been to drive to the warehouse after switching vehicles, lie low for twenty-four hours, and then move onto a safe house that Joe had organised.

The drive had taken a little over three hours. Joe had spent half the journey wondering who wanted the isotope – and why.

Ben was more pragmatic.

'Who cares, as long as we're getting paid?' he'd said. 'As soon as this is delivered, I'm off to the airport and out of this shit-hole.'

Joe had conceded the point. They were, as their safe deposit boxes could testify, being paid handsomely. In cash. More importantly, in used bank notes. Half before the job and the second half upon delivery.

The safe house, as Joe called it, was simply his mother's council flat. She'd been taken into a nursing home six months ago and never returned. The paperwork backlog at the council was so large, the tiny apartment hadn't yet been transferred out of her name and back onto the 'available' list after her funeral eight weeks ago. Joe reasoned that as long as he had a key, it was theirs to use.

It made sense.

Ben glared at a small group of kids that passed the car; they took the hint and ran off, shouting abuse towards the vehicle as they scattered.

He glanced down at a nudge from Joe.

'Here. Take the key. I need to dump the car.'

'Which one is it?' He peered through the window at the dimly lit entrance to the nearest block of flats.

'Second block back. Third floor. Take the stairs on the left side of the building.'

'Shortcut?'

'Less chance of stepping on a needle,' Joe scowled. 'Fuckin' junkies have taken over the other stairwell.'

'Jesus.' Ben opened the door and stepped out onto the pavement, slipping the key into the pocket of his jeans, before wrenching open the back door of the vehicle and sliding the silver case towards him. He looked over his shoulder and swore.

Two blocks back. Third floor up. Carrying a lead and concrete-lined box. On his own.

Joe chuckled. 'You need the exercise. Get moving. I'll be there within the hour.'

Ben braced himself to take the weight and then lifted the case out of the car and placed it on the kerb at his feet. He bent down and glared at Joe.

'You'd better be right about this.'

He slammed the door shut on the burst of laughter from the front seat and then stepped back as the vehicle pulled away from the kerb.

Joe steered the car in a tight arc and then accelerated back to the road junction and drove away.

Ben cursed and then bent down to pick up the case, hefted its weight between his arms, and walked towards the stairwell.

A concrete path curled round what had once been a grassy area laid out for the residents of the housing estate.

Ben's lip curled up in disgust at the smell of dog shit as he passed, and he noted the discarded beer bottles and cigarette packets strewn over the dirt.

At the far end, some kids had built a small wooden ramp, no doubt to act as a jump for their bicycles, and he wondered what sort of childhood they faced.

He shook his head to clear the thought and shifted the weight of the metal case between his hands as he approached the enclosed staircase.

A wave of nausea made him stumble before he'd had a chance to start climbing the stairs, the sensation so sudden it caught him off guard.

He bent down, put the case on the second step, and remained leaning over, his hands on his knees.

His eyes watered, and he wiped the back of his sleeve across his mouth, saliva forming at the back of his throat.

The moment passed, and he eased himself upright.

Automatically, his thoughts turned to the greasy takeaway meal he and Joe had consumed only a few hours ago and cursed the fast food establishment they'd bought it from.

He exhaled, lifted the case once more, and began climbing the stairs, hoping he reached the apartment – more importantly, the toilet – before his stomach decided to have another go.

His nose wrinkled as he reached the first landing, the stench of urine and someone else's vomit assaulting his already frayed senses.

He held his breath, promising himself that next time he'd put himself in charge of finding a safe house.

One that didn't resemble a war zone, for a start.

By the time he reached the third floor, the nausea had returned; sweat was streaming down his face, and his heart was hammering. He took great heaving lungfuls of air as he staggered along the passageway and then swerved away from a door as a dog threw itself against the other side, barking before being yelled at by its owner. A faint whimper was followed by a muttered curse, and then the noise was drowned out by a television in the next apartment he passed.

Finally, he saw the apartment he'd been directed to, a brass number six screwed to its surface, the paintwork peeling under a tag that had already been graffitied across it in the owner's absence.

Ben lowered the case to the tiled floor of the corridor, pulled out the key from his pocket, and unlocked the door.

He pushed it open and then, realising an automatic closer had been fitted, positioned himself until he could wedge his foot against it and bent down to retrieve the case.

The next bout of nausea was so vicious, he nearly dropped the case.

He almost cried out in hurt and surprise at the spasm that wracked his abdomen before instinct kicked in and he bit his lower lip, drawing blood.

Sick or not, he didn't need a nosey neighbour opening their door to find out what the noise was coming from their dead neighbour's apartment.

He staggered over the threshold, waited a moment to ensure the door closed under its own momentum, and then hurried through the shabby home before dumping the case on the kitchen bench.

He spun on his heel, opened a door that led to the old woman's bedroom, cursed, and tried another door.

He groaned with relief, pulled the cord to the left of the door frame, and stared in shock at the sight of his own pale face in the bathroom mirror.

Then another spasm gripped him, and it was all he could do to launch himself at the toilet bowl and sink to his knees.

He wasn't sure how long he stayed there, the motion in his abdomen subsiding in gradual waves until he felt able to stand.

He leaned against the wall while he tore strips of toilet paper from the roller next to him and then cleaned himself up and flushed.

He shuffled across to the small sink, careful to avoid looking at his reflection, and ran his hands under the cold tap, splashing his face and cupping the cool liquid to his lips to wash the acidic taste from his mouth.

Cursing Joe's penchant for crap food, he walked back through to the kitchen and searched the cupboards until he found a glass. He filled it with water from the tap, silently grateful for Joe's foresight not to alert the Council to his mother's death.

He sipped at the liquid, careful not to gulp it, and then set the glass down on the bench and turned his attention to the case.

He checked his watch. By his reckoning, it'd be another thirty minutes before Joe showed up, and curiosity was eating at him.

He shrugged. 'Might as well,' he murmured and flicked the combination lock until the correct numbers were displayed.

He paused before raising the lid and then chuckled as he realised he'd been holding his breath.

'Let's see what half a million quid's worth of isotope looks like,' he murmured and lifted the lid.

Afterwards, he couldn't remember how long he'd stared at the contents while his brain tried to comprehend what he was seeing.

When he did finally snap out of his thoughts, he dropped the lid back into place and backed away from the kitchen bench, a sudden urge to piss catching him off-guard.

Part of his mind was screaming at him to get help, the other part chastising him for even thinking of phoning the emergency services.

How the hell had it happened?

They'd been so careful, making sure the box had been secure in the vehicles, never jolting it the few times they'd had to pick it up.

His head snapped to the side at the sound of a key turning in the front door, and then it opened, the automatic closer hissing until Joe pushed the door shut.

Ben heard him lock it, the rattle of the security chain jangling his nerves, and then the smell of fish and chips wafted into the room seconds before Joe appeared.

'Dinner,' he beamed and then frowned. 'Mate, you look like shit.'

Ben pointed at the case. 'One of the vials is broken.'

'What do you mean, it's broken?'

'We've got a fucking radiation leak.'

Chapter 23

Hugh Porchester took a deep breath and turned his attention to the four people who sat around the conference table.

Above their heads, the Prime Minister's gaze frowned down upon them, his normal healthy pallor bleached by the video-conferencing camera's harsh light.

'Could everyone leave the room, please?' said Porchester. 'I'd like to talk to the Prime Minister in private.'

He ignored the raised eyebrows and muttered responses, placed his palms on the table, and waited while his colleagues filed out of the room.

His eyes found a speck of dust suspended in the air, and he watched fascinated as it spun in the glow from the projector above his head.

He fought down the panic that was threatening to surface, knowing he had to remain calm if he was going to make this work.

He had to be convincing.

He clenched his jaw as the door was closed behind the last person to leave the room and then lowered his eyes to meet the camera under the video-conferencing screen.

'What's going on, Hugh?' demanded the Prime Minister.

'There's been a problem with the project,' said Porchester. 'And I don't think you'd have appreciated my drawing it to the attention of our colleagues.'

'What sort of problem?'

Porchester sighed, threw his pen onto the table, and leaned back in his chair. 'The radioactive isotope that the drilling crews use to test the boreholes has been stolen.'

'What?' The Prime Minister jumped forward in his chair, his eyes wide. 'When did this happen?'

'Three days ago. The drilling crew were shot,' said Porchester. He held up his hand to stop the leader of the country from interrupting. 'I didn't want to tell you until I had more facts.'

'Are the police involved?'

'Yes, of course – it's a murder investigation,' said Porchester. 'But more significantly, it appears that a case of radioactive isotope used in the geological testing process at the drill rig has been stolen,' he added. 'As it was, no-one realised the significance of the attack until Dan Taylor stumbled across it by accident.'

'Taylor? They found him then?'

'Yes. A covert team was used.' Porchester glared at the Prime Minister. 'I would have appreciated being briefed on the matter prior to his rescue.'

The PM waved a dismissive hand. 'There wasn't time,' he said. 'What's the latest on the isotope? Have you managed to contain news of the theft from the press?'

'So far.' Porchester nodded. 'And that's the way we want to keep it. If word gets out that we've managed to lose a consignment of radioactive material before we've even begun the fracking programme, the public are going to crucify us.'

'Quite.'

'Not only that, Prime Minister, but I've been going over the financial projections for this work, and I must again warn you that the costs of fracking for shale commodities far outweigh the benefits while OPEC continue to over-supply on oil.'

The Prime Minister sighed. 'The oil price will sky-rocket again, Hugh, I can promise you that. As soon as the Saudis and their cronies have proven their point to the United States and ensured any shale gas projects in North America are declared non-viable, we'll be back to square one.'

'Which brings me on to the other matter I wanted to talk to you about,' said Porchester. 'Think of it as a back-up plan, if you like.'

The Prime Minister's eyebrows knitted together as he listened.

Porchester ploughed on, despite the other man's increasing look of incredulity as he spoke.

'So, you see,' he ended, ignoring the sweat he could feel trickling between his shoulders, 'if we can introduce this into the discussions with the other member States, we place ourselves in a very strong position with voters.'

The Prime Minister blinked. 'Exactly *how* did you manage to come to that conclusion?'

'Well, looking at the results from the last election and opinion polls carried out over the past two months, much of your ongoing support comes from the older generation,' said Porchester. He cleared his throat. 'Much less from, say, the eighteen to twenty-five-year-old age group.' He glanced up from his notes. 'So, the people faced with increased fuel bills leading up to and into their retirement would probably support such a notion.'

'Probably?'

'Yes.'

'Hugh?'

'Sir?'

'I think it's probably best you leave the discussions to me and my delegates, don't you?'

'Sir?'

The Prime Minister shook his head. 'I take your point about cheaper fuel, Hugh, but what you're suggesting is preposterous. I'll be a laughing stock in The Hague.'

'But—'

'No, Hugh. That's my final word on the matter, understood?'

Porchester sighed. 'Understood.'

'Good. Now, for Christ's sake – find that isotope before the press get wind of it.'

The Prime Minister leaned forward, pressed a button on the keyboard in front of him, and the screen went black.

Porchester copied the motion, ensuring the camera in front of him was switched off, and then leaned back in his chair and wiped at his forehead with a shaking hand.

'Shit.'

Chapter 24

Alan Wright licked his lips, slowly opened his eyes, and groaned.

He turned his head, fighting the nausea that immediately welled in his stomach, and then rolled to his side and lifted his head.

It was later than he'd imagined; the sparse street lighting outside cast shadows against the opposite building.

He swallowed, his throat parched, and reached out for the water bottle he'd left next to his makeshift pillow.

Empty.

He cursed and then eased up into a sitting position. He checked over his shoulder, and his heart lurched.

More hair covered the old jacket he'd been lying on.

Alan sniffed the air; he stank and hated himself for it. Once, he'd been a proud man. That was before his gambling had destroyed his life, his wife walked out, their young daughter in tow, and the bank took their home.

A convulsion shook him, taking him by surprise, and he cried out at its viciousness. Pain shot through his abdomen and crawled up his spine.

No more excuses, he thought. *Hospital. Now.*

The thought of dying, alone, in the abandoned warehouse was enough to make him stagger to his feet, grabbing onto a steel supporting pillar while the wave of dizziness threatened to knock him to the ground.

He reached into the top pocket of his threadbare cotton shirt, his fingers brushing against the welfare identification card that he'd retrieved from behind a broken brick in the warehouse wall the previous night. He didn't usually carry it around with him, its significance to a would-be thief too evident. It was his last tentative thread to the real world, and he wanted it with him when he got to the hospital. It was the only way they'd be able to contact his wife. If he lost the identification card, they'd never connect the dots in time.

He desperately wanted to see her, to apologise, if he got the chance.

He coughed, a wracking spasm that made him double over in pain. While he caught his breath, he cast his eyes around the mezzanine level, looking for something to lean on. There was no way he'd be able to walk to the hospital unaided.

His gaze fell to a piece of timber that had been discarded alongside one wall, and he shuffled towards it, fighting the urge to return to his bed and curl up.

I don't want to die like this.

And he was dying; he had no doubt of that.

He'd ruled out food poisoning several hours ago. Whatever the two men had taken from the vehicle yesterday had made him sick; he was sure of it.

If it was something that had been in the building that was causing his symptoms, word would have gotten out onto the street. The homeless looked out for each other like that, and the warehouse would've been avoided.

No, those two men were hiding something.

He groaned as he leaned down, his fingers brushing the surface of the timber. As his grip tightened, another bout of nausea consumed him, and he turned his head to one side just in time.

Panting, he wiped his mouth with the back of his sleeve, before forcing himself upright. He turned and began to stagger towards the steel staircase that led down to the warehouse level, his pace slowing as he reached the top step.

What if I break my neck?

A manic gasp of laughter escaped his lips as he realised a broken neck was the least of his worries.

He made his way down the staircase, one tread at a time. By the time he reached the warehouse level, sweat was pooling at his collar, bubbling at his forehead.

He paused to get his breath back, his lungs clawing for oxygen in the stale air. He leaned on the piece of timber, squared his shoulders, and shuffled towards a metal panel behind the staircase.

It was how he'd first entered the building. The doors had been chained and bolted by the owners, or whomever the two men had obtained their garage door key from, but he'd noticed a panel bent backwards on one of his regular walks through the estate. Taking advantage, he had peeled it back, crawled through the gap, and found his new temporary home.

Now, he pushed the panel away and threw the piece of timber onto the pockmarked asphalt beyond before getting down on his hands and knees.

He was through the gap and outside the warehouse, cowering under the halo of a streetlight, before he realised he was crying.

***

Heather Stevens shoved her hands into the pockets of her denim jacket and scowled, kicking her heel against the kerb.

It was bad enough that her salary was so crap she had to rely on public transport; it was even more annoying when the bus was running late, and she had to be home within the hour before the babysitter's fees doubled.

She shrugged her handbag farther up her shoulder and sighed.

Sometimes, she wondered if walking out on her husband had been the right thing to do, but then she recalled the years of abuse and reminded herself she wanted a better future for her daughter.

She shifted from foot to foot, trying to keep warm in the cool night air, before she became aware of movement off to her right.

A man shuffled towards her, his gait unsteady. His hair appeared to stick out on end in great tufts, and his clothes resembled the rags she kept in a box under the kitchen sink at home for when she was doing housework.

She swallowed, her heartbeat going up a notch as she gripped the strap of her bag, and then glanced back the other way.

Traffic rumbled past in each direction, but it was a busy road, and none of the drivers would be able to see if she was in trouble.

A group of people were walking slowly in her direction, but they were still several metres away, laughing and joking.

A sudden longing to be out with her friends, having a good meal and a giggle on the way home crossed her mind, before she turned her attention back to the homeless man.

In time to see him collapse onto the pavement.

Heather ran towards him before she'd even had time to question her own sanity in approaching a complete stranger who could be drunk or, worse, under the effects of drugs.

Instead, as she neared him, she dropped her bag to the ground and pulled out her mobile phone, dialling the emergency services as she felt under the man's collar.

His pulse was weak, faint – but there.

She punched the button for the loudspeaker, placed the phone on the pavement next to her knees, and rolled the man over into the recovery position.

She wasted no time when the operator answered.

'My name's Heather Stevens. I'm a cleaner at East City Hospital,' she said, retrieving the phone and putting it to her ear. 'I'm on the junction of Belvedere and Grange. I've got a man here with me who needs an ambulance – now.'

She rattled off the few details, her basic first aid training locking in as she swept her gaze over the man's still form, ignoring the questions of passers-by that now stopped and stared.

She glared at them over her shoulder.

'Will you give him some room?' she snapped. 'Unless one of you is a doctor, get out of the way – you'll block the ambulance's view, and they won't see him.'

The small crowd dispersed, evidently happy they wouldn't have to help.

'Sorry – crowd control,' she mumbled into the phone. 'How far away are they?'

She listened as the dispatcher informed her that an ambulance was leaving the hospital forecourt immediately and asked her to stay on the line until they reached her.

'Understood.'

She crouched closer to the man, listening as the dispatcher relayed her location to the ambulance crew, their siren now audible at the far end of the road.

'Who are you?' she murmured.

She leaned forward, wrinkled her nose, and methodically searched the man's pockets.

He stank, and she wasn't sure if it was a permanent feature of his or one caused by his current ailment – whatever *that* was.

Finally, in a pocket that had been re-stitched to the front of his shirt, she found something.

Turning it over between her fingers, she read the front of the card.

'Alan Wright, eh?' she said. 'You poor bastard. What happened to you?'

She sat back on her heels, the emergency vehicle's flashing lights in her peripheral vision as it bore down towards them, scattering traffic and pedestrians in its way with an extra blast on the siren by the driver.

Tucking his identification back into the man's pocket, she frowned, and leaned forward once more, her interest piqued.

Blisters covered the man's hands, and as she pushed his sleeve up his arm, the raw pustules continued.

She snatched her hand away, the sudden thought that he might be contagious leaving her mouth dry.

The ambulance slid to a halt at the kerb next to her, and she looked up at the sound of running feet.

'They're here,' she said to the dispatcher and ended the call before standing up and facing the paramedic.

'We'll take it from here, thanks,' he said.

Heather stepped back as he and his colleague began slipping gloves over their hands, before pulling a stretcher over the pavement towards their patient.

'Listen,' she said, tugging the paramedic's sleeve. 'I think you need to be careful. There's something wrong with his skin.'

The man frowned. 'His skin?'

He stepped past her, crouched down next to the tramp, and gently lifted the sleeve away from his arm.

Heather saw him bite his lip, and then he placed the man's arm across his chest and straightened.

'Excuse me,' he said and pushed past her, climbing back into the vehicle and slamming the door shut.

Heather watched as the young paramedic spoke into his radio, his tone urgent.

His words were muffled through the closed door, but she caught his eye when he turned his gaze in her direction, a worried look on his face. He appeared to listen to instructions and then spoke once more and hung the radio in its cradle.

She stepped back as the door opened. 'What is it?' she demanded. 'What's going on?'

She frowned. He looked scared and paused as if unsure what to say to her.

'What's the matter?' she said.

'I'm sorry,' he said, 'but you're going to have to come with us, too.'

'Why?' Heather's fingers tightened around the strap of her handbag. 'I mean, I can't – I've got to go home. I've got to get back before the babysitter's fees go up,' she said and then bit her lip, realising how she must sound. 'Why?'

'Those are my orders,' said the paramedic. 'Look, I'm sorry – but they want us all to report for a check-up as soon as we get our patient to the hospital.'

Chapter 25

Malikov glanced up from the latest report and frowned at the shouting that began emanating from the living area of the house.

After a few minutes, it appeared that the argument hadn't subsided, so he threw his glasses onto the desk, pushed back his chair, and stalked towards the noise.

Two of the security men stood in the hallway, their jaws set, hands on weapons as they guarded the front door and tried not to show their interest in the raised voices.

'What the fuck is going on?' growled Malikov.

It was unusual for Krupin to lose his temper. If he did, he could be unpredictable, something Malikov couldn't risk. Not now.

'We're not sure,' replied one of the guards. 'It all started when Alexsei Krupin entered the room. The others were watching something on television, and then the shouting began.'

The two men stood aside to let him pass, and Malikov pushed the door open. He repeated his question.

'What the fuck is going on in here?'

Five faces turned to him. One didn't.

Krupin.

Instead, he continued to glare at the man in front of him, their noses almost touching. The other man's face was red with anger, veins sticking out at his forehead, and spittle on his chin.

'Alexsei? What is going on?'

In reply, Krupin held up a mobile phone. 'This idiot left his mobile phone upstairs,' he said, his voice little more than a whisper.

Malikov swallowed. 'Were any calls made from it?'

Krupin shook his head.

Malikov allowed a sigh of relief to escape his lips, and he finally pulled a handkerchief from his pocket and dabbed his forehead, before carefully folding the silk square and putting it away.

'I thought I made it clear when we began this operation that no mobile phones were to be left lying around? Were my instructions not clear enough?'

The four men standing nearest the walls of the living room nodded and tried without success to avoid his gaze.

Malikov glared at the fifth man, whose composure was slowly slipping away, his arrogance and anger turning to fear.

'I am sorry, Mr Malikov,' said the man. 'It won't happen again.'

'No,' said Malikov. 'You are right. It won't.'

He took Krupin's gun from him, and shot the man in the chest.

'I'll see you in my office,' said Malikov, handing the gun back to Krupin. 'Now.'

He made his way back to his room and helped himself to a large whiskey, took a sip, and placed the tumbler on his desk.

He rolled up his shirtsleeves and spun the laptop computer round as Krupin entered the room, closing the door behind him.

'We may need a change of plan,' said Malikov and pointed at the computer screen. 'I just received this.'

Krupin picked up the laptop and read the short message. He checked his watch.

'Nothing will happen tonight,' he said. 'There will be paperwork, too many people involved.'

'How could this have happened?'

Krupin shrugged. 'They were careless.'

Malikov fought down his frustration and clenched his fists. 'You assured me they were competent.'

'They are,' said Krupin. He placed the laptop back on the desk. 'I'm sure there is an explanation.'

Malikov held up his hand. 'It's too late for that. We sever all communication with them, now.'

'And achieve what?' demanded Krupin. He raised his eyes to the ceiling. 'We still have bargaining power.'

'And we'll use it,' said Malikov. 'But I need assurances that this won't come back to me.' He pointed at the message on the screen. 'And, at the moment, he's the only one that knows.'

Krupin pulled his mobile phone from his pocket. 'Let me make some calls,' he said. 'But, please, Vasili – be patient. It's not going to take long now.'

Malikov picked up his drink and glared at Krupin over the rim of the glass.

'Don't lecture me on patience, Alexsei,' he warned. 'I've been waiting twenty years for this.'

Chapter 26

Dan snorted, his vision blurred, and then he jerked his head upright, his mobile phone ringing in his ear from its perch on the bedside table.

He extracted his arm from under Sarah's slumbering body and rolled over, pressing the 'answer' button before it went to voicemail.

'Mel? What time is it?'

'Three a.m.'

'Do you ever sleep?'

'Evidently not while I'm working for you.'

'What's up?'

'About two hours ago, a homeless man was admitted to the East City Hospital with burns to his face and hands,' she said, her voice trembling. 'He was taken in for examination and was violently sick.'

A chill wormed its way down Dan's spine. 'Radiation poisoning?'

'Exactly. That's what the hospital has informed the police.'

Dan glanced over his shoulder as Sarah rolled over and sat up, the sheet held against her chest, her hair mussed up by sleep.

She frowned at him. *Who is it?* she mouthed.

'Hang on, Mel; I'm going to put you on speaker phone. Sarah's here,' he said. 'You can trust her. She's the one that found out about the attack at the project site in the first place.'

'Okay.'

'Any more detail?' Dan asked and placed the phone on top of the sheets before turning up the volume.

'The police spoke to the man as soon as the hospital let them. He says he'd been sleeping in a warehouse off Commercial Road. It's a regular haunt of his. Except this time, two men arrived with a large four-wheel drive vehicle yesterday.'

'The stolen one from the project site?'

'Yes. He had the sense to write down the licence plate.'

'What else?' Sarah leaned forward.

'The two men unloaded what the homeless man called a large silver-coloured box. Apparently a second vehicle – a car – had been left under a tarpaulin. The homeless man didn't see that get delivered; he goes out begging every morning, so it must've arrived then. The men left with the car late yesterday afternoon.'

'Licence plate?'

'No,' said Mel. 'He never got a chance to get near it before the two men left. But the homeless man gave the police a description of the car and the two men, and they're running it through the traffic camera system to see if they can track it.'

'Shit.' Dan pushed the sheets away and reached out for his boxer shorts. 'That isotope could be anywhere by now.'

'What happened to the homeless man?' asked Sarah. 'Surely he didn't get sick from watching at a distance?'

'The men left the four-wheel drive behind,' said Mel. 'It seems he got too nosey for his own good. He had a dig around in the vehicle to see if there was anything valuable in it. It sounds like he got contaminated then.'

'Where's the homeless guy now?' asked Dan as he hopped on one foot, trying to put his jeans on as fast as he could. 'Can we talk to him?'

There was a pause at the end of the line before Mel answered.

'Sorry, boss. He died twenty minutes ago,' she said. 'But you might want to call Dr Michael Draper.'

'He was treating the homeless guy?'

'No,' said Mel. 'He's the leader of the radioactive hazard team who are on their way to the warehouse.'

Chapter 27

Dan wrapped his hands around the polystyrene takeout cup and blew across the surface of the coffee.

Across the street, a tape fluttered in the breeze between two posts, its surface depicting the three-pronged international symbol for radiation.

At each end of the industrial estate, far away from the warehouse, police vehicles blocked access to the public and media. Road closure signs diverted all traffic away from the area. A press conference had been held half an hour ago at the nearby town hall, the spokesperson taking no questions and citing the UK's expansive anti-terrorism campaign as the reason for the closure.

The press hung around anyway, hopeful for a last-minute scoop, while the workers turned their cars round and headed for home, grateful for the free day off and for the fact they hadn't been caught up in whatever was going on.

Dan watched as the first of the HAZMAT team members emerged from the building.

The man's shoulders were slumped; it had been an early start for all of them and not one that they'd welcomed.

179

Any threat of a radiation leak was cause for concern, especially when it occurred in a location where the public had been exposed.

His movements were precise, clinical, as he walked towards the staging area and then entered a specialist wash unit, its blue plastic walls a stark contrast against the greyness of the buildings that towered over it.

The rest of the small team of experts began to emerge from the warehouse and waited patiently next to the shower for their turn, their colleagues keeping a respectful distance. One by one, they trooped through the process, discarded overalls being pushed into sealed containers, ready for incineration.

The lead scientist emerged from the last plastic cubicle, now dressed in jeans and a polo shirt emblazoned with the government agency's logo. He glanced up, raised a hand at Dan, and began to walk towards him.

Dan dropped his coffee cup into a plastic bag and deposited it in a biohazard bin before calling out to the scientist.

'You're not hot, are you?' he asked, a frown creasing his forehead, the temptation to back away stronger than he'd like to have admitted.

The scientist chuckled. 'No. Not now. I'd hate to think what those shower chemicals are doing to my immune system, but given the alternative…' He ran a hand through wet hair. 'Are you the chap from the government?'

'Sort of. Dan Taylor.'

'Mike Draper.'

They shook hands and then turned to watch the rest of the team file through the shower system.

'Did you find anything?'

'Significant traces of radioactive activity in the four-wheel drive vehicle,' said Mike. 'Certainly more than I'd expect if the vials were intact. You were right – you've definitely got a leak on your hands.'

'Jesus.' Dan squinted down the road, looking at the graffiti that adorned other abandoned warehouses, his mind turning to the homeless man that had died. 'Thank god no kids found it first.'

'I know.'

'What do you think happened here?' Dan jutted his chin towards the warehouse.

'My best guess is that they have no idea the vials are leaking,' said the scientist. 'I think they're simply following their pre-arranged plan. Lie low here, knowing the second vehicle is already hidden, and then wait a day and move on.'

'And wherever they're hiding, if there are other people around, they're going to get sick, too, aren't they?'

Draper nodded. 'Absolutely.'

'Shit.' Dan watched as, one by one, the team of scientists emerged from the showers, freshly dressed in more casual wear. 'What do you do now?'

'We'll keep the area closed off. It's going to take a while to get the place decontaminated,' explained Mike. 'And by that, I mean months, not days or weeks.' He cleared his throat. 'Look, it's not my place to enquire too closely about what people like you do for the government, but you have to understand – the people that have those other vials? They're going to start getting sick and quickly.'

'How quickly?'

'The homeless man that reported this probably succumbed to the symptoms a lot faster as he wasn't that healthy to start off with.'

'What about a healthy person, say, someone like me?'

Draper shrugged. 'At best, they've got a day or two. After that, they're going to go downhill fast.'

Dan exhaled, his mind working overtime.

If the thieves had radiation poisoning, they were likely to start acting more erratic, perhaps bringing their plans forward in light of the fact they were going to die soon – or be under arrest as soon as they entered a hospital with symptoms.

And he was still no closer to finding out who they were or what those plans entailed.

'It does make you wonder whether they have any contingencies in place,' said Draper.

'What do you mean?'

The scientist shrugged. 'A "Plan B",' he said. 'You don't carry this stuff around with you and not have a back-up plan.'

Dan rubbed his chin. 'Between you and me, I don't think they're the ones that will use it,' he said. 'I'm getting the distinct impression they really are just thieves –

stealing things to order. Otherwise, they would've opened the case here and discovered the leak.'

'Well, I hope they got a good payout to leave in their wills.'

'So it's a suicide mission?'

'With the levels of isotope they've been exposed to?' said Draper. 'It is now.'

Chapter 28

'Dan? Dan!'

Dan's eyes shot open, his heart racing. His fingers immediately sought out the gun on the bedside table, the pale afternoon light filtering through the curtains and across the sheets where he'd kicked them off in his sleep.

As he realised where he was, and who was calling him, he relaxed, pushed the gun away and checked his watch.

Two in the afternoon.

The effect of the painkillers and the early morning start had played havoc with his body clock.

'Dan?' Sarah appeared in the doorway, her face anxious. 'You need to see this.'

Groggy from sleep and the painkillers Sarah had insisted he take when he'd returned from the warehouse, Dan climbed from the bed and pulled on his jeans. 'What's wrong?'

'Television. Now.'

Sarah disappeared from the door, and he heard her footsteps padding back down the stairs to the living area.

He tucked the gun into his waistband, grabbed his t-shirt, socks, and shoes from where he'd tossed them on the floor before collapsing with exhaustion only four hours before, and hurried after her. The faint aroma of coffee wafted up from the kitchen on the ground floor, and his stomach rumbled.

He ignored it, grabbed the bannister at the bottom of the stairs to slow his descent, and jogged across the landing and into the living area.

Sarah was standing in front of the large television, the remote in one hand while she tugged at a fingernail on the other with her teeth.

She pointed at the TV with the remote. 'Look.'

Dan joined her, read the headline that screamed across the foot of the screen, and felt his mouth drop open in shock.

Radioactive isotope stolen from top-secret government project site.

'Oh, shit,' he murmured. 'How the hell did that get out?' He turned to Sarah. 'Any of your contacts know who broke the story?'

She shook her head. 'I had the radio on in the kitchen,' she said. 'I was going to make some coffee before I woke you.' She jerked her head at the television. 'As soon as I heard, I made some phone calls. No-one knows who leaked the story. Apparently, Hugh Porchester's going to make an announcement within the next few minutes.'

Dan folded his arms and frowned at the screen.

On it, a row of television cameras and reporters were set up facing a backdrop with the logo of the government's latest initiative blazed across it. A small lectern and microphone stand had been placed in front of it.

'Where is this?'

'Milton Keynes,' said Sarah. 'Apparently Porchester was visiting businesses in the area, promoting the new government tax rebates for small businesses when this blew up. This is the local Party office.'

They fell silent as the news announcer's voice washed over them.

'And here is the Right Honourable Hugh Porchester,' said the woman. 'Let's hear what he has to say about this breaking story.'

The noise in the Party office lessened to a hum on the screen, broken only by the sound of cameras and reporters clearing their throats in readiness for the surge of questions that would be aimed at the PM's senior advisor.

Hugh Porchester walked to the lectern with a prepared speech in his hand, and cleared his throat.

'Thank you for being here at short notice,' he began and then found his cue and looked straight down the camera lens in front of him.

'The government has been made aware that a small amount of radioactive material has been stolen from a project site in the north of England,' he said, ignoring his notes. 'At this time, the emergency services and government departments are working together to locate the perpetrators of this crime and would ask that the public remain vigilant and report any suspicious activity immediately to the police.'

A reporter started to interrupt, but Porchester held up a hand to silence him. 'At present,' he continued, 'we have reason to believe that the suspects removed the material from the site in a secure container and are currently in hiding.'

He checked his notes and then cast his eyes round the room. 'We would ask that all media outlets use whatever means necessary to help us locate the stolen material. Use your contacts, your informants, and contact the police immediately if you believe you have information that can help them.'

'Can this be used to make a dirty bomb?' called out one of the reporters.

Porchester sighed. 'What we are *trying* to do,' he said, glaring at the journalist, 'is convey to the public that only a *small* amount of radioactive material has been stolen. The risk to public health is minimal.'

'He didn't answer the question,' Sarah murmured.

'What about the man who died in the hospital?' called out another journalist.

All the faces in the room turned to see who had asked the question and then back to Porchester, who appeared to gather his wits before answering.

'He didn't see that one coming,' said Dan.

'Late yesterday afternoon, a homeless man was rushed to hospital, where doctors confirmed he had been subjected to radiation, yes,' said Porchester. 'Police spoke with him to ascertain what his movements were, and an area of east London is currently under specialist investigation.'

There was a flurry of activity on the screen as reporters surged nearer to the lectern, peppering the politician with questions. He held up his hands to try to calm the onslaught.

'Ladies and gentlemen, if you please,' he said sternly. 'As you will appreciate, this is still an open investigation, one which the emergency services and government departments have been working closely together to resolve.'

'Where's the Prime Minister, Hugh?'

Dan watched as Porchester seemed to sway at the lectern and then shook his head slightly and cleared his throat.

'The Prime Minister is keeping a close eye on the situation, I believe,' he said. 'In the meantime, he is continuing with his commitments in Europe and meeting with the leaders of France and Germany over the coming days.'

Dan cocked an eyebrow at Sarah, but she shook her head and put her finger to her lips. He turned his attention back to the screen, where Porchester was wrapping up the press conference.

'That's all I've got time for,' he said. 'We'll keep you up to date as we find out more.'

Sarah muted the television as Porchester left the lectern and disappeared out of shot.

Dan already had his mobile phone out and punched in Mel's number.

She answered on the first ring. 'Boss.'

'How the hell did that story leak?'

'We're trying to find out the source,' Mel said. 'It was an anonymous call to the *Guardian*. Untraceable, of course, but I'm doing my best.'

'Good of them to give the government the heads up.'

'Serious situation,' said Mel. 'I think they realised they had a live one.'

'Anyone contacting the PM yet?'

Mel sighed. 'I don't think it's a case of us contacting him, boss. It's more like his office will tell us when he wants to meet with us. In the meantime, we've got orders to liaise with Porchester, same as usual.'

Dan tucked the phone between his ear and shoulder, perched on the edge of the sofa, and began to pull on his socks and boots. 'This changes everything,' he said. 'Whoever leaked the story just screwed up any deadline these suspects may have had. They'll panic. Act irrationally.'

'Do you think Porchester was right?' asked Mel. 'About a dirty bomb? It *is* only a small amount of isotope that's been stolen, right?'

'A dirty bomb doesn't have to be big, Mel,' said Dan, raising his gaze to meet Sarah's. 'It just has to be big enough. Even if it's a small explosion, with a low fallout radius, the panic it'll cause will cripple the country.' He ran a hand over his face, frustrated that he'd have to wait for Porchester to return from Buckinghamshire. Even with a police escort, it could take a couple of hours, and then he might have to wait until the man had been briefed by several agencies before he had time to talk. 'I'm coming in,' he said. 'We'll keep working the angles, see what we can do.'

He ended the call, stood, and tucked his phone back into his pocket before reaching out to Sarah.

'I need you to stay here. I've got to go.'

'I'll go with you.'

'No,' he said. 'I'm sorry, but you can't. Please,' he said and ran his fingers down her cheek. 'Do as you're told this time.'

'Where are you going?'

'I've got an idea,' he said. 'But if I'm wrong, I need to know you're safe, okay?' He swallowed. 'I don't know what I'd do if something happened to you.'

'Okay. I promise,' she sighed. 'What are you going to do?'

'I'm going to try to speak to the PM – if I can find him.' He turned towards the door. 'Someone around here has to know what the hell is going on.'

She followed him, her stockinged feet quiet on the tiled floor. 'Dan? What happens if there is a bomb?'

He stopped, his hand on the door latch.

'Hope that we find them before they get that far.'

Chapter 29

Malikov ground out the last of his cigarette into the stone tiles of the terrace beyond his office and turned his head slightly, blowing the smoke between his lips.

He watched as it curled into the air before the breeze caught it, the remnants of nicotine teasing his senses as it filtered away.

He caught movement at one of the windows on the top floor of the house; a curtain fell back into place, and a shadow moved out of sight.

He coughed, shoved his hands into his pockets, and began what he hoped appeared to be a leisurely gait towards the barbeque area.

Despite the pool being cleaned prior to his arrival, late summer leaves already floated on the water.

He wondered whether he would keep the house after his business was concluded.

He suspected not.

He preferred the sights and sounds of the capital, not the countryside, with its wide open spaces, rolling meadows, and prying eyes.

Despite what people thought, it was much easier to hide in the city; people ignored the activities of their neighbours. Here, the slightest change would be commented upon, analysed, and reported if the locals were in any way suspicious.

Malikov made a mental note to call his real estate agent as soon as his guests had departed.

It would soon be time to move on to new challenges.

He turned at the sound of the back door closing.

Krupin hurried towards him, and Malikov noticed the mobile phone clutched to his chest.

Krupin ignored the two armed bodyguards that kept a respectable distance from Malikov and waited until he stood next to him before he spoke, his voice an undertone.

'It's him,' he said.

'How is he?'

'He sounds scared,' said Krupin. He moved to hand over the phone to Malikov and then seemed to change his mind and pushed it closer to his chest. 'With respect, we need to be careful,' he said. 'If he panics, he may do something that will expose us, despite the guarantees we have in place.'

Malikov nodded and beckoned for the phone. He took it from Krupin's hand and then walked a few paces away, took a deep breath, and put the phone to his ear.

'You have been told not to call me unless there is an emergency.'

He listened to the caller, the man's words tumbling over each other.

'Slow down,' grumbled Malikov. 'Tell me, does anyone suspect you? Are you being followed?'

He waited and watched a flock of starlings arc over the woodland beyond the house. The air was beginning to cool as twilight began to settle over the countryside.

He realised the caller had stopped talking and was waiting for him to respond.

'Stick to the plan,' he said. 'And don't call me on this number again.'

He ended the call and passed the mobile phone back to Krupin before pulling a handkerchief from his pocket and wiping his hands.

'Do you think he suspects anything?' asked Krupin.

Malikov pursed his lips and shook his head. 'I don't think so. He's panicking about how to contain the rest of the story and wondering who leaked it to the press.'

He tucked his handkerchief back into his pocket and then pointed at the phone. 'Destroy that. I want no trace of that call, understand?'

'Understood.'

'Good.' Malikov turned back to the house and then paused. 'Are there any more loose ends we need to discuss?'

'None,' said Krupin. 'I will make the necessary arrangements.'

'See to it that you do,' said Malikov. 'I hate surprises.'

Chapter 30

Dan heaped extra sugar into his coffee, stirred the hot liquid with enthusiasm, and grabbed his cup and a second one for Mel and hurried from the kitchen back to the conference room he and Mel now commandeered.

It hadn't been difficult – the rest of the EPG analysts, led by Neil Evans, had been busy with briefings and other assorted meetings since Porchester had arrived back in the city.

The whole office had mobilised following the press conference, yet Dan and Mel had been largely ignored, despite being the ones who had effectively led the investigation to date.

'You've definitely pissed off someone,' Mel had complained. 'There goes my chance of a career-enhancing opportunity.'

Dan had spent the first four hours pacing between the conference room and Mel's desk and hovering outside Evans's office, pestering the man's assistant until she'd allowed him five minutes with him, exasperated.

Evans had been stoical.

'You're still technically off duty,' he'd explained. 'You've done more than enough. Go home and get some rest.'

Dan had ignored him, returning to the conference room in a blacker mood than before.

Mel had lasted another thirty minutes of his grumbling, until she'd handed him a twenty pound note and sent him in search of food.

Luckily, there was a takeaway pizza shop two blocks from the office that still served food late into the evening.

Now, Dan sipped on his coffee and stared out the window, watching the lights from a large aircraft as it took off from Heathrow and then banked across the urban sprawl.

His mind was a jumble of thoughts, but one kept rising to the surface, refusing to go away.

Until the story about the stolen isotope had broken, Porchester had kept him close, asking for regular updates. Now, he and Mel had been cast aside, despite the fact that they offered expertise the government could use.

'It's just politics,' Mel had said when he'd first voiced his thoughts an hour ago. 'They're still dealing with the fallout of the PM nearly losing his job.'

'Bad choice of words.'

Mel had ignored him and had turned her attention back to her laptop screen.

They'd decided to pursue another angle. Instead of waiting for Porchester or the PM to reach out to them, Dan wanted to find someone who could get a message to the

PM on his behalf. Or tell him where David and Mitch were, given that the government was dealing with a crisis the founding members of the EPG were well-equipped to support.

'This guy might be worth checking out,' said Mel, her mouse working across the biographies under the photographs. 'He's got a reputation for being one of the PM's longest-running supporters.' She turned the laptop to face Dan. 'Maybe he knows a way to get in touch with him without going through the usual channels.'

'Will he help us?'

Mel shrugged. 'It's worth a shot, I guess. I've made some enquiries – discreetly,' she said, before he could interrupt. 'And he's rumoured to be the one that uncovered the plan to oust the PM last month.'

Dan took the mouse from her and clicked on the photograph of the Member of Parliament. A new webpage opened, with more detail.

'George Heatherington. Currently the Member for Whitton-upon-Thames. He's written or co-authored several articles about the European Union debate and has a reputation for clearly setting out the pros and cons without being biased.'

Dan straightened and stretched his back, before he started to pace the small space behind Mel's desk. 'Pros and cons,' he muttered. 'I guess on the one side, there's the expense of leaving it, and on the other, plenty of opportunity to explore trade deals without the restrictions of the EU.'

'Do you think he'll know how to contact the PM?'

'I hope so,' said Dan. 'Maybe we can ask him to get a message to the PM for us. I can't understand why he isn't more involved in this business with the stolen isotope. Usually, by now, the phone here would be ringing off the hook with his office demanding updates.'

'All right,' said Mel and pulled out her mobile phone. 'Let me see if I can persuade Heatherington's office that you need to meet with him.'

'Tell them it's urgent,' said Dan, leaning over to hit the 'print' button on the open webpage. 'I've got a feeling we're running out of time.'

Chapter 31

Dan hitched up the handbrake and sat forward, leaning his arms across the steering wheel.

Exhaustion had driven him from the conference room at two in the morning to one of the first aid rooms on the second floor of the building. He'd crawled into the narrow bunk, rolled onto his side, and slept fitfully until a cleaner had discovered him at daybreak and shooed him from the room.

He yawned.

Beyond the windscreen, the asphalt of the car park gave way to a grassy bank that sloped gently towards the river. Wooden bench seats had been installed along the grass, linked together by a concrete path that snaked next to the river, weaving in and out of ancient trees that cast dappled shadows in the summer light.

An official-looking car was parked a few metres away from where Dan sat, two security men standing next to it, their arms crossed over their chests, their eyes obscured by sunglasses. One faced him; the other's attention was given to a man hunched on one of the wooden benches next to the river.

Dan checked his watch and then slipped from the car, stretched, and slammed the door shut.

He knew from experience that it would be better not to approach the man on the bench without checking in with his security team first, and he withdrew his identification card from his wallet as he walked towards them.

The shorter of the two men took his card, nodded, and then handed it back and gestured towards the bench.

'He's waiting for you.'

'Thanks,' said Dan.

He pocketed his wallet and made his way across the last of the asphalt and then stepped over a low chain linked between the posts that separated the car park from the river.

A mist had formed in the early hours of the morning and was now beginning to lift from the water course and surrounding landscape. The aroma of the riverbank reached his senses as he drew closer to the bench.

For a fleeting moment, he was reminded of childhood adventures on homemade rafts, and then his attention snapped back to the present as he reached his destination.

'Mr Heatherington?'

'That's correct. You must be Dan Taylor.'

'Thanks for seeing me at short notice.'

The man looked up but didn't stand. 'Your friend said it was urgent.'

'It is.'

'Sit down.'

Dan did as he was told and stared out at the river flowing past, copying the stance of the man he sat next to.

The Right Honourable George Heatherington was a stalwart in the Prime Minister's cabinet, a back-bencher who had, according to Dan and Mel's research, been an active Member of Parliament since his late twenties. Never one to make too much noise, he had a reputation for fairness, thoroughness, and a keen sense of loyalty. Now in his late sixties, he sat with his hands folded in his lap, a beige coat folded on the seat next to him, his thinning white hair lifting gently in the breeze.

'Why here?' asked Dan.

'I like it. Gives me space to think,' said the politician. 'What do you want to know?' he asked after a moment's silence, his pale blue eyes boring into Dan.

'I'd like to know where the Prime Minister is,' said Dan. 'Apparently he's not been seen in the UK for several weeks now.'

Heatherington chuckled. 'Oh, he's around,' he said, gazing across the river to the opposite bank. 'Just very busy at the moment.'

'Did you know anything about the EPG?'

'Your lot? Not really, no. Can't say I do.'

'So you wouldn't know where I can find David Ludlow or Mitch Frazer either?'

Heatherington locked eyes with him. 'No, no I can't.'

Dan exhaled and looked away. He was being played; he was sure of it. 'What *can* you tell me? You agreed to this meeting, so you must believe there's something I need to know.'

'I have a message for you,' said Heatherington. 'From the PM. He says to be patient, and that you should stall your enquiries for a day or so, until he can bring you up to speed personally.'

Dan twisted round to stare at Heatherington. 'We have a rogue terrorist gang on the loose with a stolen isotope. Why the hell would he want me to stand down?'

'There are other matters at play here, Mr Taylor,' snapped the older man. 'Matters that you're not privy to, and that must be dealt with by other means than your typical gung-ho methods.'

'Gung-ho methods?' Dan fought down his anger. 'Is that what the PM thinks of our successes?'

'Calm down,' said Heatherington and held up his hand. He glanced over his shoulder towards the cars. 'And keep your voice down.'

Dan kept his eyes on the elderly politician. 'Then explain to me what the hell is going on.'

'Lately there's been talk of another attempt to overthrow him.'

'What does that mean?'

Heatherington sighed. 'Even before the failed spill last month, there were people in the Party who weren't happy with the Prime Minister's view that this country remain in the European Union. Or his insistence on going ahead with coal-seam gas fracking, even if it's simply because he wants to show the public that this country should stand on its own two feet when it comes to energy production. Too controversial, especially in the year leading up to the next General Election. Likely to lose it for us, you see?'

Dan nodded, not wishing to interrupt.

'Well, a few of the old boys decided that enough was enough. Better to cut ties with the European Union and seek out a new oil and gas deal with the Russians. With or without the blessing of the PM.'

'Hang on – what?' Dan frowned. 'Isn't that a bit extreme?'

Heatherington squinted at the horizon while he seemed to contemplate his answer. 'What you have to understand, Taylor, is that the media are being used to convince the general public that it's very *detrimental* being part of the European Union. Especially for us British. We're too scared to say no, you see?'

'No, I'm not sure I do.'

'Look at it this way. If the French disagree with an EU directive, they simply ignore it. We British, on the other hand, go all out to obey. We love a bit of bureaucracy.' He snorted. 'It'll be our undoing, if we're not careful. Especially with the EU Human Rights Act binding our hands so we can't even kick known terrorists out of our country. On top of that, we're obliged to our immediate neighbours to share energy supplies. You know as well as I do the sort of situation *that* can lead to.'

'So, go back to your comment about the Russians,' said Dan. 'What's all that about?'

'It's the damn EU sanctions against Russia,' explained Heatherington. 'Britain has a few of its own sanctions against trading with Russia, but they're not as stringent as the EU's. Actually, they're as weak as all hell.' He cleared his throat and checked over his shoulder to see where his security men were and then, satisfied they were out of earshot, turned back to Dan. 'There are always *loopholes*, if you catch my meaning.'

'So, if Britain broke away from the EU, however long that would take, what's Russia got to do with the current situation in Parliament?'

'The PM's got it into his bloody head that the only way to stop this beloved country of ours from facing an energy crisis every year is to explore the possibility of using coal seam gas fracking to supplement our supply from the North Sea. Try to keep everything *British*,' said Heatherington. 'Although we've developed ways to get to oil and gas deeper under the seabed than ever before, it's still going to run out one day. And no-one wants a nuclear reactor in their back garden.'

'There are a few people that aren't too keen on fracking, either,' said Dan.

Heatherington held up a finger. 'And that's my point, m'boy. Hence why the PM was most insistent the project in Northumberland went ahead in secret – to get the results in and prove to the general public that there was nothing to fear from it.'

Dan leaned back on the seat and then jerked forward as the wooden slats rubbed against his stitches.

So that's why the isotope was stolen, he thought. *To embarrass the PM, and expose the project as being too dangerous.*

He kept his thoughts to himself and instead scratched his chin before asking his next question. 'And the Russians?'

'Lining up to sign new gas contracts with us,' said Heatherington. 'As soon as Britain leaves the EU, it can get its gas supplies from whoever it damn pleases – and the Russians are desperate to sell. The EU sanctions are crippling them. We'd be able to name our price on the first swathe of gas contracts and ensure supply for the next twenty years at a fraction of the normal cost.'

Dan whistled through his teeth. 'So it's got nothing to do with a dirty bomb, and everything to do with embarrassing the PM into cutting a deal with the Russian gas companies.'

'Precisely,' said Heatherington. 'Cheap gas would help win the election – energy prices are going up year on year and will only get worse.' He squinted at the horizon as a swan began its graceful descent towards the water. 'For the past decade, the government has been handing out winter payments to pensioners,' he said and then turned to Dan. 'With an ageing population, how sustainable do you think that course of action is?'

'Do you think recent events have been encouraged by the Russians?' asked Dan, his thoughts turning to the Russian assassin he'd fought off in the hospital.

'I'm certain of it,' Heatherington said. 'The PM's fracking plans are very unpopular and have a lot of his fellow party members nervous; even though the split was avoided, there's still a lot of tension in the ranks. I suspect the Russians are encouraging the discord with promises of lucrative back-handers if the party members can persuade the PM to drop the fracking programme, split from the EU, and buy cheap Russian gas instead.'

'And if they can't convince him?'

Heatherington sighed. 'Then I fear they'll do whatever it takes to get rid of the PM.' He glanced up at movement to their left. 'Looks like I'm being summoned,' he said and stood.

Dan looked over his shoulder and saw Heatherington's security men advancing towards them. He got to his feet, collected Heatherington's jacket for him, and extended his hand.

'Thanks for taking the time to talk with me,' he said. 'I appreciate it.'

'You're welcome,' said Heatherington. He slipped his jacket over his arm, nodded, and turned to walk towards his security men, before he stopped and looked over his shoulder.

'Use the information wisely, Mr Taylor,' he said. 'There are people willing to kill to make this deal with the Russians happen.'

Dan began to follow Heatherington, his hands in his pockets as he walked up the slope towards his car. His thoughts churned with what the man had told him, and he began to hurry, keen to get on the move and phone Melissa and tell her everything he learned, before he forgot a precious detail.

As he unlocked his car and slipped behind the wheel, he glanced up and saw Heatherington standing next to the chain link. The taller of the two security men reached out and steadied the older man as he lifted his foot over the fence and then stood back as the politician ambled towards his car.

Dan raised his hand in farewell, started the engine, and steered the car away from the park.

As soon as he reached the main road, he dialled Melissa's mobile number.

'It's me. Can you phone Mike Draper and get me a copy of his team's preliminary report? And then you'd better get me a meeting with Hugh Porchester as soon as possible. There's been a development.'

Chapter 32

Ben flushed the toilet and turned to look at his face in the small mirror above the tiny bathroom's sink.

A bird twittered cheerfully on the gutter outside, a stark contrast to the stink pervading the air in the room.

Ben leaned over and pushed open the window, a welcome burst of fresh air filling his nostrils.

That was the only problem with two blokes sharing a house with no women around, he thought. None of that fancy air freshener around.

'Are you done in there?'

He turned his head at a pounding on the door.

'Be right out.'

He unlocked the door and opened it.

Until yesterday, he would've been shocked at the sight of Joe's face with its bright red pustules and grey skin.

Until yesterday, he'd been telling himself it was just flu; it had nothing to do with the broken vial they'd discovered in the metal case.

Until this morning, when he could no longer pass off his own symptoms as a simple virus.

'Move,' Joe growled, seconds before his eyes opened wide, and he pushed past Ben. He made it to the toilet bowl just in time, heaving on an empty stomach.

'We're screwed,' said Ben. 'We're dead men.'

He pulled the bathroom door closed and then made his way towards the kitchen and poured a glass of water. He collapsed into a chair next to a small square dining table and clutched the chipped glass in shaking hands before taking a sip.

They'd argued last night. It had been Joe who had shot Mark just as the man had been trying to tell them something.

At the time, they'd laughed it off, recalling the man's look of surprise and terror as he'd realised he'd been double-crossed.

Of course, they didn't *have* to shoot him. He was in on the original deal. It just worked out that way – a conversation between Ben and Joe as they'd driven to intercept the case that led to an agreement the pay-off was better split two ways, not three.

And now, the press had caught wind of the theft. The silenced television in the corner of the room replayed the images from the politician's speech, while a headline screamed under the flickering image.

Radioactive isotope stolen!

Ben cursed under his breath and fought the urge to lower his head onto his arms and sleep at the table.

Instead, he unfurled one hand from around the glass and reached out towards the mobile phone he'd left plugged into the wall.

The buyer still hadn't phoned.

The bathroom door opened, and Joe emerged, his face paler than before.

'We need to talk,' he said, shuffling towards the table and slumping into a chair opposite. 'We're screwed.'

'It's radiation poisoning.'

'It might not be.'

Ben dropped the phone back onto the table and glared at the man opposite. 'You know it is.'

Joe jabbed his finger in the direction of the phone. 'Call him. Find out what the fuck is going on. He was meant to phone us last night.'

'No.'

'Then I will.'

Ben slapped Joe's hand away. 'No. You won't. The arrangement was he'd call us, never the other way around.'

'We should ask for more money. Danger money.'

'You're the one that shot Mark before he could warn us.'

'Fuck off.' Joe leaned back in his seat and crossed his arms over his chest. 'It might not have been enough to kill us. We'll get better.'

'Hair loss, sickness, blistered skin,' said Ben, counting off the symptoms on his fingers. 'Which part of radiation poisoning *don't* we have?'

Joe looked away, his gaze falling on the silver-coloured box on the floor next to the back door. 'Remember that Russian in London years ago? It's like that, isn't it? *Fuck*.'

'Like I said, we're dead men.'

Chapter 33

Dan looked up at a flurry of movement outside the door and spotted Hugh Porchester flanked by two aides, both looking harried as he entered the meeting room.

He shook hands with Dan and then turned to Evans. 'I understand you have an urgent situation you wish to speak to me about?'

'I'll let Taylor explain,' said Evans. 'Thank you for coming over at such short notice.' He ran a hand through his thinning hair. 'We didn't feel this was something that could be discussed over the telephone or conveyed via email.'

'Okay then, Dan. Bring me up to speed,' said Porchester.

'When we last spoke, sir, we discussed the possibility of the isotope being stolen to create a dirty bomb,' Dan began. 'Since then, I've got a copy of the preliminary findings from the warehouse where the homeless man said he'd seen two men arrive days before he got sick. I've also made some additional enquiries,' he said. 'And on the basis of that, I'm inclined to think that the isotope has been stolen for political purposes, rather than being an immediate terrorist threat.'

'How close are you to finding the people that have this isotope?' asked Porchester.

'The homeless man, Wright, had the sense to note down the licence plates of one of the vehicles at the warehouse,' said Evans. 'The police found it written on a scrap of paper in one of his pockets.

'The vehicle that was left at the warehouse had been stolen in Norwich a week before,' said Dan. 'And the licence plates had been changed.'

Porchester frowned and tapped his pen on the surface of his leather-clad diary. 'So, that's not much use to us at all.'

'True,' said Dan, 'but we're hoping that the description of the second vehicle, the one that's missing, will turn up something. We're waiting on the results from the police investigation using the APNR system.'

'Traffic cameras?' said Porchester. 'Are you sure that will work?'

'It should do,' said Evans. 'The UK's got the biggest network of CCTV cameras in Europe. And, I believe Taylor has had some success using that system in the past?'

Dan nodded. 'It works. It'll take our analyst a while to programme all the potential routes they could have taken to drive south, though. Once we find them on a main road passing through a town or on a motorway, we can easily track them. Finding that first point of contact is the hardest part.'

'Are we any the wiser as to who the thieves are?'

'We're not,' said Dan. 'But, we do know they're going to be sick – very sick – from radiation poisoning.'

'How will that help us?'

'We're hoping one of them will seek help; after what happened to that Russian guy in London a few years ago, the general public is fully aware of what radiation poisoning can do to a person.'

'Have you got anything you can give me now, so that if the PM asks, I can bring him up to speed?'

'Of course,' said Dan as he reached into his pocket and withdrew a thumb drive. He'd been reluctant when Mel had handed it to him that morning.

'Take it,' she'd said. 'I'm presuming he's going to want as few people as possible finding out about this. If you hand him a heap of photocopies, there's more risk it'll be seen by one of his minions and it'll be all over the six o'clock news before you know it.'

Dan had had to agree with her, and as he passed the USB stick to Porchester, he spotted one of the man's two aides outside the meeting room quickly turn his head away, as if he'd been watching.

'You might want to keep that to yourself, sir,' he said and jerked his head towards the door.

Porchester's lips thinned. 'That bad?'

Dan shrugged. 'I'm presuming this is very sensitive for the government at the moment,' he said.

'A fair point,' agreed Porchester and slipped the thumb drive into his jacket pocket. 'You'll keep me fully informed of developments, of course.'

'We will,' said Evans. 'Your office will receive a twice-daily briefing as usual, and we'll phone directly we have anything new to report.'

Porchester slipped his notes into his briefcase and stood. 'Where are you staying if my office wants to get in touch with you, Taylor?'

'Somewhere safe, sir.'

Porchester raised an eyebrow.

'It's better that's all I tell you, at the moment,' Dan explained. 'Until I find out who tried to kill me at the hospital and is following me.'

'You're still being followed?' Porchester's eyes narrowed. He turned to Evans. 'Were you aware of this?'

'Dan reported it this morning. He's been too busy tracking down the stolen isotope to worry about it.'

'It *is* a concern, though,' said Porchester, rubbing his chin. 'Are you armed?'

Dan paused for a heartbeat. 'No, sir. Not until after the psych evaluation next week.'

'What can you do about providing him with some armed support?' Porchester asked Evans.

'No,' said Dan, holding his hand up. 'Don't. They'll slow me down. Not to mention no-one will talk to me if I've got a couple of thugs following me around.'

Porchester sighed. 'I had a feeling you'd say that.'

'Sir? Is there any way you can get me to the Prime Minister?' asked Dan. 'No disrespect, but there are some issues I'd like to discuss with him, to see if they have any bearing on my investigation.'

Porchester sighed. 'Look, I'll see what I can do,' he said. 'But I can't promise anything. There are a lot of things going on behind the scenes at the moment, Taylor, which is why the PM's entrusted this business to me.'

'I understand, sir. Anything you can do is appreciated.'

Porchester shifted his briefcase in his hand. 'All right. I think we're done here, gentlemen. Do make sure you keep me posted, though.' He paused as Evans opened the door for him. 'I think you'll find I'm a bit more hands-on than our Prime Minister, so don't hesitate to call my office, morning or night. I'll make sure I'm within easy reach until this situation is resolved.'

'Thank you, sir.'

Chapter 34

Hugh Porchester waited until his chauffeur-driven car had merged seamlessly into the traffic before he raised the soundproof glass between the driver and the back seat.

Pulling his laptop out of its case, he gazed out of the window as it powered up and then reached into his pocket and withdrew the USB stick Dan Taylor had handed to him.

He had to give the man credit where it was due. Only three weeks ago, he was rotting in a forgotten Eastern European prison. Now, he was actively pursuing a story that Porchester still couldn't fathom how he'd stumbled across.

Without back-up.

Porchester's lips thinned as he inserted the thumb drive into the laptop.

It was also evident from his meeting with Taylor that he had no idea where his colleagues were, either. Which was disappointing, to say the least.

Since the attempt to overthrow the Prime Minister's cabinet had failed six weeks ago, the party was in turmoil.

Deals had been struck, new allegiances made, but suspicion amongst the ranks remained.

There were just too many damn secrets.

He sighed and then began to scroll through the files now displayed in front of him.

After he'd glanced at the copies of local newspaper stories, he moved onto the official project reports Dan had obtained through his contact, and finally Dan's own report on his findings to date.

Porchester broke out in a sweat as he began to read and raised his gaze to the glass partition. He'd been told it was soundproof, but was it really?

He shook his head and tried to concentrate on the report.

After another five minutes of re-reading paragraphs, trying to work out what to do, he made his decision. It was no good; he'd have to say something, even if it would anger them.

His briefcase slid a little on the seat as the car turned left, following the convoluted one-way system that led back to his office at the House of Commons, and his right hand shot out to steady it at the same time as his left foraged in his jacket pocket for his mobile phone.

He dialled a number from memory and didn't bother to introduce himself when the call was answered.

'I've just left a debriefing with Neil Evans and Dan Taylor,' he said, barely able to keep the tremor from his voice. 'I think they're onto us.'

He paused, listening to the person at the other end of the phone, and then closed his eyes before he spoke.

'I have to admit I was surprised to see him earlier this week. His recovery has been remarkable.'

He gazed out the window, the passing buildings and people a blur.

'It was an accident,' he snapped. 'There was nothing I could do about it.'

He clenched his left hand into a fist and beat it against the bulletproof window.

'I understand,' he said. He closed his eyes. 'Please, that's not necessary.'

He listened and ran a hand over his face before opening his eyes.

The man at the other end of the phone stopped talking, and Porchester pinched the bridge of his nose. 'I'll see what I can do,' he said. 'I just need more time.'

Porchester ended the call and then wiped the phone record from the call history and tucked the phone back in his pocket, his hand shaking.

He tried to keep his face impassive, aware that the driver would check the rear view mirror every few minutes to make sure his passenger was comfortable.

Porchester knew the man on the other end of the phone had been serious.

Only six weeks ago, Nigel Finckley, the Minister who had set out to overthrow the PM, had been found hanging in his garage.

Porchester didn't care what the official report said. Malikov had arranged the killing, both out of spite and as a warning to others, he was sure.

He was also sure there would be more victims if the oligarch's plans went wrong.

He stared through the tinted glass, ignoring the famous landmarks the car travelled past, his mind elsewhere, trying to fathom how the hell he was going to keep Taylor on a short leash without causing suspicion.

Chapter 35

Dan elbowed his way into the conference room, kicked the door shut, and planted the two steaming mugs of coffee on the table.

Mel glanced up as he approached and threw her mobile phone onto the desk.

'Any news?'

'Nothing,' she said and then pointed at the mugs and raised an eyebrow.

Dan pushed the one on his left towards her and then eased into one of the chairs and began flicking through the notes they'd been making.

Sometimes, he found writing out the known facts sparked inspiration and a new angle to be investigated.

Sometimes.

For the past four hours, they had gone through everything, trying to work out the suspects' route from the warehouse to wherever they were now hiding.

They both looked up as the door to the conference room opened, and Neil Evans walked in.

'Ah, they said I'd find you in here.'

'What's wrong?' Dan slipped his mobile phone into his pocket and closed the file in front of him.

'We just received a phone call from the police,' said Evans. 'Apparently there's one very sick suspect in custody in hospital.'

'One of the suspects?' asked Mel, her eyes open wide. 'Really?'

Evans nodded. 'It seems so. Handed himself in half an hour ago.'

Dan pushed his chair back from the table and stood. 'I'll go.'

'Wait.' Evans held up his hand. 'It's not that simple.'

Dan frowned. 'Why?'

'The man is dying, Taylor. From acute radiation poisoning.'

'So, the sooner I go, the better.' Dan moved towards the door.

'There are procedures that have to be followed,' said Evans and leaned against the door.

'Such as?'

'Full protection suit, and the treating doctor will only let you have ten minutes with the patient.'

'Protection suit?'

Evans nodded. 'Apparently, he's highly radioactive. It's just as well he stole a car to get to the hospital, because if he'd gone near public transport or a taxi, we'd have an even bigger problem on our hands.'

'We *do* have a bigger problem on our hands,' said Mel, as Dan gestured to Evans to move aside.

'What's that?'

'There were two suspects,' said Dan. 'So, where's the other one, and what have they done with the isotope?'

***

Dan waited while the specialist hospital team prepared their patient, reassuring him that the man would be conscious, but on a high amount of painkillers.

He leaned forward on the chair in the waiting area and leaned his elbows on his knees. As he stared at the beige tiled floor, he ran through in his mind what he needed to find out; often, it was easier to start with the answers he sought rather than try to come up with a list of questions that would lead nowhere.

And sometimes, it was simply better to try to build a rapport and let the interviewee talk at his own pace.

He sighed and then straightened. Whatever he did, he had only one chance. According to the doctor he'd spoken to on his arrival, the man in the room wasn't expected to survive for long.

His thoughts turned to the homeless man that had died. The doctors weren't sure about the exact dose of radiation he'd been exposed to, but had to agree that his already ill health had contributed to his quick demise.

And the man in the sealed room beyond the waiting area had been *carrying* the damn stuff.

Dan couldn't imagine the terror the criminals would have felt at their discovery. Despite the fact they were intent on stealing the isotope, then selling it on, he would have rather they were found in good health, with the canisters intact, not like this.

The door at the far end of the waiting area opened, and Dan turned at the sound of a busy hospital corridor. The door shut, and the silence returned, save for the footsteps of the tall greying man in a white coat that approached him, his face grim.

'I wish you'd change your mind,' he said as he approached. He held out his hand. 'I'm James Howard. I understand you want to go in there to speak with him, rather than use the video link we recommended?'

Dan nodded and realised his throat was dry. 'Yes, that's right.' He shook the man's hand. 'I'd prefer to talk to him face to face, rather than be another face on a screen.'

'You understand the risks?'

'Yes. But this is a matter of national security, Mr Howard. And I don't believe we're going to get the chance to do this twice, do you?'

Howard exhaled. 'No,' he conceded. 'You're not.' He checked the clipboard in his left hand. 'All right. Come with me. I'll hand you over to my colleague, Jennifer Hayes. We'll get you suited up, and then you can go in.'

'Thanks.'

Chapter 36

Dan fought down the urge to panic in the claustrophobic atmosphere of the radiation protection suit and instead turned his attention to the comms equipment, testing it to ensure he'd be able to record everything the man in the treatment room divulged.

The sound of his breathing filled his ears, and he realised he was sweating already. He couldn't work out if it was from the confines of the suit or his fear that somehow some of the radiation emanating from the man would seep through the clothing.

'Okay, we're ready,' said the female doctor. She waited until he turned to face her. 'What I'm going to do is lead you into the room through a series of air locks,' she explained. 'At the second air lock, I'm going to open the door so you can go through to the third one on your own. When I've closed the door – and *only* when I've closed the door, you can open the last door that leads into the treatment room, do you understand?'

'Loud and clear.'

'All right, let's go.'

Hayes spun on her heel, evidently more comfortable in the bulky plastic clothing than Dan felt, and punched in a security code next to a steel door.

It hissed open, and lights flickered on across the ceiling of the small enclosure.

As the door slammed shut behind him, Dan's throat constricted.

Calm down, he told himself. *These guys know what they're doing.*

He stood to one side as Hayes stepped past him, careful that their suits didn't touch or snag on each other, and made her way to the second door.

She glanced over her shoulder at him, her face partially obscured by the angle of the large visor.

'Last chance to turn back,' she said.

Dan raised an eyebrow. 'Like I've got a choice,' he murmured. 'Let's do it,' he said, louder and more confident than he felt.

She nodded and then reached out and punched a different code into the keypad next to the door and pushed it open.

As Dan followed, he noticed small holes covered the walls and moved closer to take a look.

'Water jets,' explained Hayes, 'with a decontaminant agent included. When you come back from the treatment room, make sure you've shut the door securely. A green light will go on here,' she said, pointing to the bulb fitted above the door. 'Then I'll let you back in from the control room.'

'Okay.'

'Once the door closes, you strip off the suit, push it all through that hatch in the wall there, and the water jets will come on.' She held up a packet. 'This is a special soap. Make sure you wash everywhere thoroughly.'

Dan turned his head to the camera fixed to the wall in the corner and then pointed at it. 'No privacy?'

'No privacy,' she confirmed. 'We can't risk you infecting us, so we make sure you're clean before you're let through to the first airlock. Your clothes will be waiting there for you.'

'Right.' Dan exhaled, trying to let go of some of the nervousness that was beginning to cloud his thoughts.

'Breathe normally,' said Hayes. 'The regulator will take care of the rest. Try to relax; you don't want to hyperventilate in one of these.'

'Okay.' Dan closed his eyes and concentrated on getting his breathing under control. When he opened his eyes, the doctor was watching him.

'Hey,' she said. 'You'll be fine. Just make sure you remember everything I've told you.' She pointed to the ceiling. 'This place is wired anyway, so if I see any problems, or if I think you're panicking, I'll talk you through it.'

'Thanks.'

'No problem. Ready?'

'Yeah.'

'Come on then.'

Dan followed her towards the third door in the airlock sequence and waited while she punched in a third code, opened the door, and stood aside to let him through.

He nodded at her as he passed and then stepped into the next chamber.

The steel airlock swung shut behind him with a dull *thud*, and then he was alone.

His breathing still sounded heavy to his own ears, and a trickle of sweat began at his hairline, tickling as it made its way down his forehead. He automatically lifted his hand to wipe it away and then cursed under his breath.

'Everything okay in there?' said Hayes.

'Yes. Just getting a new appreciation for what you guys do every time there's a situation like this.'

'Thankfully it doesn't happen too often.'

Dan eased himself towards the final door and peered through the reinforced glass that acted as a window through to the treatment room.

The view was limited, but he could make out a single, standard hospital-issue linen covering the occupant, who was surrounded by an assortment of machines. Wires looped across the space between the machines and the bed, disappearing under the covers.

The patient was propped up slightly on pillows, and even from the distance at which he observed him, he could see the blisters that covered his pale face.

He noticed the man was bald and then remembered the lead doctor explaining that the patient had told him that both of the criminals kept their heads shorn, so they hadn't noticed the typical hair loss that so many other victims of radiation poisoning suffered. It was partly why the men had taken so long to notice their symptoms, compared with the homeless man.

Dan took a deep breath, spun the steel handle on the inside of the door, and then stepped over the threshold, trying not to let any fear show in his face.

Stay calm, he told himself. *Get the answers.*

He made sure the door shut behind him, giving it a firm push with the palm of his gloved hand, and then padded across the tiled floor towards the bed.

He noticed that a curtain could be pulled around the patient to separate him from a second bed, already set up by the medical team in case the other criminal was located, and a fleeting thought of what it would be like for the last man to die crossed his mind.

He blinked, shook off the mental image, and flicked the comms equipment so the man could hear him.

The patient opened his eyes as Dan approached, and Dan had to stop himself from automatically recoiling at the sight of the man's bloodshot eyes. The man's frame seemed shrunken as well, as if the whole effort of trying to stay alive was consuming his body.

'Hello,' said Dan.

'Who are you? You don't look like a doctor,' the man croaked.

'My name's Dan Taylor. I'm from an organisation called the Energy Protection Group.'

'What do you want?'

'I'm hoping you can help me.'

'Why should I?'

'How about I ask some questions, and you decide if you want to answer them?'

The man chuckled, a death rattle that shook his shoulders. When he smiled, Dan noticed the man's gums had been bleeding, staining his teeth.

'Go on, then,' he said. 'But make it quick. I don't know how long I'm going to be around for.'

'Yeah. I heard about that,' said Dan. 'When did you find out when you were in trouble?'

'Night before last,' said the man. 'When we arrived at the apartment. I'm Ben, by the way. I'd say 'nice to meet you', but, y'know–'

'Yeah,' said Dan. 'I know. Where were you staying?'

'Someone's mother's,' said Ben. 'She died nine weeks ago. Council couldn't organise a piss-up in a brewery, so the house is still in her name.'

'What happened at the drill site?'

Ben groaned, and Dan saw the man's thumb punch a button attached to a drip that led into a vein in the back of his hand.

The man shuffled under his blankets and then sighed. 'We didn't know one of the canisters was leaking, okay? It was a last-minute decision. More money to split between us.'

'Who shot Mark?'

'I did,' said Ben. 'I've already given my statement to the police.'

Dan narrowed his eyes. He was sure the man in front of him was lying. 'Where's the other guy? There are two of you, right?'

Ben frowned and turned his head to glare at the second bed. 'He refused to come with me,' he said. 'Reckoned he'd take his chances.'

'But you gave yourself up?'

The man turned back to Dan, tears in his eyes. 'I hurt, man. All over. I just want it to end.'

Dan hovered at the foot of the bed. He wanted to reach out to the man, but his bulky suit and common sense prevented him from moving too close. He simply couldn't risk snagging it on the machines or have the man reach out and try to tear it.

'Where is he now?'

'I can't. I promised.'

'Who paid you for the job?'

'I can't tell you.'

Dan gritted his teeth. 'Where's the isotope now, Ben?'

The man shook his head, his mouth downturned.

'Fuck,' Dan hissed under his breath. 'You do realise that there's a danger of other people being contaminated?' he said, his voice louder. 'Don't you give a shit about them?'

Ben wiped at his eyes with the back of his hand, and then his jaw tightened, and he looked Dan in the eye.

'No,' he said. 'I don't.'

His hand moved under the blanket, and as he removed it and crossed his arms over the bed linen, an alarm started to go off above Dan's head, the sound making him spin round to see if he'd knocked against one of the machines and ripped his suit.

He patted the surface of his arms and legs, cursing as he tried to peer through the restricted view the visor provided.

When he realised the alarm hadn't been caused by him, he turned back to face Ben to see the man watching him, his head lolling to one side, a serene expression across his face.

'Oh, shit.'

Dan realised what had happened a split second before the air lock door swung open and three of the medical team led by Howard hurried into the room, slamming the door shut behind them.

He stepped out of the way so they could reach their patient, utterly helpless as they moved around the bed, checking machines and stripping the bed linen away from the man's body.

One of them began chest compressions as the female doctor inserted a long needle into the man's neck, their frantic activity sending Dan's own heart racing.

Dan tried to make out what they were saying, but they were operating on a different frequency to his during the emergency, and their suits kept their voices muffled.

A single loud beep began to fill the room, droning on until Howard leaned across and flicked a switch on the front of one of the machines, and the room fell silent.

Dan ground his teeth, the urge to punch something only tempered by the need to keep his suit intact.

Howard turned and raised his eyes to a clock on the wall before speaking.

'Time of death, three twenty-four.'

Chapter 37

'What happened?'

James Howard tossed the clipboard onto his desk and played with the metal clasp of his wristwatch. 'Morphine overdose.'

'You let him self-administer morphine?'

The doctor's eyes bored into Dan's. 'Yes, we did. I don't think you can imagine the pain he was in, Mr Taylor.'

Dan held his hand up. 'Sorry. It's just that – couldn't anyone foresee this happening?'

'Maybe if you'd been less insistent on meeting him face-to-face instead of using the video link as I suggested, we wouldn't be having this conversation,' snapped the doctor. He sighed. 'I'm sorry. That was out of order.'

'He mentioned nothing to you or your team about where he and his accomplice were hiding?'

'No.'

'Damn. Then we still have one very sick criminal and a leaking container of isotope to find.' Dan stood and held out his hand to Howard. 'Thanks, anyway,' he said. 'I know you did all you could.'

'I'm surprised he lasted as long as he did,' said the doctor as he opened his office door and led Dan down the corridor in the direction of the elevators. 'If I were in his shoes, I'd have hit that morphine tap a lot sooner.'

'Mr Taylor?'

Dan glanced over his shoulder and saw one of the nurses hurrying towards him. He instinctively took a step back, just in case this one tried to kill him as well. 'That's me.'

'You need to call your office. The woman who phoned our reception desk said it was urgent.'

'Thanks.'

He excused himself from the doctor and hurried down the corridor, away from the biohazard area and towards the elevators. He pushed the button and pulled his phone out of his pocket as he waited.

Sure enough, there were three missed calls from Melissa, each ten minutes apart, starting half an hour ago. Whatever it was, it evidently couldn't wait until he reached his car.

There was a soft *ping*, and then the doors to the elevator on his left slid open, and he stepped inside, hoping his phone signal wouldn't be lost within the depths of the hospital.

Thankfully, he had the elevator car to himself. He hit the speed dial for Melissa's mobile number as the doors slid shut.

She answered on the second ring.

Dan didn't waste time with niceties. 'What is it?'

'George Heatherington has been found dead,' said Melissa, her voice barely above a whisper. 'Suspected drowning.'

Dan leaned against the wall, clutching the phone to his ear. 'What? When?'

'This morning,' Melissa said. 'At the river where you met him the other day.'

'Hold on.'

The elevator doors opened, and Dan rushed through the lobby of the hospital and almost wrenched the sliding glass doors off their hinges as he waited for them to open. He raced across the forecourt, aimed his key fob at his car, and ripped the door open.

He thrust his phone into the hands-free bracket, turned the key in the ignition, and dragged his seatbelt across his chest.

'All right,' he said. 'Talk to me.'

'I can't right now. I'm at my desk,' hissed Melissa. 'Evans has got me running some analytics. It's taking me forever.'

'So how did you find out about Heatherington?'

'Because it's been all over the bloody news since he was found three hours ago,' she replied. 'Gotta go.'

Dan's eyes flickered from the road to the phone as she disconnected.

'Shit.'

He banged the steering wheel with the heel of his hand and concentrated on weaving the powerful car through the rush-hour traffic.

He'd had no idea he'd been at the hospital for so long; the procedures to get him in and back out of the radiation treatment room had been so thorough he'd lost track of time.

He pushed a switch on the wheel under his forefinger, and the radio flickered to life, and then he skimmed through the channels until he found a national BBC station, which guaranteed him news headlines every fifteen minutes.

It turned out he didn't need to wait for the next quarter of the hour; Heatherington's death was the top story of the afternoon.

He toggled the volume up and swung the car into the overtaking lane, pointing the vehicle towards the office.

'Police say they have interviewed Mr Heatherington's security detail and confirm that he had spent the morning attending to constituency issues and various meetings, before choosing to take a walk beside the river,' said the male reporter.

'It's tragic that someone generally considered to be in the twilight years of his life would choose to end his life this way,' said the female programme presenter.

'Indeed it is, Michelle. Mr Heatherington is a family man, who leaves a wife, four children, and six grandchildren.'

Dan frowned. *Were they reporting this as a suicide?*

He indicated left, moved into the next lane, and pushed the accelerator to the floor.

He turned up the volume.

'How do the police think this tragedy happened?' the female announcer was asking.

Good question, thought Dan. *Two bloody security guards, and he drowns himself?*

'According to police reports, Mr Heatherington dismissed his security detail and told them to wait by his official car while he went for a walk,' said the reporter. 'The men have told police that they argued the sense of this with Mr Heatherington, but he was adamant. He told them he'd only be ten minutes. He walked out of sight, away from them along the towpath. When he didn't return after twenty minutes, they went to search for him.'

Dan spun the wheel, steered the car up an exit ramp and pulled over to the side of the road as soon as he was able.

Something isn't right.

The female presenter had moved onto other news, and Dan switched the radio off so he could concentrate.

When he'd reached the car after his meeting with Heatherington, he'd looked across the car park to see the old politician being helped across the chain linked between the fence posts. He'd walked towards his car as if every step was an effort.

A man who struggled to walk a few paces from a park bench to a waiting car wouldn't then decide to go for a stroll along a towpath on his own.

And his two security guards, who knew the man's frailty better than most, simply let him.

'Something about this stinks,' he murmured.

He checked his blind spot and then swung the car back out into the traffic.

As he pointed the vehicle in the direction of the office, he couldn't help but recall the politician's parting words to him.

There are people willing to kill to make this split from the EU happen.

Chapter 38

Mel reached out and turned down the volume on her phone and then tore the earphones away and tossed them to one side.

She stared at the computer screen, her mouth dry. It was exactly as she'd expected.

She took a shaking breath, her hand hovering over the mouse before her forefinger depressed the button.

'Oh my god,' she whispered.

She checked over her shoulder. The conference room door remained shut, the red light on the electronic locking mechanism blinking at her.

She'd re-programmed it before she'd started work so that no-one could enter the room without her authorisation.

She was safe, for a while.

Dan had told her about his mission in Eastern Europe, skimming over the detail of his capture, but hell-bent on finding out who had betrayed his mission.

Mel had grown to like him in the short time they'd been working together. Sure, he could be infuriating, but he'd given her a chance when no-one else would work with her, so she owed him.

The least she could do was use her considerable computer skills to trace his movements, and those of others, in the lead-up to his orders being handed down.

With the stolen isotope taking precedence over their workload, though, she hadn't had a chance to investigate.

Until now.

Her fingers stabbed at the keyboard as her eyes traced the flickering code across the screen. So far, she'd completed a systems check of all the people employed by the EPG. It was a small, specialised group, so the initial search hadn't taken long. She'd become frustrated upon finding the records for David Ludlow and Mitch Frazer. Their profiles had been locked away from prying eyes, so she moved onto Dan's, looking for clues.

There was nothing.

True to his word, Evans had even prohibited anyone from noting details of Dan's rescue or the hospital where he'd been sent to recuperate, so their traitor was definitely an outsider.

Mel exhaled with relief.

She minimised the window and turned her attention to the next display, a familiar crest at the top of its page above a single word.

Password?

Her fingers hovered above the keyboard. Beyond the door, she heard muted voices in the corridor growing louder as the people approached the conference room.

She jumped in her seat, fighting down the urge to cry out as the door handle turned.

A muffled curse quickly followed and then footsteps retreated back along the corridor, and a door slammed shut.

Mel waited until her heartbeat had calmed a little and then turned back to her screen, her fingers a blur.

She began working through the system, using the programme she'd created, and was secretly pleased that it worked so well.

She slowed, her jaw slack as she read the text in front of her, and then stabbed the mouse key onto the next message.

She checked her watch and then, with a shaking hand, reached out for her mobile phone and pressed the speed dial for the only number saved to its memory.

As the ringtone began, she suddenly wondered if Dan Taylor was the only one that was in danger.

Or whether she should be worried as well.

Chapter 39

'Okay, what's wrong? What couldn't wait until I finished interviewing the suspect?'

Mel rubbed at her eyes with a knuckle.

He noticed how she leaned against the windowsill, her hands gripping its surface to try to hide the way they trembled. Her face was strained, her shoulders slumped, and he realised she'd lost a lot of her normal swagger.

'Mel? You're starting to worry me. What's going on?'

She took a shaking breath. 'Remember how you asked me to look into how your mission was compromised?'

He nodded.

'This afternoon was the first chance I'd had to do anything about it,' she said. 'I didn't really know where to start, so I thought I'd check our systems, see if anything had been compromised there. It hadn't,' she added, holding up her hand to stop him from interrupting. 'So, I figured I'd take a look at individual emails, see if anyone's accounts had been compromised.'

'You mean you hacked the accounts?'

'Not ours. I've got administrative rights for those.'

Dan frowned. 'But you *did* hack someone's accounts.'

She nodded, her face miserable.

'Whose accounts, Mel? What have you done?'

She looked away. 'The House of Commons.'

'What?' Dan strode across the room towards her. 'What the hell were you thinking?'

She turned to face him, a sneer on her face. 'I was *thinking* I'd really like to catch whoever dropped you in the shit.'

Dan took a step back and forced his anger down. 'Did you get caught?'

'No.'

'Will anyone know you were poking around in there?'

'No.' She jutted her chin at him, her eyes defiant. 'I'm good, Dan. *Really* good. It's what David's been paying me for.'

He narrowed his eyes. 'What did you find?'

She sighed. 'It's easier if I explain how email works, first,' she said. 'You understand that every internet connection is assigned an Internet Protocol address, yeah?'

'Uh-huh. That's what gives your location, right?'

'Right. So if you try ordering a book online from here but the site is in the USA, the retailer's website will probably have a pop-up message that tells you to buy from your country's own specialised site for that service, got that?'

'Yes.'

'Okay. This is where it gets interesting. A lot of organisations, governments included, will introduce a Virtual Private Network, or VPN, to protect those IP

addresses. A VPN hides your location from nosey people.'
A faint smile crossed her lips. 'After all, we don't need to
know what the Minister for Agriculture is buying his wife
for her birthday, right?'

'Right.'

'So, a lot of people take the whole VPN theory on face
value. They think it protects their emails. They see their
own organisations put it into practice, so they think 'I
know – I'll do that for my personal emails, too', are you
still with me?'

'Yes.'

'What they don't realise is that all website browsers
have a fatal flaw. That's why IT departments in large
organisations program the VPN alongside the router, not
the web browser. It's safer. If you link it straight to the web
browser, the flaw means that anyone with a bit of coding
knowledge can bypass the VPN and access the IP address's
true location.'

Dan leaned against the windowsill next to Mel and
rolled his neck, frowning. 'That all sounds fine, but how
does it help us?' His eyes met Mel's. 'And what does it
have to do with you hacking into the House of Commons's
network?'

He noticed her shoulders sag a bit further.

'I just wanted to make sure that anyone associated with
the Energy Protection Group hadn't been compromised,'
she explained. 'So once I eliminated the computers in that
network, I knew it had to be someone linked to you. I
know a lot of your missions are covert, and they don't get

discussed outside of the ops centre, but there was no other explanation as to why your mission failed. You were acting alone. Only a select group of people knew about it, right? There's not even a written record.'

Dan nodded. 'It was put together fast. I got called into the office at nineteen hundred hours on the Thursday, and only David and a handful of other people were there—'

'Don't tell me,' Mel snapped.

Dan cocked an eyebrow at her.

She closed her eyes and took a wavering breath. 'Hear me out. I want to test my theory. Don't tell me who was there until I've finished.' She opened her eyes and held his gaze. 'Okay?'

'Go on.'

'I've got a rough idea of the government officials who've been dealing with EPG from time to time,' she said, 'so I started with their IP addresses. I accessed their emails and took a look at what had been going on for about a month leading up to your mission being activated and for a week after. Starting with the Prime Minister.'

'You hacked the Prime Minister's email?' Dan exploded. 'Are you fucking *crazy*?'

'Hey!' she said, backing away, her hands held up. 'Do you want me to tell you what I found or not?'

Dan's nostrils flared as he fought to keep his temper under control. Images of Mel and him being found out and disappearing for good flashed through his mind; at the same time, he worked out the different ways he could strangle her and make it look like an accident.

'Go on,' he said through gritted teeth.

She shrugged. 'It wasn't him.'

'Get on with it.'

She swallowed. Her voice shook when she spoke. 'Three hours after you were given your operational orders, an IP address located at the House of Commons received an email, confirming orders had been received and that all necessary steps would be taken to ensure the disappearance of a covert operative by the name of Dan Taylor.'

The hairs on the back of Dan's neck prickled, and a chill carved a path down his spine as Mel's words sunk in.

He rubbed his hand over his face and looked out the window, contemplating his next question. 'And you think the IP address belongs to someone associated with the EPG?'

Mel shook her head, her eyes downcast. 'No, Dan. I *know* the IP address belongs to someone involved with the EPG.' She raised her head slightly until she could look him in the eye. 'I just want to corroborate what I've seen. I need to know if he was sitting in that room with you the night you received your mission orders.'

Dan exhaled and steeled himself for her answer. 'Okay, who was it?'

'Hugh Porchester.'

Chapter 40

Dan blinked. 'Are you sure?'

Mel nodded, her face miserable. 'It's him.'

'You're absolutely sure? How did you manage to do this, anyway?'

'The USB stick you gave to him had a virus on it.'

'What? What sort of virus?'

'A worm,' said Mel. 'I wrote it. It enables the user to access other people's computers. I just had to wait until he put the USB stick in his personal computer and connected to the internet.'

'Why didn't you tell me this at the time?' demanded Dan.

Mel withered under his glare. 'Because you wouldn't have done it,' she whispered. 'Would you?'

Dan hissed through his teeth and turned to face the window. He leaned his forehead against the cool glass and closed his eyes.

Porchester?

But the man had been so concerned when he'd returned from the army hospital; he'd been the first to offer the PM's condolences on the man's behalf, apologising that they hadn't been able to organise the rescue operation sooner. Surely it couldn't be true?

Or had the PM somehow found out about the betrayal and organised the rescue mission?

If his life was on the line, then what about Mitch and David? Where were they?

And who exactly could he trust?

He felt sick as his mind returned to the confines of the dark, dank prison cell, and the thought he'd been betrayed by someone who was supposed to be on *his* side.

Someone he'd almost grown to respect since his return. Someone who was as desperate as he to find out where David and Mitch were.

He opened his eyes and tilted his head towards Mel.

'Did you find anything else?'

She shook her head. 'Just that email. Whether he was in a rush and forgot to use a safe channel of communication or...' she broke off and then shrugged.

'Or he knew I wouldn't be coming back and therefore didn't have to worry about it,' Dan finished for her. He slammed the windowsill with the palm of his hand. 'The arrogant little prick.'

'I don't understand, Dan. If he tried to have you killed, why would he be so nice to you once you were rescued?'

Dan scratched his chin and frowned. He'd been wondering the same thing. Unless —

'He's using me to find out where David and Mitch are,' he said. 'I don't know what's going on, but they're in trouble, too.' He swore under his breath. 'How could I have been so stupid?'

He glared out the window at the mist lifting off the river, a steady flow of traffic beginning to build up in both directions across the bridge that spanned the water course below him.

'Dan?' Mel moved beside him, her hand on his arm. 'What are we going to do?'

'Have you got somewhere you can go? Somewhere safe?'

He turned to face her. She looked petrified.

'What do you mean?'

'With your computer skills, can you disappear?'

Her eyes widened. 'You mean off the grid?'

He nodded.

'I – I don't know. I've never really thought about it.'

'Think about it now.'

'You think we'll have to?'

He raised an eyebrow.

'Shit.' She turned away from him, pulled out one of the chairs that had been tucked under the meeting table, and sank into it. 'Shit.'

'Sorry, Mel.' His voice softened. 'I had no idea it'd come to this.'

She shook her head. 'Blimey, neither did I.' She snorted. 'I was just trying to keep my head down, keep out of trouble.'

'Yeah. You were probably doing quite a good job of it, too.'

She took a deep breath and tipped her head back, stretching her neck muscles, before her gaze found his once more. Her eyes narrowed. 'If I'm supposed to disappear, what are you going to do?'

'I have to find David and Mitch somehow. They're either in hiding or in trouble.' Dan glanced towards her. 'You've heard nothing?'

She shook her head. 'Not recently.'

'Okay. I'll have a dig around. Check some of our old haunts. See if anyone's seen them.'

'What else?'

'We can't use the email you found as evidence.'

'Why not?'

'Because we obtained it illegally.' He drummed his fingers on the table. 'We have to find another way to prove it.'

Mel wound an end of her hair around her finger and stared out the window for a moment. 'There might be a way.'

'Go on.'

She leaned forward. 'All government mobile phones are supplied by the same company. Those phones are obviously loaded with the best encryption codes the manufacturers have got up their sleeves.'

'That doesn't help us.'

A faint smile crossed Mel's lips. 'Actually, it does. The manufacturer makes the SIM cards to GCHQ specifications. The same specs that the NSA likes to use.'

Dan scratched the stubble that grazed his jaw. 'You're going to tell me something else I wish I didn't know, aren't you?'

She grinned. 'Yes. But it'll work to our advantage.'

'Explain.'

'If you know the GCHQ SIM card codes, you can trace the user's phone calls and text messages.'

'Can you do that without being seen in the system? I mean, will you be able to look at Porchester's records without leaving a trace?'

'If you've got the codes, yes.'

'*Have* you got the codes?'

Her gaze dropped to her hands. 'Not right at this moment.' Her eyes met his. 'But I *can* get them.'

'How risky is it?'

She shrugged. 'Not too bad.'

He reached across the table and stabbed his finger on the surface. 'You promise me now, if you have any suspicion you're going to get caught, you pull the plug, understand?'

She nodded. 'Understood.'

'Can you still do this and stay in hiding somewhere?'

'Yes. I've got some equipment of my own that'll do the job. And there's a room I can use; it's pretty basic but it'll do.'

Dan held up his hand. 'Don't tell me where it is.'

She frowned.

'Just in case,' he explained.

'Okay,' she said, her voice wavering. 'What are you going to do?'

'I think I'd better go over to Portcullis House and have a word with the Right Honourable Hugh Porchester, don't you?'

Chapter 41

'Dan, good to see you.'

Dan turned from the senior policy advisor's secretary in time to see Porchester stride from his office, his hand outstretched.

He set his jaw and returned the handshake. 'Thanks for seeing me at short notice.'

'No problem at all. I got the impression it was rather urgent.' Porchester handed a leather-bound signing case to the bewildered-looking woman behind the desk, who seemed as surprised as Dan to see the politician emerge from his office in such a hurry. 'See to those, will you, Hannah?' He returned his attention to Dan without waiting for a response from her.

'Is there somewhere we can talk in private?' asked Dan.

Porchester checked his watch. 'I've got another two hours until I have to hold a press conference. Let me show you something I think will interest you,' he said and gestured towards the door.

Dan blinked, caught off-guard by the man's casual demeanour. What if Mel had been wrong?

'Um, sure,' he managed.

'Excellent,' said Porchester. 'Follow me.'

Dan glanced at the secretary, who looked as confused as he felt before she averted her gaze and busied herself with the contents of the folder that had been thrust at her, and then he spun round and hurried to catch up with Porchester, who had already left the reception area and was stalking towards the elevators.

The politician waited for him to catch up and then pressed a button that showed a below-ground level designation, and the doors closed.

'I've heard you're quite a good marksman,' he said.

Dan shrugged. 'I'm not bad. I've been lucky.'

Porchester snorted. 'You shouldn't be so humble,' he said. 'I've read the unofficial transcripts of your exploits, remember?'

The elevator eased to a standstill, and then Porchester led the way along a brightly-lit passageway.

Dan frowned and tried to get his bearings. 'I didn't know Portcullis House had a basement this big,' he said.

Porchester chuckled. 'This passageway runs under Bridge Street,' he said. 'It leads straight under the Palace of Westminster. Saves one getting rained on before facing the television cameras at Prime Minister's Question Time.'

He stopped as they reached a closed steel door, pulled out his security card and swiped it across the panel to the right of the doorframe. He waited for the lock to click open, and then pushed against the door.

'Let's see what you're like on a range,' he said.

As Porchester flicked switches on a panel to the right of the open door, Dan's eyes widened.

He'd heard the rumours, but he'd never imagined the Palace of Westminster housed such a state-of-the-art rifle range as was illuminated in front of him.

He decided at once that whatever happened, he'd let Porchester win. Despite his competitive nature, Dan realised he'd have to play to the man's ego if he was going to fathom how he fit into the theft of the radioactive isotope and why he'd deliberately sabotaged Dan's mission.

He followed the politician across the concrete floor towards a locked cabinet, their footsteps muted by the soundproofed walls.

'The worst-kept secret in the Palace of Westminster,' said Porchester. 'They finished constructing it in 1916.' He pointed to a brass plaque on the wall. 'It was opened by Prince Albert. Seems everyone thought it was a much better arrangement than holding competitions at Bisley.'

Dan lifted his chin and looked up at the wooden roll call of competition winners that had been mounted on the wall. Porchester's name appeared twice in the past ten years, but not in the last annual round.

'I haven't had much time to practise lately,' explained the politician. 'But I'm hoping I'll do better this year.'

He swiped his security card against the panel on the cabinet, and Dan heard the faint *click* of the lock mechanism. Porchester swung the door open, reached inside, and handed Dan a set of ear defenders and plastic glasses for eye protection.

Dan looped them around his neck and took the pistol that Porchester handed to him. 'I thought only .22 rifles were used down here?'

Porchester smiled. 'That's for the newcomers – and the media.' He pulled out a second gun. 'I'll use the same. Keeps it fair, isn't that right?'

'I think you'll be fine,' said Dan.

'Come on then,' said Porchester and pointed back past the door. 'Range One has better light. Let's use that.'

Dan looked around the room as they made their way towards the range, while Porchester paused at another locked cabinet to retrieve a box of ammunition. The facility didn't appear to get much use, and he wondered how much money had been wasted on it.

'Does no-one else come down here?' he asked.

'Sometimes,' said Porchester. 'It's just what with the attempted ousting six weeks ago, the Prime Minister's made it clear he wants his ministers in the office at all times. It plays havoc with one's social life.'

Dan cleared his throat. 'Well, hopefully you'll all get some more free time soon,' he said.

'Here we are.' Porchester stopped next to a partitioned booth at the far end of the room and put his gun on the shelf that separated them from the range before passing a handful of rounds to Dan.

He took a cardboard target from a rack on the wall next to him, slotted it into place, and flicked a switch. The target fluttered as the wire pulled it back towards the far wall while Dan readied his gun, inserting the now full magazine into the pistol grip.

'Twenty-five metres only, I'm afraid,' said Porchester. 'There's limited space for anything else under here.'

'No problem,' said Dan.

'Off you go, then.'

Dan put on the safety glasses, wiggled the ear defenders into place, and then lifted the pistol in a familiar two-handed grip. His feet slightly apart, he waited a few seconds to settle his breathing and fired.

He squinted at the target and then frowned.

His aim was slightly off. He cricked his neck, exhaled, and then raised the gun once more and fired the remaining rounds in quick succession.

'Oh, bravo,' said Porchester.

Dan felt the slide lock back on the empty chamber, and then reached out and flicked the switch to return the target.

Apart from the errant first shot, all of the rounds had found their mark, the last three a tidy grouping that overlapped each other.

He unclipped the target, replaced it with a fresh one, and flicked the switch. He placed the now empty gun on the shelf and stepped aside.

'Good luck, sir.'

Porchester chuckled. 'I think I'm going to need it, Taylor.'

Dan watched patiently, his hands clasped behind his back as Porchester took aim, and then fired his gun in quick two-shot bursts until the clip was empty.

'Excellent, sir,' said Dan as the politician waited for the target to return on its static wire. 'I can see why your name is on the roll of honour.'

He wasn't being sarcastic; all of Porchester's shots had found their mark, a tidy grouping that clipped the bullseye of the target card was visible from several metres away.

Porchester reached up and changed over the target card for a new one, then turned to Dan.

'So – what did you want to talk to me about?'

'I've been looking through the findings so far,' said Dan. 'There's something that doesn't make sense to me.'

Porchester raised his eyebrow as he fed rounds into the magazine, and then pushed it back into place. 'Care to elaborate?'

'The people who stole the isotope. They went to so much trouble to plan the theft, even infiltrating the project team months ago,' Dan said, shaking his head. 'For them to go and make a mistake, to not have a contingency plan in place in case there was a leak – it doesn't seem right, does it?'

'It does seem careless of them.'

'I'm also wondering how they obtained so much detail about a supposed secret government project,' said Dan. 'It's almost as if someone was passing information to them.'

He watched the Deputy Prime Minister, waiting for the man to bluster, to make some far-fetched theories, or suggest Dan pursue another path of enquiry.

Instead, Porchester picked up Dan's empty gun, and held it out to him.

When Dan reached for it, his fingers wrapping around the proffered hand grip, Porchester didn't let go.

'Now,' he said. 'Why don't you tell me why you're *really* here?'

'I think you know why I'm here,' snapped Dan. 'You've been keeping an eye on my activities for a long time, haven't you?'

'You're known for having a plain disregard for authority,' said Porchester and shrugged. 'It's perfectly natural for me to take an interest in all your missions.'

'There's taking an interest and then there's using that information to your advantage, isn't there?' said Dan.

Porchester's eyes hardened. 'What do you mean?' he said, his voice giving nothing away.

'Why the *fuck* did you compromise my mission in Eastern Europe?'

Chapter 42

Porchester held up his hand. 'Before you go any further, Taylor, let me show you something.'

Dan's thumb ran across the trigger guard of his gun as the politician put down his weapon and reached into the inner pocket of his jacket. He relaxed as the man pulled out a mobile phone, swiped his forefinger across its surface, and then turned it so Dan could see the screen.

On it, a bright red banner ran across the bottom.

Breaking news!

A video played on a repeating loop.

Dan felt his jaw drop as he watched.

The news channel showed a biohazard team taping off a run-down apartment block, and then the camera panned out to show residents being herded through showers similar to those he'd seen when the warehouse had been discovered.

Stolen isotope located. Second suspect found dead. Residents evacuated.

Dan's head jerked up, and he stared at Porchester. 'I don't understand.' His mind raced. 'When did this happen? How did the police find him so quickly?'

Porchester checked his wristwatch and then picked up his gun once more. 'I believe the police received an anonymous tip-off half an hour ago,' he said, before he stared at Dan. 'A few moments before the press received the same message.'

'Why are you doing this?'

'It's quite simple,' said Porchester, his gaze flickering over the screen. 'This isotope was stolen nearly a week ago. Yet the Prime Minister has done nothing, *nothing*, to warn the general public. He hasn't attended any briefing sessions. He hasn't even bothered to contact *you*.'

He sneered. 'All he's done is continue his grand tour of Europe, grovelling to its leaders to let the UK have more control of its own destiny. It sends a clear message that he doesn't care about the people that elected him to lead them. He isn't *fit* to lead them. I am.'

'What?'

'Let me make you a proposition,' said Porchester, holding his finger up to silence Dan. 'You're good at what you do. I can arrange it so that you'll never have to worry about money again.'

'What do you mean?'

'Work for me,' said Porchester. He jutted his chin at the news feed. 'After this, the Prime Minister's reputation will be damaged beyond repair.'

He chuckled. 'Allowing a government project to proceed in secret? Knowing that a radioactive isotope had been stolen – and not telling the public? Endangering their lives while criminals spread radiation around the country at will?'

'Wait a minute.' Dan pinched the bridge of his nose and tried to keep up with the direction the conversation had taken. '*You* organised the theft of the isotope?'

Porchester jiggled the gun between his hands and played with the hem of his rolled-up shirtsleeves, his eyes darting left and right.

Dan concentrated on keeping his breathing calm.

The politician hadn't denied the accusation, but instead had veered off into unknown territory, and Dan was at a loss to keep up or guess where the conversation was going. The man was visibly sweating now and bordering on incoherence.

'Hugh,' he said, his voice calm. 'What's going on?'

'You wouldn't understand,' Porchester snapped.

'I'm trying to,' said Dan. 'Did you organise the theft of the isotope?'

'Don't be preposterous!'

Dan took a step back and raised his hands. 'Sorry, but I'm a bit confused,' he said. 'What's the problem with the PM? Why isn't he fit to lead the country? Isn't he in Europe right now, trying to negotiate better legal and trading terms within the EU for the United Kingdom?'

Porchester clutched the gun in his right hand and wiped the back of his left hand across his brow. He ignored Dan's questions.

'When the public find out what's happened, they'll crucify him,' he crowed. 'He hasn't made a public appearance in over a week. They'll be looking for someone to lead them. Someone with integrity and a better understanding of what it takes to run this country. They're going to need a new leader, Dan.'

Dan narrowed his eyes. 'What, you?'

Porchester nodded. 'And I'll need a new man to head up the EPG. Not David Ludlow. Someone I can trust.' He checked his watch and put his phone in his pocket. 'Join me, Dan. I'll be forwarding a motion to the Party in an hour.'

'You *did* have something to do with the theft,' Dan exclaimed. 'Why the hell would you do that?'

Porchester blinked at him. 'It doesn't matter, Taylor.' His hand began to steady, and Dan kept a wary eye on the weapon in the man's grasp. 'Join me, Dan.'

'Fuck off. I'm not working for a madman,' Dan snarled. 'Do you realise how many lives you've put at risk with your little stunt? Just so you can fuel your own selfish ambitions?'

Porchester shrugged. 'I thought you might say as much. That's why the investigating team being sent to that apartment block where the suspect's body has been located will find traces of your DNA.'

'What?'

'Call it an insurance policy,' said Porchester, a gleam in his eye. 'We had a feeling your self-righteousness might be a problem. So, you see, you might want to reconsider your answer. Because, right now, you're looking at a *very* long prison sentence with no chance of a court appeal. The evidence is simply too compelling.'

'Fuck. Off.'

Porchester stepped back and then raised his gun until it was level with Dan's chest and smirked. 'Such a shame. Two lives down already, Taylor.' His hand began to shake, and he pressed the gun against Dan's t-shirt. 'I don't think you'll get a third chance.'

Dan took a step back. 'You *did* set me up?' He was incredulous. 'Wait – you said "a third chance". You organised the nurse at the hospital as well?'

'You just won't die, will you?' said Porchester. 'I needed you out of the way, Taylor. Ludlow and Frazer had disappeared. You were the only threat left to deal with. You have an uncanny knack for turning up when you're least expected.'

'But the nurse – she was Russian. What the hell have the Russians got to do with this?'

A muscle under Porchester's eye twitched. 'Absolutely nothing,' he said, his gaze shifting to the left and then back. 'She was merely doing a job for me.'

'Wait a minute,' said Dan. His memory flashed back to his conversation with George Heatherington. 'You're *helping* them?'

Despite wanting to leap forward and throttle the man who stood in front of him, Dan's mind worked, calculating the odds.

If he rushed forward, he'd be dead before he got the chance to take a second step. If he tried to duck and run,

Porchester would simply keep pulling the trigger until the clip was empty.

Instead, he slowly closed the space between them, ignoring the gun that pressed once more into his chest, and used his height to try and intimidate the other man, waiting for a chance to snatch the weapon away.

'Have you ever shot someone, Hugh?' he said, his voice calm, despite the adrenalin that filled his veins. 'Ever pulled the trigger when you're looking someone in the eyes?'

Porchester took another step back and blinked. 'Stay where you are.'

'What? Or you'll shoot?' Dan forced a laugh, hiding his fear. 'I don't think you've got the balls,' he spat and edged closer to the politician. 'And I'm dying to know what arrangement you've got going with the Russians. What is it? You get the top job if you buy their gas cheap?'

He kept his movements slow, precise, looking for an opening, anything that would give him a way to disarm Porchester without actually harming him, if possible.

Somehow, he had to have proof that the man in front of him had almost single-handedly exposed the country to a nuclear threat.

A door slammed in the background, beyond the realm of the rifle range.

The noise echoed through the bowels of the building, closely followed by the sound of running feet along the passageway from the stairs, drawing closer.

There was only one thing Dan knew of that could create such a racket.

Military-issued boots.

Porchester must have somehow raised the alarm when he was using his phone, and Dan was running out of time.

He resisted the urge to turn his head and instead caught the moment Porchester's eyes flickered towards the locked door to the range.

Dan rushed forwards, his left arm smacking the inside of the politician's hand that held the gun. The motion caused the gun to arch away from his chest, away from danger.

He followed it up with a quick, sharp slap with his right hand directed at the man's left ear, sending him tumbling towards the floor in shock.

The weapon discharged, the report deafening within the enclosed space.

Startled, Porchester struggled to regain his balance.

Dan aimed a kick to his stomach, and the gun flew from his hand, skidding across the floor.

'Right, you bastard,' Dan muttered. 'Let's have some answers.'

He reached down for the weapon, emptied the remaining rounds from the magazine, and then returned to Porchester, who was crawling on all fours across the floor, wheezing. Dan stood over him, and then kicked Porchester's arms out from under him.

The politician rolled onto his side and then pushed himself up into a crouch and raised his hands above his head.

Dan realised he'd have seconds before the range would be secured by armed force. His mind raced. Perhaps there was a way he could use the incursion to his advantage – convince them that Porchester was somehow connected to the isotope theft.

He knew his own evidence was tenuous – he had to get hold of Porchester's phone, to prove the connection to his own failed mission and a potential threat to the PM.

'Stop,' Porchester pleaded. 'Please. Don't shoot me.'

'Get up,' he said, leaning down and dragging Porchester to his feet. 'You're not going to convince anyone with that act.'

'Oh, but I will,' said Porchester, a gleam in his eye. 'You see, I haven't got a choice.'

'I'm not going to shoot you,' said Dan. 'But I want some answers. *Now.*'

He didn't get a chance to ask a question.

With a crash, the door to the rifle range caved inwards under the force of a well-aimed battering ram, closely followed by three figures in black fatigues who stepped through the breach, their faces covered by black protective helmets and goggles, and all brandishing assault rifles.

'Don't let him shoot me!' screamed Porchester. 'He's a madman! Arrest him!'

'No – wait!' yelled Dan.

It was too late.

The men launched themselves across the rifle range, all shouting at once, their voices muffled by scarves they'd wrapped around their faces.

'Down, down!'

'Drop your weapon!'

Dan slowly loosened his grip on the gun and dropped it to the ground, where it landed with a metallic clatter.

As he straightened, the apparent leader of the three men shot forwards, brandishing his rifle at Dan's chest, the respirator over his mouth giving his voice a mechanised cadence.

'On your knees, soldier!'

Dan laced his fingers behind his head and did as he was told.

Stay calm, he told himself.

'Cover me,' instructed the guard over his shoulder.

His two comrades swung their rifles in Dan's direction, and he gritted his teeth as the man grabbed his wrists, lowered them behind his back, and then slipped plastic zip ties around them and pulled tightly.

'My name is Dan Taylor,' he said, keeping his voice calm. 'I'm an operative with the Energy Protection Group.'

No response.

'Listen to me,' he urged. 'This man is a danger to security. He's a terrori—'

A hand slapped the back of his head, and he cursed as he bit his tongue.

A hood was shoved over his head, pulled down under his chin, and secured.

Tasting blood in his mouth, his mind raced.

Christ, what's going on?

A hand snaked under his arm and pulled. 'Get up.'

Dan concentrated on standing up without losing his balance. His heart chilled at the next words spoken.

'Dan Taylor, you're under arrest.'

Chapter 43

'Move, move!'

Dan concentrated on not tripping as he was hauled forward and out of the rifle range, Porchester's voice receding into the background as the armed guards took control.

He heard their leader mumble something to Porchester about him returning to his office and that someone would be in touch to interview him, and then he was shoved sideways to his right before a hand clamped on his shoulder.

'Stairs.'

He nodded to show he understood, before allowing the man to guide him down the flight of steps.

Behind, he heard a door slam shut and then an electronic *beep* filled the space.

He guessed a locking mechanism had been activated.

'Hurry,' he heard one of the men say.

How deep does this place go?

At the foot of the stairs, the guard steered him to the left.

Even behind the confines of the hood, Dan sensed a change in the air. It felt stagnant, humid, as if it had been a long time since anyone had been there.

He heard a heavy steel door swing shut behind him, the noise echoing off the walls.

Where the hell are they taking me?

He forced down the panic, instead planning what he would do once the hood was removed. Instinctively, he twisted his wrists within the plastic ties, but they were held firmly in place.

He tried to work out from the sounds of the guards around him how many there were. Three had entered the rifle range, and after they had ushered him down the stairs, he guessed there were no more.

Three against one.

A rush of air filled the space beyond the material of the hood, and he realised the passageway had ended, and he'd been led to a large space. The air was musty, so he was still underground.

He recalled the Palace of Westminster was built on marshland, with tunnels underneath that led to Whitehall and other places of government, to save politicians and their minions having to walk above ground in inclement weather or at times of heightened national security. There were other tunnels, too. Secret places that even politicians might not be aware of.

Were the guards simply going to shoot him and dispose of his body in the Thames?

'Stop.'

Dan's shoulder was shoved as someone pushed past him, and then he heard sounds of boots on metal, a muffled curse, and then a hand gripped his arm.

'Step forward. Mind the gap.'

Dan frowned, but did as he was told, his mind racing.

His head twitched to the left at a noise behind him, before the hood was ripped from his head.

He hissed through his teeth as his hair caught in the material and then blinked to adjust his eyesight as quickly as possible to his gloomy surroundings.

Confusion filled his senses as his mind tried to process the scene in front of him.

He was standing between two of the armed guards, one slightly shorter than the other. He appeared to be in what could only be described as a steel cage, its dull yellow paint rusted away in places.

Dan glanced over his shoulder, back the way he had been forced to walk, and then his jaw dropped.

A dark opening in the wall was obviously the entrance to the passageway along which he'd been pushed and shoved, but it was the faded markings on the wall that held his attention.

I'm in an old underground station.

He turned back to his captors, but their faces were still hidden behind their goggles and makeshift masks.

He twisted his head back and forth, a new realisation hitting him.

He wracked his memory; he'd heard about the old underground lines that still lurked under the city, derelict

272

and unused, but he hadn't known the trains were still in working order. Or that they intersected with the working railway that transported commuters and tourists alike under the bustling metropolis.

'Move. Sit.'

The tallest of the three masked guards pulled him into the narrow space and forced him down onto a low bench.

Dan tucked his long legs out of the way and grimaced as his shoulders locked under the duress of the cuffs. He twisted in his seat until he could take some of the pressure off his arms.

In the dim light from the vehicle's headlight, he squinted at the markings on the steelwork next to his hands and realised he was riding on one of the old Mail Rail trains operated by the Royal Mail. It made sense now; the low bench he and the other men sat on had been designed for mail bags and parcels, not human passengers.

The leader of the guards pushed past his comrades and moved towards the front of the small locomotive. He turned his head and nodded at the guard next to Dan, before his attention was drawn back to the control panel he sat in front of.

Within seconds, the driver flicked the headlights off and the machine started moving forward, its wheels turning silently on the rails.

The tall guard edged closer to Dan.

'Lean forward,' he said.

Dan did as he was told.

To his surprise, the man extracted a knife from the webbing that covered his chest, then reached behind Dan and sawed through the cuffs.

Dan exhaled, loosened the plastic from his wrists, and rubbed them to get the circulation working again.

'Hold on,' said the man, his voice gruff.

Dan gripped a steel railing fixed to the side of the machine as it began to slide faster along the tracks.

Soon, they were travelling at such a speed that Dan's hair ruffled in the breeze, the damp, slick walls of the tunnel slipping past before he had a chance to try and read any of the markings on the surface.

He had no sense of direction, whether they were moving north or east, or how deep the tunnel ran under the city.

The vehicle shook as it travelled over a series of criss-crossed tracks, and Dan twisted his neck sideways as a bright light shone in his eyes from another tunnel, before the vehicle he was travelling on plunged once more into the darkness.

Holy shit. That was a train!

He'd lost all sense of time and, with it, distance. He had no idea where he was being taken.

He cursed his own stupidity, his haste in confronting Porchester without back-up. The man was unhinged, blinded by ambition, and there appeared to be no way of stopping him now.

Not unless he could evade his captors.

Their silhouetted forms surrounded him; the shorter figure opposite him, weapon slung across an arm, black goggles staring sightlessly at him through the gloom.

The taller one sat further forward, peering over the driver's shoulder, checking on Dan from time to time as the vehicle powered along.

Dan watched as the driver appeared to speak to the second guard, who nodded before clambering back towards Dan.

The man gestured to the guard opposite Dan to move forward, and he watched as the driver swapped places and began climbing towards him.

The mail cart was approaching some sort of widened area – Dan couldn't make out whether it was an old platform or an underground maintenance yard for the old trains, but light filtered through air vents in the ceiling.

The vehicle slowed, and Dan realised they must be approaching a space where the line ran directly under a street. The new driver eased off the throttle and the mail cart slowed, gliding beneath the air vents under its own momentum. The shafts of light created a strobing effect, and Dan averted his eyes to counteract it.

When he raised his head once more, the taller guard had reached him.

He crouched next to him and held out his weapon. 'Hold that.'

'What?'

'Hold it.'

Dan did as he was told, the hairs on the back of his neck standing on end as he realised his fingerprints were now on a weapon that had, in all likelihood, at some point been fired. Porchester was making sure there would be no escape for him, no matter what he told his prosecutors.

If he even got a chance.

His gaze shot upwards as the man leaned back, reached up, and then wrapped his fingers around the elastic that held his goggles to his face. Dan watched, confused, as the goggles were removed, closely followed by the respirator around the man's face.

Next, the black head covering was removed, and a familiar face grinned at him.

'Mitch?' Dan turned his head to look at the second figure next to him, who also ripped off his mask. 'David?'

He felt his jaw drop, and then his brain caught up.

'Where the *hell* have you two been?'

Chapter 44

Hugh Porchester pulled a silk handkerchief from his pocket, wiped his brow, and then stalked across the firing range towards the secure gun cabinet, emptying the unused rounds from his gun.

He swiped his card in the lock and then used a corner of the handkerchief to rub the gun's surface and placed the gun back in the rack.

Next, he hurried back to Range One, used his handkerchief to retrieve Dan's gun from the floor where it had fallen, and emptied the blanks from the magazine.

Finally, he wiped each of the live rounds and slotted them into the magazine before pushing it back into place with the heel of his hand.

He stood, a little unsteadily, and shook his head, his breathing finally returning to some semblance of normality.

That was too damn close.

He knew Taylor was good, but the fact that the man had only escaped prison mere weeks ago, a prison to which he'd been purposefully sent in order to disappear for good, and then survived a second assassination attempt was nothing short of miraculous.

The fact that the man had then *stumbled* upon the theft of the radioactive isotope was incredible bad luck.

As soon as Taylor had appeared in his office, he knew he'd been exposed. Somehow, Dan Taylor had linked him to the isotope theft.

And the debacle that had been Eastern Europe.

Porchester gritted his teeth. With any luck, by the time Taylor's case came to court, he'd be so far up to his neck in criminal charges, he'd never see the light of day again, which gave Porchester enough time to appease those he reported to and reassure them that everything was still under control and that he was going to be able to meet their deadline.

He turned, frowned at the sound of running feet, and strode towards the entranceway to the range, the door now obliterated.

As he drew closer, stepping carefully over the splintered wood, two men in navy fatigues and masks over their faces appeared, their weapons raised, aimed at his chest.

Behind their masks, their eyes mirrored the confusion that wormed its way through his mind.

The man to his right lowered his weapon and shoved his mask up onto his head.

'Sir? We received your panic button signal two minutes ago.' His jaw went slack as he cast his eyes over the remains of the door and then fell back to Porchester. 'What's going on, sir?'

Porchester pushed past him, shoving the second man out of the way, and glared at the four other masked armed guards lining the corridor. All of them kept their weapons steady, their bodies poised, ready to shoot.

He spun round, taking in the empty passageway that led back to the elevator and fire exit stairs, and then turned back and squinted through the dim light to the other end of the corridor.

It was empty.

His attention settled on the men's leader.

'Where are the others?'

'Others, sir?'

'The three men that were here, the ones that rammed that door down,' he said, pointing at the damage and then quickly lowering his arm as his hand started to shake. He forced himself to remain calm.

Surely there had to be a simple explanation.

The men's leader looked over his shoulder at his men, who all shook their heads, and then turned back to Porchester.

'Sir, it's just us. There's no-one else on duty tonight.'

'No, that's not right,' said Porchester. 'When I pressed the panic button, three guards dressed exactly like you appeared in less than a minute.'

The leader frowned and then pulled a comms microphone from the collar of his blue uniform shirt. 'Base, this is leader one. Confirm any others on duty tonight?'

Porchester watched the man's face as he listened to the response, his finger pressed to his earpiece. A frown began at his brow, confusion etched across his face, and Porchester clenched his fists, fighting down the urge to rip the comms equipment from the man and speak to the head of the security detail himself.

'Okay, copy that.'

Porchester folded his arms across his chest and raised an eyebrow, waiting for the man to tuck the comms microphone back into his collar.

'Well? What did they say?' he urged. 'Did they find out who they were?'

'Not exactly, sir.' The leader scratched his head. 'They said you personally requested the additional security by email an hour ago. Something about wanting a team close to the rifle range as you wanted to practise tonight.'

***

Porchester dismissed the security guards, managing to coerce the leader of the group to arrange to have the damaged door replaced with as little fuss as possible, promised to launch a full investigation upon his return to the office the next day, and then hurried towards the elevator and punched in the number for the upper level.

His gut twisted as he recalled the promises he'd made, the deals he'd struck, and the fact that if he wasn't careful, the whole lot was going to slip through his fingers before he'd had a chance to finalise his plans and set the whole lot in motion.

He silently cursed Dan Taylor, keeping his features smooth, aware of the security cameras that hung in the uppermost corners of the elevator.

As the doors opened, he dashed forward, his suit jacket flapping behind him as he hurried towards a doorway off to the right of the secured reception area.

'I'll call your driver, sir,' called out one of the security guards.

'No need,' said Porchester, holding up his hand as he dashed past. 'I'll take my own this evening, thank you.'

He pushed through the door and ran down two flights of stairs and then across the wide expanse of the underground car park, sliding to a stop next to a classic grey sports car, its paintwork gleaming under the fluorescent lighting.

Fumbling with the key fob, he tried to steady his shaking hands and then wrenched open the door and collapsed into the driver's seat. He stabbed the key into the ignition, shoved his mobile phone into the hands-free holder on the dashboard, and rested his hands on the steering wheel, his breathing laboured.

His heart hammered so hard, he felt sick. Sweat ran down the back of his neck, yet he resisted the urge to rest his forehead on his hands, knowing the garage was peppered with CCTV cameras.

He pressed the buttons on the dashboard-mounted mobile phone and pulled the seat belt across his chest while he waited for the call to be connected.

After three rings, the call went through, the person that answered sullen, reluctant in their duty.

He persisted and then waited.

Eventually, he was handed over to the person he wanted to speak to most.

'You're so bloody-minded,' he exploded. 'Why leak the story of the isotope theft to the press?'

He closed his eyes, leaned his right elbow against the car window and massaged his temples as he listened to the response.

'Couldn't you see?' he finally snapped. 'All the time he was looking for the isotope, he was distracted from finding out why his mission had failed.'

He leaned forward in his seat, his chest straining against the nylon restraint that crossed his chest.

'No, please.' He sighed and waved a pacifying hand in the air. 'I'll do whatever's necessary. Please.'

He stared at the phone, the dialling tone loud within the confines of the leather upholstery, and then pressed the 'end call' button and stared at the blank display.

He turned the key, the engine roaring to life, and then threw the car into gear and eased it from its parking space.

As he turned away from the building and out onto the city street, his mind raced.

He'd have to put contingency plans in place to appease them, especially as he'd already ensured that the first half of their payment had already been secretly stored in an overseas bank account, but it was still possible to carry out their plans. A few adjustments were necessary; that was all. He was sure they'd understand.

And he still had options as far as Dan Taylor was concerned.

Plenty of options.

Chapter 45

'What's going on?'

'No time now,' said David. 'I'll explain when we get there.'

'Get where?' Dan yelled over the noise of the small train powering along the tracks beneath it.

David shook his head, beckoned to Mitch, and the two of them crawled back towards the front of the train.

He ran his hand over his eyes, relief turning to fatigue and frustration, then leaned back against the steel rail and tried to gauge where David might be taking him.

As the train clattered over a set of points, it swung into a narrower tunnel, and Dan ducked his head as the roof height dropped by several centimetres. He craned his neck, to see David and Mitch crouching on the floor of the train, and he copied their stance, easing himself from the shelf he'd been sitting on and kneeling on the steel floor, his hands gripping the seat to counteract the swaying of the vehicle as it began to slow.

Dan craned his neck to see beyond the driver hunched over the controls and then held his breath.

The mail train's lights flickered to life, revealing a dead end.

Now what?

As they drew closer, his ears picked up a metallic scraping sound. It began as the train approached the end of the tunnel at a slow crawl, and then his eyes caught movement in the middle of the tunnel.

His jaw dropped.

The whole end of the tunnel was moving apart, revealing an opening.

Dan moved into a crouching position and edged forward, his interest piqued further when he realised he was staring at a large steel door.

He leaned across and tapped Mitch on the shoulder. 'What the hell is that?'

'Flood defence door from the Second World War,' came the reply. 'We tweaked it a bit.'

Dan leaned back on his heels and wracked his memory. He'd heard of the underground train stations being used during the war for bomb shelters, but had no idea the government at the time had gone to such lengths to protect its citizens and infrastructure.

Mitch turned to face him. 'You've got the same look on your face that I think I had when I saw this for the first time,' he grinned.

'It's amazing.'

'It worked using hydrophones,' said Mitch. 'If they picked up any noise over a certain amount of decibels, such as a bomb hitting the river or a building near one of the lines, the doors closed automatically so the people sheltering down here didn't drown.'

Dan shook his head in wonder as the doors slid into their housings at each side of the tunnel, and the mail train passed through.

Mitch held up a remote and pressed a button, and then the doors began to close once more. 'Enhancement,' he explained and tucked the remote control back into the webbing at the front of his jacket.

They turned back to the front of the train as it moved forward at a walking pace.

Lights began to flicker to life above their heads, and the platform of an abandoned station was revealed, its old wall tiles yellowed with age, the familiar logo and station name faded almost beyond recognition. Old posters peeled away from the tiled walls, ancient advertisements for wartime propaganda, cigarette companies, and theatre shows.

The driver of the train eased it to a standstill and leapt across the gap, before hurrying across the platform towards a spiral staircase, its steel surface glinting under the lights, and began to climb.

Dan clambered from the train, stretched his legs, and then walked across the platform and peered at the name across the middle of the logo on the wall. He turned to David. 'Where —'

'This one doesn't even appear on any historical maps,' David winked.

'Then how did you…' Dan stopped himself. He figured there were some things David would never reveal, and his insight was rewarded with a knowing smile.

'Come on,' said David. 'We've got a lot of work to do, and we're running out of time.'

'Nearly there,' said Mitch cheerfully and slapped Dan on the shoulder as he walked past, gripped the railings of the spiral staircase, and began to climb.

Dan followed and then glanced over his shoulder as the lights on the platform began to dim, before the area was plunged once more into darkness.

'We tweaked it,' Mitch called down to him.

'Don't tell me,' muttered Dan. 'Another enhancement.'

He concentrated on putting his feet one in front of the other as the staircase wound upwards, careful to ensure his boots landed squarely on the small steel treads.

'Who built this? Bloody pixies?' he muttered and ignored the snort of laughter from Mitch as he joined him on a gantry at the top of the stairs.

'No joking now,' said Mitch, his face serious. 'No talking. This last part of the route's dangerous.'

He beckoned Dan forward and led the way along a passageway, its walls covered with pipes and electrical wiring.

Dan jerked sideways as a thunderous rumbling passed behind the wall to his left-hand side and nearly swore out loud until he remembered Mitch's instructions. He hurried after the man, who stood next to an open door to the right of the passageway, his finger to his lips.

Dan walked past him and then waited while Mitch carefully pushed the door back into its frame, locking it shut with a faint *click*.

He pointed behind Dan, who turned and saw another, shorter, spiral staircase.

As he reached the top tread, he stumbled in surprise.

David stood at the entrance to a room off to his left and beckoned Dan closer.

'Welcome to our new headquarters,' he murmured and stood aside to let him pass. 'Keep your voice down.'

Dan stepped over the threshold, his thoughts in turmoil.

Before him, a fully-functioning operations room was laid out, while off to the right-hand side, he saw a conference room and an office – evidently much in use.

He swung round at the sound of the door closing and faced David and Mitch.

'Okay, we're clear now,' said David.

Dan watched in astonishment as the third masked man turned from the computer he'd sat in front of, whipped off his black hood and mask, and shook out a mane of blond hair.

'Mel?' He spun round to face David. 'What the hell?'

'We felt it safe to leave Melissa in place. That is, until you went storming off after Porchester and nearly blew our whole mission. She's the only other person to know about our operation here.'

'You scared the crap out of me,' Melissa grumbled. She scowled at Dan and then turned back to her computer screens.

'What the hell is this place?' Dan asked. 'Where are we?'

David raised his gaze to the ceiling. 'We're in a concrete and steel reinforced bunker below the pavement outside Waterloo,' he said. He tapped his foot on the floor. 'Below us, probably another metre down, is the tunnel for the new underground line.'

Dan tried to concentrate, to get his jumbled thoughts into some sort of coherent order.

'How did you know where to find me?' he managed.

'I tracked you,' said Mel. 'Button on your jacket is wired.'

Dan spun round to face her and then raised his hands and began to tug at each of the buttons on his leather jacket.

'Bottom one,' said Mel.

'Thanks,' he said and then wrenched the button away and threw it across the room at her.

She caught it one-handed, grinned, and then turned back to her computer.

'I suppose I have you to thank for finding me before Porchester's security team?' he said to her back.

'Sure do.'

'Thanks.'

'You're welcome.'

'How—'

'Hacked into his email,' she said over her shoulder. 'Remember?'

'When Mel contacted us to say you'd gone after Porchester, we figured you'd go straight to his office to confront him,' explained David.

'Predictable,' called out Mitch from the other side of the room.

Dan flicked his finger up and then turned on his heel to stare at the equipment the small team had managed to squash into the tiny space they now occupied.

'How the hell…,' he began and then shook his head. 'I don't understand – why aren't you using your own office back at the EPG?'

David dropped his equipment on a table in the middle of the room. 'Because there are too many secrets, Dan. And we're one of those secrets.'

Chapter 46

'When we heard that your mission had been compromised, we knew something was wrong,' explained David. 'Except we kept being stalled. We weren't allowed access to the file, which raised a stink – I pointed out you report to me, but was told I wasn't to be made privy to that operation.'

'We were given another mission twenty-four hours after you left the country,' added Mitch. He looked at David. 'It stank. We were trying to raise hell to get you back, and there we were, being sent on a mission three thousand miles in the opposite direction.'

'What happened?'

'I had a quiet word with the Prime Minister,' said David. 'Turns out he hadn't authorised either of the missions – yours or ours.'

'So Porchester tried to set you up as well?'

'He's a bastard, all right,' said Mitch.

'How did you escape, then?'

The corner of David's mouth twitched. 'We didn't escape. We never went.'

'What?'

'Hence all the secrecy,' said David. 'We went AWOL. We're wanted men in some circles of the British establishment. For the moment, anyway,' he shrugged. He held his hand up as Dan began to protest. 'It's okay. The Prime Minister knows how to contact us. No-one else does. It's safer that way. Until we can work out what's going on.'

'How did they find me in Eastern Europe?' asked Dan. 'Why rescue me and then try to kill me again?'

'The Brigadier organised the rescue mission,' explained Mitch. 'No-one was told about that operation. Apparently you were spotted being stretchered away from the helicopter at the airfield in Germany, though, so someone found out you were being transferred to the hospital here in England.'

'Jesus.' Dan paced the small room and scratched at the stubble forming on his chin. 'Why would someone try to kill all three of us? Have you gone through all our old mission reports?'

'We did,' said David. 'It's the first thing we got Mel onto once we set up down here.'

'What did you find?'

'Absolutely nothing. It's got nothing to do with an old mission, Dan.'

'Then what's going on?'

His senior officer leaned against the desk and held his stare. 'This isn't about retribution. They're not trying to pay us back, Dan. They're trying to prevent us from *stopping* them.'

'Stop them from doing what? Break the UK away from the European Union?'

'That,' agreed David. 'But there are others pulling strings behind the scenes. It's not just Porchester and his cronies in Parliament trying to overthrow the PM to get their own way. Nor are they alone in their endeavours.'

Dan's eyes narrowed. 'Russians.'

David held up a finger. 'Precisely. Or, more to the point, *some* Russians.'

'Why?'

'European Union embargoes are starting to cripple the Russian economy,' explained David. 'Internally, there's a lot of disquiet in the Kremlin, wondering where the President's aggression is going to lead. No-one knows for sure, and it's making them nervous.'

'One thing is certain, though,' he added. 'Russia will likely be a broken country economically if something drastic doesn't happen – and soon.'

'But – Porchester?' said Dan. 'Why the hell would he betray us?'

Mitch dropped his Kevlar vest on the desk next to them. 'Because we monitor everything to do with energy services and infrastructure in the UK,' he said. 'And he probably knew that if he was going to attempt to strike a deal with the Russians, he'd need to make sure we were out of the way first.'

'What sort of deal?'

'The sort that ousts the current PM, puts Porchester in a position of power within a new government, and breaks the UK out of the EU.'

Dan sighed. 'I get it now. It's what Heatherington said. It'll free up the UK to buy cheap gas from a Russian government and any companies desperate to sell it to us,' he said.

'Got it in one,' said Mitch, mimicking a gun and firing it in Dan's direction.

'But why the stolen isotope?' said Dan. 'I don't understand why that was necessary.'

'Smoke and mirrors,' said David. 'Porchester got that one right. A radioactive isotope stolen from a government fracking project? It's a massive public relations disaster for the PM. Although I think the leak blew that part of their plan out of the water.'

'If Porchester could show that he could lead the country in a time of crisis in the absence of the PM, it'd probably make a more convincing transition in the event of a bloodless coup,' said Mitch. 'You've got to admit, the man's a natural in front of the cameras.'

'But then it leaked,' Dan murmured and sank into one of the chairs next to Mel's computer. 'And I made them panic.'

'You did,' said David, 'but without you doing that, we would've had a much larger number of members of the public seriously ill from radiation poisoning.'

'Er, guys?'

They turned at the sound of Mel's voice. She was staring at one of the monitors on the wall that had been linked to a twenty-four hour news channel.

'We have a problem,' she said, her voice shaking. She pointed at the monitor.

On it, a photograph of Dan was being displayed, the caption underneath screaming out its headline.

Wanted by police.

'Ah, shit,' sighed Dan.

'Turn it up,' David commanded.

They gathered round Mel's chair as she increased the volume.

'Police have been warned that this individual is extremely dangerous and probably armed,' the newsreader said. 'Under no circumstances should members of the public try to apprehend him. Instead, they should dial nine-nine-nine.'

The photograph disappeared and was replaced by a shot of the newsreader.

'To repeat,' she said, the excitement in her voice palpable, 'Police wish to question this man, Dan Taylor, in connection with the stolen radioactive isotope found earlier today. He is considered dangerous and probably armed.'

'Porchester,' Dan spat. 'He set me up.'

'She's pretty,' Mitch murmured.

Dan glared at him and then pointed at the screen. 'I'm a wanted man.'

Mitch shrugged. 'We were a good team while it lasted.'

'Fuck off.' Dan turned to David. 'I need to contact Sarah,' he said. 'She could be in danger.'

'Where is she?'

'The safe house, at Eaton Terrace.'

'Mel, take the car and get Sarah from the safe house,' said David. 'He's right. I don't want Dan's enemies using her to get to him.'

'On it.' Mel leapt from her computer, swiped a set of keys from the desk, and turned to go.

'Hang on,' said Dan. 'She doesn't know you.' He turned to David. 'I left her with instructions to keep the door to the house locked unless I phoned first.' He withdrew his mobile. 'I'll give her a heads up.'

Mel shifted from foot to foot while Dan spoke to Sarah, then when he ended the call and nodded at her, she disappeared through the door, pulling it shut behind her.

'We didn't know about the plan to steal the isotope,' David admitted, turning down the volume on the television feed. 'Since the attempted overthrowing of the Prime Minister last month, we've been trying to collate information on his enemies – with all our resources under scrutiny from them, the three of us have been somewhat limited in our abilities.'

'Where's the truck?'

A few years ago, David had insisted on a mobile back-up office, enabling the team to travel anywhere around the UK and Europe and still maintain a working ops centre. Now, he looked pained.

'We destroyed it,' he said. He pointed at the equipment Mel had been working on. 'This is everything from the truck. We stripped it, brought it down here in stages over a few nights, and then took the truck apart piece by piece and scrapped it.'

'Seems a bit extreme.'

'We're being hunted, Dan.' Mitch took a step forward. 'And, until now, we haven't been sure who's after us. We didn't have a choice.'

Dan raised his gaze to the television, his photograph now plastered across the screen with a flickering red banner at the foot of the image.

He ran a hand over his face and then looked at the David and Mitch. 'And now I'm a wanted man, too.'

Chapter 47

Forty-five minutes later, Dan rose as Sarah walked through the door, closely followed by Mel.

Her worried expression softened as she saw him, and he gave her a quick hug.

'Everything okay?'

'Yes,' she said. 'I wondered what on earth was going on.'

Mitch walked towards them. 'I need to apologise for scaring you the other day,' he said to Sarah.

'What?'

'It was Mitch that followed you from your apartment,' said David. 'You were getting too close to the truth before we were ready to confront Porchester.'

Sarah spun on her heel to face Mitch, her face thunderous. 'You scared the hell out of me.'

Mitch held up his hands. 'It had to be realistic.'

'It's true,' said David. 'I'm sorry, but it was the only way we could make sure you backed off without exposing our plans. We still weren't sure where Dan's investigation was leading.'

He turned to Dan. 'Mel was keeping us up to speed,' he explained. 'If you and Sarah had gotten too close to Porchester and scared him off before we had enough evidence, we'd have already lost.'

'What evidence *have* you got?'

'The USB stick Mel gave you that you passed onto Porchester means we've got everything on his personal computer,' said David.

'Did it work?'

'Oh yeah,' Mel grinned. She pointed to a stack of paperwork clipped together in the middle of the table. 'It worked *really* well.'

'But we agreed you couldn't use the email alone to prove Porchester's involvement,' said Dan, confused. 'So what use is that?'

'It's never been simply about exposing Porchester,' said David, handing him the print-outs. 'There are names in these emails – people who are supporting him and, more importantly, people who are *sponsoring* him to overthrow the PM.'

'We were about to bring all this to the Prime Minister's attention when you decided to jump the gun and confront Porchester yourself,' said Mel. 'You nearly blew our whole covert operation out the water.'

'You should've seen Mel's face when she turned up here and said you'd gone to see him,' Mitch snorted. 'I think she would have killed you herself, given the chance.'

Mel glared at him. 'You said you wouldn't tell him.'

'It's like the tip of an iceberg,' said Dan, ignoring both of them as he fanned through the pages. 'You think you can see it all, but when you look under the surface, it's huge.'

'It certainly is,' agreed David. 'Plus, with Mel's hacking skills, we've managed to obtain copies of Porchester's bank accounts – the ones he doesn't report.'

'Swiss?'

'Of course.'

'Can you trace who's paying him?'

'Working on it,' said Mel.

'We've got to convince the PM his life continues to be in danger,' said David. 'After that, we have to move fast to prove who Porchester's paymasters are.'

'That could take months.'

'We don't have months. We have hours.'

Chapter 48

'I'm not too concerned with the first few names at the moment,' said David, tapping his finger on the page. 'I *am* interested in this guy.'

'Vasili Malikov,' said Dan and then frowned. 'Where have I heard that name before?'

'Russian mafia,' said Mitch. 'Old school. Grew up during the Yeltsin era. Took over from his father in his twenties and turned out to be even worse than the old bastard.'

'Yeah, I remember now,' said Dan. 'What the hell is he doing in the UK?'

'Diplomatic immunity,' said David, ignoring a snort from Mitch. 'Apparently, Malikov decided to go legitimate ten years ago, severed all ties with his old way of life, and re-established himself as a businessman specialising in capital investments.'

'Bollocks.'

'Indeed.'

'Thoughts?'

'Probably the man who owned the prison you were being held in.'

Dan reached forward and snatched the photograph from the file, his knuckles turning white as he held it in his grip.

'Then I owe him one.'

David tweaked the photograph from Dan's fingers. 'All in good time,' he said and dropped it back in the folder. 'Right now, we need to find out what he and Porchester are up to. And fast. I've got a video conference with the PM in less than an hour.'

'Where do you want us to start?'

David jerked his chin at the television screen. 'I've got a contact in the Metropolitan Police who's keeping me up to date when he can. Let's try to get him on speakerphone, see if he can shed some more light on this news about the isotope being recovered.'

He turned to Sarah. 'Help Mel if you can. With your investigative skills, an extra pair of eyes on this would be appreciated.'

'Okay.'

David pointed at Dan. 'And you'll have to stay quiet. As far as the police are concerned, I'm AWOL. I don't want them to know I'm also harbouring a wanted man.'

Dan slumped in a chair out of the way while David dialled a number and asked to be put through to his contact.

'There was one male suspect in the building,' said the detective. 'Already dead, so no use trying to question him.'

David appeared to ignore the dark humour and instead rubbed at his earlobe. 'Radiation poisoning, too?'

'Actually, no,' said the man on the end of the phone, his surprise still evident. 'We've got to wait for the official forensic report, but first impressions are that he was smothered to death.'

Dan grabbed a pen and notepad and scrawled across the page before spinning it round to face David and jabbed his finger at the writing.

David nodded. 'Do we know yet if the fingerprints match those of the suspect that died at the hospital earlier today?'

'Not for sure, but it could be,' agreed the policeman. 'He could've put his accomplice out of his own misery before turning himself in.'

'Or took matters into his own hands if his accomplice refused to get help,' said Mitch.

Dan pulled the notebook back and wrote two words on it and then shoved it across the desk to David.

Kill switch?

'What if Ben Hicks was acting on orders from someone else?' asked David.

'What do you mean?'

'They must have been reporting to someone,' said Mitch. 'If that person found out both Ben and this second guy were at death's door with radiation poisoning, maybe the person they were reporting to instructed Ben to kill his accomplice while he was too weak to do anything about it.'

'Or before they were found,' David added.

Dan heard the policeman swear under his breath.

'We'll need to find out if Ben said anything to Dan Taylor when he interviewed him at the hospital,' he finally said. 'From the transcript I read, it appears Ben refused to give up his accomplice, but it's certainly worthy of further investigation.'

Dan gave David a thumbs up and then wrote once more on the page.

Porchester?

David nodded, but kept his thoughts to himself.

'Well, if you've got anything else for me, use my private number,' said David and ended the call after the policeman assured him he would.

'What do you think?' he asked.

'Ben was either reporting to Porchester or Malikov,' said Mel, turning from her computer. She leaned forward, balancing her elbows on her knees. 'Except I don't think Porchester was running the two thieves.'

Dan frowned. 'What makes you say that?'

Mel shrugged. 'It doesn't seem his style,' she said and glanced down at her hands.

'Explain,' said David. 'And don't be shy about it.'

Mel took a deep breath. 'Okay. Well, Porchester seems to only deal with people on the same level as him – psychologically, you know? I can't see him lowering his own perceived standards to deal with a low-life like Hicks.' She looked at each of them in turn. 'Yes, he'd be able to provide information about the government project, but organising the theft of an isotope?' She shook her head. 'No way.'

'So, the Russians, then?' asked Dan.

David pointed at the paper trail that Mel had started to accumulate. 'Apart from that one email you found from Porchester to Malikov, have you found anything else?'

Mel turned and jabbed her forefinger on the keyboard to wake up the computer. 'I've been trying to get into his bank accounts,' she said. 'I found one that has me worried. I can't see it listed on his assets register.'

'Why has it got you worried?' Dan prompted. 'What can you see?'

'This,' she said and beckoned them closer. She ran her finger down the screen.

Mitch whistled under his breath. 'That's a *lot* of money.'

'Where's it coming from?' asked Sarah.

Mel moved her hand up the screen to the more recent account activity. 'Look at this. Until three weeks ago, there were regular payments going into the account. Same amount, every week. Then,' she said, tracing her finger down the screen as she spoke, 'those same amounts were transferred again, twenty-four hours after being received.'

'Porchester moving the money,' said Dan.

'Right,' Mel nodded. 'What I'm trying to trace is where that money was coming from – and why.'

'A payoff?' suggested Mitch.

'Then why did it stop?' said Sarah.

Dan leaned forward. 'I got rescued.' He turned to David and Mitch. 'And you two went into hiding.'

'It's still only circumstantial,' said David. 'Unless you, Mel, can verify the money was coming from Malikov.'

'And where Porchester was transferring it to,' said Dan, calculating the amounts in his head. He straightened and stared at David. 'There's more than half a million quid over the past four months.'

'*Pounds*,' said Mel, unable to keep the smirk off her face.

Dan glared at her and then continued. 'I'm presuming we'll find it's all been transferred to Switzerland or another tax haven that has a reputation for asking no questions.'

'Porchester getting ready to take his family and run for the hills if his plan doesn't work?' suggested Mitch.

'We need to tell the PM,' said David. 'If Porchester's been receiving bribes from Malikov for compromising your mission and is trying to influence the PM's European policy to favour the Russians, he needs to know about it.'

He reached into his pocket and pulled out his mobile phone.

'Hang on,' said Dan. 'I thought you were in hiding, too? How are you going to reach the PM without compromising your position?'

David glanced sideways. 'The PM has had his suspicions that there's been something going on behind the scenes still, despite surviving the 'no confidence' vote,' he finally said. 'He didn't know who to trust, so I agreed with him that Mitch and I would go into hiding instead of following orders passed down by Porchester,' he said. 'We've been trying to get this breakthrough ever since.'

Dan crossed his arms over his chest. 'And how do you know you can trust the PM?'

'He was the one that authorised your rescue,' said David.

Chapter 49

'Get the PM on the line now,' said David, pointing at Mel's computer. 'We'll meet you in the conference room.'

'I thought you didn't want me present?' said Dan.

'This changes everything,' said David. 'Strength in numbers. We need to convince the PM that Porchester is trying to overthrow his efforts in Europe.'

He led the way to the cramped room that had been set up with basic conferencing equipment, and the three men sat down at chairs facing a camera and screen.

As Mel powered up the system and fought her way through the PM's bureaucratic outer circle, Dan leaned forward.

'I didn't stumble on the story about the isotope theft,' he said. 'Someone sent the information about the theft to Sarah – the same day I discharged myself from hospital.'

David tugged his ear lobe. 'Malikov.'

'Why him and not Porchester?'

'Because Malikov probably can't be tied to the isotope theft – he *can* be linked to the prison where you were being held. Only Porchester could be associated with the project.'

'Hell of a risk, though.'

'Not if Malikov wanted to keep Porchester under control,' said Mitch. 'Sounds to me like the knowledge of the theft sent you both on a wild goose chase.'

'And distracted you from investigating who knew about your mission and held you captive,' said Sarah.

'But why hold me captive? Why keep me alive?'

'I'm sure there are a few people who'd like to get their hands on you – for a price,' said David.

Dan shivered.

'Coming online now,' Mel called.

The screen in front of them lit up, and the team turned their attention to it as one.

'Prime Minister,' said David. 'Thank you for talking to us at short notice.'

The PM's camera shook a little, the image quality poor, and Dan realised the man was holding a tablet computer.

'Best make it quick, Ludlow,' said the PM. 'I'm about to get on a helicopter to City Airport. 'I've got a press conference to attend.'

David's gaze shifted to the door as Mel appeared. 'Where's Evans?' he asked. 'Can you get him to dial in?'

She held up her mobile phone and shook her head. 'No answer.'

David turned his attention back to the PM. 'We've reason to suspect the theft of the isotope was carried out to embarrass you and force your resignation.'

The PM frowned. 'Go on.'

'The radioactive leak ruined that plan,' said Dan. 'They couldn't control it, so in an attempt to use it to their advantage, they broke the story to the press, implicating me in the process.'

'Who's 'they'?'

'Vasili Malikov and Hugh Porchester,' said David.

'Porchester?' The PM fell silent for a moment, a frown creasing his brow. 'Are you sure?'

'We've got evidence to show he was receiving large sums of money on a regular basis,' explained David. 'We've got emails tying him to Vasili Malikov.'

'Good grief.'

'Prime Minister, until we can substantiate the evidence in greater detail, we have to assume that your life is in danger,' said David. 'These are desperate men, motivated by power and corruption. I'd respectfully recommend that you hold your press conference there, rather than return to London.'

'The problem is,' said the PM, 'After the events of the past week, it would be political suicide if I didn't return.' His eyes shifted to the right, and he nodded to someone off camera. 'As it is, my press secretary and I have decided that we'll hold the press conference in Covent Garden – we need to show the public that they're safe to go about their daily lives, and there's nothing to fear.'

'I really don't think that's a good idea,' said David.

'Pass on all your information to MI5,' said the PM. 'They can assess what you have, and then we can convene a meeting to discuss how best to deal with what you think you have.'

'With respect, sir,' said David through gritted teeth, 'that doesn't address the fact that now is not the time for you to be making a very public appearance.'

'Hand over the information, Ludlow,' said the Prime Minister. 'That's an order.'

'Sir.'

The PM checked his watch. 'Hugh Porchester is due to meet my flight in less than an hour. If he is guilty of conspiring to overthrow my government, then I don't want to alert him to the fact that we're onto him, not until MI5 have corroborated your findings – is that understood?'

'Yes, sir.'

'Good. I'll see you in London.'

'What have you told the other security services?' asked David. 'Who do I liaise with?'

The PM held up his hand. 'I've asked them to keep it low-key,' he said. He raised his eyes to someone off camera and then turned his attention back to David. 'There'll be a police presence, of course, and they'll have people on top of the buildings as well, and my usual security detail will be with me. But if Malikov is planning something, we don't want to scare him off.'

'Is that it?' Dan stepped closer to the screen, his tone incredulous. 'We've just told you we believe your life is in danger, and you want to hold a press conference?'

The PM's eyes narrowed. 'Harbouring a fugitive, Ludlow?'

'He's been set up,' said David. 'I'll explain, but he's right. You must reconsider.'

'It has to be done,' said the PM. 'You look like you're healing well, by the way, Taylor.'

'Thank you, sir,' said Dan. 'But I still think this is a mistake.'

'We can't assure your safety if you go ahead with this,' agreed David. 'We have no idea to what extremes Porchester will go now. Or whether he's even in control of the situation any more.'

'I understand,' said the PM, 'but that's my final word on the matter.' He glanced up as someone approached his right side, and a woman bent down to whisper in his ear. He nodded and then dismissed her. 'My helicopter is ready. I'll be back in the country within the hour.' He reached forward, his hand hovering over the screen. 'Do your best.'

His image disappeared.

David swore under his breath, before he spun his chair round to face the team.

'Okay, notwithstanding the fact that our Prime Minister appears to have completely lost his mind, let me have your suggestions.'

'He's up to something,' said Dan, wagging his finger at the blank screen. 'He's not telling us everything. There's no way he'd be going ahead with this press conference otherwise.'

'I agree,' said Mitch. 'As a tactician, our Prime Minister is usually more open to suggestions.'

'He seemed distracted,' said Sarah.

'That doesn't help us. We still need to ensure his safety, just in case he *has* missed something,' said David. He began to pace the room. 'Mel – do as the PM ordered. Send everything we have on Porchester and Malikov to MI5. I'm sure they'll be pleased to hear from you.'

'Maybe,' said Mel, then hurried to her computer.

'Right, you two. Put yourselves in Malikov and Porchester's shoes,' said David. 'The PM's on his way back, he's going to make a very public appearance in a crowded place, and no-one has a clue what he's going to say.'

'Porchester will show support for the PM,' said Dan. 'He's a survivor. He'll wait for another chance. If the PM plays this right, Porchester will never know he's under suspicion, because he thinks he's got me out of the way.'

Mitch frowned. 'Why would the PM keep him close now?'

'To draw out Malikov,' said Mel, joining them once more. 'I reckon the PM wants to end any Russian influence as soon as possible.'

'I agree,' said David. 'But I'm also wondering what Malikov might be planning.'

'What do you mean?' asked Dan.

'Malikov's got a reputation for being a sore loser,' said David. 'He's not going to let this go. If he was prepared to use Porchester to try to influence the negotiations with the European Union, then he's not going to give up easily.' He pointed at the documents they'd left strewn across the conference table during their video call with the PM. 'Let's face it, we already believe him to be responsible for the deaths of two high-ranking politicians. One that supported the PM, and the other who failed to pull off a vote of no confidence to oust him.'

'Er, boss? You need to look at this.'

Both Dan and David spun round to face Mel, the note of panic in her voice raising the hairs on the back of Dan's neck.

'What is it?'

She pointed at the screen, her hand shaking. 'I think Porchester's Russian friends just triggered their own kill switch.'

Dan leaned over the analyst's shoulder. 'Explain.'

'This is an email account Porchester – or his paymasters – set up, using a common internet-based email server, okay?'

'Understood.'

'Okay, well, they've been messaging each other by saving emails in the "drafts" folder, believing they can't be read by anyone else.'

'So, what did you find?' asked David.

Mel cleared her throat. 'Well, I hacked into the account before we went to fetch Dan,' she said. 'I left it running so I could hack the new messages that had been posted.' She traced her finger under the text of the message she'd clicked open. 'I've been waiting for the encryption programme to translate it.'

Dan felt his heart skip a beat, a brief moment before he heard Mitch swear under his breath next to him.

'There's no doubt of this?' asked David. 'You're absolutely sure this has come from the Russians to Porchester? No-one else is involved?'

Mel glanced over her shoulder and nodded. 'I'm sure,' she whispered. 'The Russians have just instructed Porchester to make sure the Prime Minister attends a press conference here in London to confirm the safe intercept of the radioactive isotope and the immediate suspension of the government's fracking project.'

'And as soon as the Prime Minister shows up, the Russians will kill him,' finished Dan. He straightened and then turned to David and Mitch. 'We need to stop him. Now.'

'But how on earth is Malikov going to get to the PM?' asked Sarah. 'The place will be crowded.'

Dan looked at Mitch and then pointed at the satellite image of the Prime Minister's chosen location for his speech.

'There's only one way he could try at short notice,' he said. 'Sniper.'

Chapter 50

Kevin Baxter shifted the weight of the sports bag on his shoulder and wove his way between two Australian tourists that had stopped in the middle of the pedestrianised area to take photographs.

He grunted an apology as the bag brushed against one of them and then picked up his pace.

Timing was everything.

Too early, and he could be spotted. Too late, and he wouldn't have time to set up the rifle he carried.

He'd recce'd the venue a week ago; when he'd asked how his contact had known the PM's exact whereabouts, he was assured that he wouldn't have to worry – the leader of the country would show up at the allocated place. On time and with as little security as possible to help convey an air of safety to the general public.

He glanced sideways at the crowd that filled the wide-open expanse of the square and raised his gaze to the ornate architecture that surrounded the permanent market.

Only last week, he'd been one of the contractors that worked at gently sand-blasting the surface of that building, gradually peeling away the years of dirt and grime that plastered its walls.

It had been a perfect opportunity to gauge the entrances to and, more importantly, the exits from the square.

In the evenings, at home in his one-bedroom apartment to the far east of the city, he'd pored over blueprints stolen from the work site, carefully planning every aspect of the hit.

He prided himself on his professionalism and tenacity. His services weren't cheap, and for this reason, he was able to pick and choose the work he accepted. It enabled him to keep a low profile, so he appeared to live a normal civilian life outside of his profession.

He couldn't help the smirk that twitched at the corner of his mouth.

Most weekdays, he could be found advising clients at the accounting offices of Abbott and Baker, a mid-tier firm based in Chelmsford. He'd taken his parents' well-placed advice to get his chartered accountant qualifications; 'see the world', his father had told him.

Three weeks after celebrating his graduation with them, his parents had been killed, a burglary gone wrong while he'd been out drinking with friends. The police had told him his father had tried to fight off the knife-wielding intruder, evidenced by the injuries to his hands, arms and face.

The murderer had never been caught.

After that, Baxter had joined the French Foreign Legion, disappearing off the face of the planet as far as his friends were concerned. It had been the only way he'd known how to direct his grief and anger in private.

He'd quickly discovered, however, that there was money to be made on the freelancing circuit – a *lot* of money. After a minor training incident left him with a medical discharge from the Legion, he'd accepted the order to quit and had returned back to the UK via Berlin, his first assassination job already complete.

Within three months, he'd tracked down his parents' murderer and had exacted his revenge, leaving the man's corpse to rot in an industrial bin in an abandoned parking lot.

Now, his work found him through recommendations, an arrangement that suited him well. Only people that could afford his prices would approach him, and they could only do so through a previous client. It ensured complete trust and an unspoken understanding that the work would be carried out.

Baxter didn't accept last-minute cancellations, and he sure as hell didn't give out refunds.

After completing a circuit of the square, taking his time while he milled about alongside the tourists and city workers, he stopped beside an entranceway to a narrow building squashed between its neighbours. His back to the door, he squinted up at the skyline and then let his gaze wander back to the cobbled street, all the time searching for anything that seemed out of place, dangerous, and liable to turn the plan to shit.

A few hundred metres away, close to where a stage was hastily being constructed, a collection of television news vans had congregated, the occupants standing around, talking to each other, takeaway coffee cups in one hand and mobile phones in the other.

Two armed policemen approached his position, their slow walking pace appearing nonchalant to any normal passer-by. Baxter knew otherwise. The pace enabled vigilance.

He dropped his bag to the ground beside him, reached into his pocket, and pulled out a cigarette packet. He knocked out one into his palm together with the small plastic cigarette lighter and lit up.

He pushed the packet back into his pocket as the policemen approached, blew smoke away from them, and nodded.

They turned away from him in unison to watch three youths go tearing past, their shouts suddenly muted at the sight of the two policemen, and then they were gone.

Baxter watched their backs as they disappeared round the corner of the square and then removed the cigarette from between his lips and stubbed it out on the brickwork of the building. He hawked to clear the remnants of smoke from his lungs. The last thing he needed was an unexpected cough to ruin his plans. He returned the cigarette to the packet, picked up the bag, and then turned the doorknob and entered the building.

His fingers brushed the bolt as he closed the door, and he slid the steel across before pulling a key from his pocket and securing the deadlock as well.

The actual location for him had been pre-planned; his job had been to recce the available exits. Unknown to his client, however, he undertook his own insurance policy and had broken into the derelict building three nights ago and replaced the lock.

Just in case.

He stood and listened for a good five minutes until, satisfied he was truly alone, he began to climb the stairs to the room that would give him the visibility he needed across the square.

Finally, once he was ready, Baxter reached into his pocket and pulled out a pay-as-you-go mobile phone. Once he made this call, it would be crushed under his foot, the parts collected and bagged for disposal at different locations several miles away from his current position.

He dialled the number from memory, waited until the man at the other end answered, and then spoke just six words.

'Best go and rehearse your speech.'

Chapter 51

Dan leapt from the car before Mitch had time to brake to a standstill and began running up the narrow paved street towards Covent Garden.

As he approached, he recalled the familiar landmarks in the square – the enclosed market, the church, the large sprawling pub that overlooked the street performers.

Street performers – shit.

He slid to a halt, Mitch barrelling into him, cursing under his breath.

'Why have we stopped?'

'Problem. Look.'

Dan tucked his gun into the back of his jeans so it was out of sight and then jutted his chin towards the wide expanse outside the church and began to walk over to its perimeter.

In the middle of the square, a man balanced precariously on stilts, taunting the crowd that laughed and clapped at his antics. As he lurched and wobbled in the circle created by the swelling throng, he juggled three chainsaws, the loud buzzing of the motors echoing off the surrounding buildings.

To Dan's right, people leaned over a balcony that jutted out from the side of the pub. They laughed at the street performers as they held their drinks aloft, the occasional catcall from the street crowd causing good-natured jeering between the two areas.

It was already busy, and the Prime Minister hadn't even arrived yet. It was only going to get worse.

At the far end of the square, beyond the church, a raised platform had been erected, the Prime Minister's party colours displayed by bright flags that fluttered in the gentle breeze. Camera crews from various news agencies were already milling around, waiting for the leader of the country to appear, while a sound crew tested the audio equipment.

'*One, two. One, two.*'

'Three,' Mitch muttered and then swore as a man in a clown suit brushed past him, pulling a bright red scarf from Mitch's collar as he did so. The crowd laughed, the man bowed, and continued his way around the circle of people.

'I fucking hate clowns,' Mitch grumbled.

'Smile,' said Dan. 'Don't draw attention to yourself.'

He ignored the retort Mitch mumbled under his breath and led the way to a restaurant below the pub's balcony, its overhang providing shade and a way to avoid being seen by anyone on the surrounding buildings.

Dan waved away the owner and turned back to the square, his fists clenched.

'Okay, where is he?'

Mitch checked his watch. 'We've got ten minutes before the press conference is due to start.'

Dan craned his neck to where police had congregated at the northern entrance to the square, blocking off traffic and pedestrian access to make way for the official vehicles that would soon swoop upon an unsuspecting public.

'It's going to be bloody embarrassing if no-one listens to him,' said Mitch.

Dan couldn't stop the twitch at the side of his mouth at the thought. 'I'm sure he'll get plenty of attention from this lot. It's all entertainment, after all, isn't it?'

'I just wish he'd listen to sense. He could've done this in a studio.'

'Yeah, but it wouldn't have had the same effect. Porchester knows the PM has to make a public appearance now or risk losing support.'

They broke off as the sound of a helicopter washed over the streets, its rotors chopping at the airspace above them.

Dan squinted up at the sky as the aircraft banked over the square and then passed. He tapped the microphone at the base of his throat. 'You getting this, Mel?'

'Loud and clear.'

'Are the buildings clear?'

'Nothing up top. Police have done a good job sealing off access points at short notice. They've got their own snipers covering exits onto roofs, too.'

'Right. So he's either *inside* a building or in the crowd.'

'Great, that narrows it down,' said Mitch. He turned at the sound of running footsteps. 'Shit. What does *he* want?'

Dan reached under his t-shirt, his fingers beginning to wrap themselves around the rubber grip of his weapon as the man in the clown suit and make-up barrelled towards him.

He could see the man's features contort as he drew closer before he raised his hand and called out.

'Stop. I need to talk to you.'

Dan stood his ground and kept his hand on his weapon as the man slid to a halt.

'What?'

'You're police or something, right?'

'Who wants to know?'

'Listen, mate – I've seen enough television shows, okay?' The clown glanced over his shoulder. 'I've seen the way you've been scoping the place. You're looking for someone.'

'What if I am?'

The man's eyes hardened. 'There's a dead man in a doorway over near the American restaurant. Broken neck. I thought you should know.'

Dan exhaled. '*Christ*, thank you.'

He slapped the clown on the shoulder as he ran past, calling out to Mitch as he picked up speed.

'With me!' he yelled, and kept going. He punched the clip to his microphone. 'Did you hear that?'

'Copy.' Mel's voice was breathless over the comms equipment. 'Trying to get visual.'

'Hurry. I need to know what I'm walking into.'

'You call that walking?' Mitch's voice carried over the airwaves.

'Got it!' said Mel. 'White male. Neck broken. He's been pushed into one side of the doorway. You won't see him as you approach – there's an industrial bin blocking your view.'

'Anyone else around?'

'Negative.' There was a pause as Mel continued to observe the area. 'You're clear to proceed.'

'Copy that. Mitch?'

'Here.'

Dan slowed his pace as he approached the alleyway that led to the side door of the restaurant and then peered round the corner. He glanced up at the CCTV camera that faced the industrial bin to the right of the alley, the same that Mel was using to observe the scene.

He checked over his shoulder as Mitch slid to a halt next to him. 'You ready?'

'Ready.'

Dan exhaled, taking a split second to fight down the adrenalin that was urging him forward. Ignoring the body at his feet, he reached out cautiously and pushed against the closed door.

It was unlocked, and he thought either someone had entered in a hurry or was planning to leave just as quickly.

He didn't need to check over his shoulder to see if Mitch was following; he knew he'd have his back covered as they entered the building.

Holding his weapon in a steady two-handed grip, Dan edged past the door and threw himself against the inner wall.

Discarded boxes from food supplies filled the narrow passageway to his right, beyond which filtered the sounds of the restaurant as it filled with the start of the after-work crowd. Nearer to his right, he heard the familiar noises of a commercial kitchen – shouts for food orders, pots and crockery being moved at speed, and a radio blaring above it all.

He raised a hand and signalled towards the left, where the corridor stopped abruptly before a flight of steps led upwards.

'Staircase leads to three floors,' said Mel. 'Four doors on each landing.'

'Copy that.' Dan threw himself against the wall, swinging his weapon towards the stairs.

Mitch followed, covering their rear.

Dan made his way up the stairs as fast as he dared, his head jerking left and right as his eyes drew level with the first landing.

Mitch echoed his every move, the two men working as one to clear the space. They moved swiftly, opening each door, guns sweeping the empty rooms, and then moving onto the next until they were satisfied the floor was clear.

'Clear,' Dan murmured over his mike, passing on the message to Melissa. 'We're going up to the next level.'

'Copy.' A soft clicking sound carried over the airwaves. 'I've altered the path of the CCTV cameras at the end of the alleyway now,' she said. 'Last thing we need is the police seeing that body until we're ready.'

'Copy that.'

Dan glanced over his shoulder at Mitch and then jerked his head towards the next flight of stairs.

With the noise from their moving through the rooms on the first level, they'd lost the element of surprise. Now, they moved quickly, and Dan's movements became more fluid as his training took over.

His finger hovered above the trigger guard of his gun; if he had to shoot, he wanted to injure, not kill. They needed answers – and fast.

He forced his mind away from the thought of what would happen if they didn't locate the sniper in time and instead stepped onto the second landing, Mitch on his heels.

Dan turned to Mitch and pointed at him and then at the two doors at the far end of the corridor, indicating he would take the two doors at the front of the building, and Mitch should take the other.

Mitch nodded, and they split up.

Dan forced the air from his lungs and took a deep breath. They had to split up; it was the only way they were going to find their target in time.

He hurried to the first door to the left of the corridor and steadied himself, before reaching out and grasping the door knob between his fingers. It gave way under pressure, and he pushed it, raising his weapon in a two-handed grip as it swung open.

His eyes swept the empty space, dust motes dancing in the sunlight from the pockmarked windowpanes. Footprints smudged the wooden floor in places, and he calculated a man of about his height had been here recently.

Dan swallowed and then moved into the room, stepping towards the windowsill.

Keeping his weapon raised at the doorway at the back of the room, which he supposed led to a bathroom, he glanced down at the scrape markings on the chipped surface.

Someone had definitely rested a rifle on it recently.

Heart racing, he turned his attention to the smaller space at the back of the room, his mind working overtime as he tried to fathom what was going on.

His fears were realised when he threw himself against the frame and aimed his gun to the right.

He cursed under his breath and then pulled the comms mike close to his mouth and lowered his weapon.

'Target located,' he said. He heard Mitch's boots on the linoleum floor pounding towards him.

'What is it?'

'We've got a problem.' He jerked his head towards the body on the floor. 'Someone was here before us.'

Mitch swore and then glanced at his watch. 'We're running out of time.'

'I know.' Dan crouched next to the body and kicked away the rifle at the man's side, although given the fact the man's brains were smeared up the side of the wall, he didn't think the guy would be firing it any time soon. 'Mel

– go through the CCTV footage for all cameras around the restaurant for the past twenty minutes. And get the Brigadier to check with MI5 and Six – maybe they wanted to claim this one and get the credit.'

'Copy.'

Mitch moved nearer. 'Is he our man?'

'Was. Yeah. Definitely.'

Dan ran a hand across his eyes, trying to pin down the thought that was running through his mind. He took out the comms earpiece and held up a hand to Mitch while he tried to think.

'If you shot a sniper, why the hell wouldn't you take his rifle?' he murmured. 'And why the hell wasn't this building locked down?'

Then it hit him.

He snapped the earpiece back into place and turned to face Mitch. 'Mel – are you hearing this?'

'Yes?'

'Tell David the Prime Minister's still in trouble.'

'What do you mean?' Mitch stepped closer, confusion etched across his face.

'There's more than one,' said Dan. 'This man was a decoy. We've got to find a second sniper.' He checked his watch. 'And fast – the PM's due to be here in under ten minutes.'

'Copy that.'

'And, Mel?'

'Yes?'

'Get someone to find out where that fucking clown went.'

Chapter 52

'Bastard, bastard, bastard.'

Mitch's curses carried down the stairs behind Dan as they raced through the innards of the building to the ground floor.

Dan swore under his breath as he ran. In hindsight, it had been too easy, the way the dead man had been left out as bait to draw them into the building and lose precious time.

He fleetingly wondered who the first sniper had been and then discarded the thought – he was someone else's problem now. Dan had bigger issues to worry about.

Such as, where the hell was the second sniper hiding?

And, was the second sniper working for Porchester as well or someone else?

Was Porchester even in control?

As he reached the foot of the stairs, a shadow passed the outside of the door.

In an instant, Dan had his gun up in a two-handed grip.

He heard Mitch clatter to a standstill behind him, breathing heavily after the rapid descent, but knew Mitch would automatically follow his lead.

Dan didn't hesitate. He levelled a kick at the door and stormed through the opening, aiming his weapon.

'It's me.' David held up his hands, his own weapon in one of them, until Dan lowered his gun. 'I heard over the comms.'

'We're running out of time,' said Dan. 'We're going to have to split up.'

David peered around Dan and jutted his chin at Mitch. 'Walk the perimeter. Start checking the windows that have a line of sight on the podium. If you think you see something, tell us. Don't second-guess yourself. We haven't got time.'

'Yes, boss.'

Dan watched as Mitch hurried away.

David flicked the microphone at his neck. 'Mel? Help him out. Use as many CCTV cameras as you can and alert the other services we've still got a rogue gunman.'

'Can't we get the PM to cancel?' asked Mel.

'He won't cancel,' said David. 'I already spoke to him on my way over here. He won't be told. Says if he cancels, it'll play into Porchester's hands.'

Dan watched as Mitch walked away and exhaled, trying to dispel some of the adrenalin that was building up in his system, threatening to cloud his judgement. Their task was impossible, yet he had to believe there was a chance, however slim.

'Where do you want to start?'

'The buildings directly opposite the podium,' said David and took off at a sprint.

Dan followed, ignoring the stares from people that he jostled as he raced towards the southern edge of the square.

'He's got a gun!' a woman exclaimed as he passed.

Her voice was lost amongst the shouts of the crowd watching the street performers, and Dan kept running.

David led the way, skirting round the perimeter of the square close to the buildings so as not to draw the sniper's fire towards them until they'd had a chance to find his location.

As Dan drew level with David, he tucked his weapon under his t-shirt and stood, hands on hips, as he craned his neck to survey the windows above.

'Anything?' he murmured.

David shook his head. 'I can't see any open windows – can you?'

'No.'

'Shit.'

'Hurry,' Mel's voice called over the comms equipment, her words doing little to hide her nervousness. 'We've tried phoning the PM but his aide tells me he's not taking any calls.'

'He's going to get himself killed.' David swore. 'What is it with these bloody politicians?'

'You're just worried about your annual bonus,' Mitch's familiar drawl replied. 'Get yourselves over to the building at your one o'clock position. I think I've found our man.'

Dan took off at full pelt, his long legs covering the distance around the square seconds before David caught up with him.

Mitch stood at a doorway, his lock-picking keys in his hand, patiently wiggling one of the steel wands into a brass lock.

'Are you sure?' asked David, keeping his voice low.

'Yes,' Mitch murmured. 'He's there all right.'

'Which room?' Dan took the opportunity to check the clip in his weapon.

'Third floor. Fourth window along. Where the scaffolding ends. There's some plastic sheeting hanging down the right-hand side of the window. It's flexing against the breeze, not with it.'

Dan peered out from under the doorway and up at the side of the building.

Sure enough, the plastic sheeting was exactly where Mitch said it was. He couldn't see the sniper, though.

'This is suicide,' said Dan.

The lock gave way with a small *click*, and Mitch turned to glare at him. 'Have you got any better ideas?'

'No time to waste,' said David. 'Move.'

Mitch pushed the door open, his weapon held high, while David followed, his gun trained at the midpoint.

Dan crept over the threshold behind them and pushed the door, leaving it open in case they needed to make a quick exit.

Mitch signalled to them he was going to start to climb the stairs and then gripped his gun between his hands and pushed himself against the wall next to the first tread.

Dan saw his eyes flicker upwards before they opened wide.

'Get down!' Mitch yelled and threw himself towards Dan and David.

A split second later, the sound of suppressed gunfire echoed down the stairwell, splinters of wooden balustrade and plaster showering them in the small confined space.

'Shit, shit, shit,' muttered David. 'The bastard's got a look-out.'

'It's that fucking clown,' said Mitch.

Another volley of bullets struck the wall next to the stairwell, and they ducked as one.

Mitch turned to David. 'What do you want to do?'

'Split up,' said David. 'Dan and I will keep this shooter distracted. You take this hallway. See if you can find another way upstairs.' He tapped his comms mike. 'Mel?'

'Here.'

'Tell the police covering this building to watch out for Mitch,' he said. 'He's probably going to have to use the external fire exit down the side of the building to get to the third floor to reach the sniper. Don't let them shoot Mitch by mistake.'

'Copy that.'

Dan backed away, shuffling across the floor until he could stand without becoming an easy target.

In his mind, he imagined the PM climbing from his car, making small talk with the press as he made his way towards the raised lectern. They were never going to reach the sniper in time.

He tucked his gun back under his t-shirt and ran towards the door.

'Where are you going?' yelled David.

'We're not going to make it,' Dan yelled over his shoulder. 'Time for "Plan B".'

'What are you going to do?'

Dan slid to a halt and gripped the doorframe. 'Whatever it takes.'

Chapter 53

'What is it, Paval?'

Malikov brushed past Krupin and stood next to the man staring at the two computer screens on the table.

He pushed back his chair, motioned towards the blank displays, and then turned to Malikov.

'These went dark thirty seconds ago,' Paval said, a slight tremor in his voice.

Malikov spun round to face Krupin. 'You've alerted the perimeter patrol?'

Krupin held up a transmitter. 'We tried. No answer.'

Malikov rounded on Paval. 'You see? You are blind without your technology.' He turned his anger towards Krupin. 'I told you we needed more men. It was a mistake to rely on this.' He waved his hand at the useless array of equipment.

'I am sorry, sir,' said Krupin.

Malikov's jaw clenched. He checked his watch. 'Any news?'

'Only what's on the television,' replied Krupin. 'The Prime Minister hasn't made his speech yet.'

'Are we secure?' He glanced from one man to the other. 'Where are the guards?'

'Two at the front of the house, two at the rear entrance to the building,' said Krupin. He jutted his chin towards the hallway. 'The rest are in the living area, preparing.'

Malikov nodded. 'Leave two in the living area. The others can form a defensive position along the hallway.'

'It'll be their Special Forces,' said Paval, his eyes wide as he rose from his chair. 'We won't stand a chance. We should leave, now.'

'Courage,' said Malikov. 'We don't know it's them for certain.'

He turned his attention back to Krupin, and the man gave him an almost imperceptible nod.

It would be a disaster if it were the country's Special Forces approaching the building; even more so if they were to capture Paval and discover the secrets he held.

'I'll meet you in the living room,' said Malikov. 'I want to brief everyone.'

'I won't be long,' murmured Krupin as he passed.

Malikov closed the door to the comms room, cutting off the exclamation of fear from Paval, and strode towards the living room.

As he entered, some of the men glanced up from their preparations before their attention returned to the cache of weapons laid out in front of them.

'Hurry,' said Malikov. 'The security systems are out.'

He reached down and picked up a remote control from a low table, pointed it at the television and muted the sound.

The news presenter's jaw continued to work noiselessly, while a smaller picture in the top right hand corner of the screen showed a podium set up in a corner of Covent Garden, a security cordon keeping the general public at bay.

Malikov shook his head and turned his attention back to his men. 'Concentrate,' he urged. 'We're under attack from the best soldiers in the world.'

'And yet they attack us in daylight,' muttered one of the older men. 'They're either brave or their superiors are stupid.'

'Or they're desperate,' snapped Malikov. 'In my experience, desperate men are dangerous men.'

He turned at a sound from the hallway. Krupin entered the room and made his way towards the haul of weapons, selecting a 9mm pistol.

Malikov's eyes fell to the man's bloodied knuckles, and he raised an eyebrow.

Krupin shrugged. 'He didn't want to go easily.'

'Here,' said the man next to Krupin and thrust a semi-automatic rifle at him. 'You'll want this.'

Krupin ignored the weapon, his lips curling in disgust. 'Useless in close quarters,' he snapped. He held up the 9mm. 'This isn't.'

'You'll run out of ammunition.'

Malikov smiled as Krupin pulled a knife from his waistband.

'Then I'll finish them with this.'

The other man shook his head and fell silent.

Krupin glanced at Malikov. 'Do you want me to move our guests?'

Malikov shook his head. 'No. Make sure you keep the noise to a minimum down here for as long as possible. I don't want to alert them to the fact we're under attack.' He raised his gaze to the ceiling. 'I'll deal with them.'

'Don't leave it too long.'

'How long do you think we've got?' asked Malikov.

'Two minutes,' said Krupin and jerked his head towards the door. 'You should hurry.'

Chapter 54

Dan closed the door behind him, hoping to deaden some of the gunfire so as not to alert the passing pedestrians.

Although all of them were using suppressors on their guns, those were only designed to protect the hearing of the person shooting, and he didn't want to cause a mass panic.

The area was becoming more crowded as news of the PM's impending arrival spread, and Dan was pleased to note the noise levels in the square were such that, with any luck, the gun battle that was raging in the building at his back would go unnoticed.

He briefly crossed his fingers, blinked in the bright sunlight that dappled the square, and began to hurry to where the television cameras and reporters waited.

As he walked, he heard the roar of a powerful car engine echo off the buildings, and then three official vehicles swept into the square, accompanied by motorcycle police.

The vehicles' blue lights flickered as they cleared a path and surrounded the cortege, protecting it from the throng of people that filtered from all corners of the square to stand near the raised platform.

Off to one side, a small group of protesters had gathered, placards waving above their heads as they chanted various slogans.

Some jostled against the police cordon in jest, and were pushed back with a shouted warning, before settling down once more as the cars passed.

The people that had been watching the street artists had surged towards the podium, some craning their necks over their shorter neighbours to see what was going on, the rest milling about at the fringes, feigning disinterest.

Dan had to slow as the wall of people grew more packed and used his height to track his progress. He pushed through, apologising under his breath, smiling at people as they let him through, trying to keep his features calm so as not to cause alarm.

Ten metres.

In his earpiece, he could hear the report of gunfire and, at one point, pulled the small piece of equipment from his ear, sure the noise would carry through the crowd from the building at his rear.

Satisfied the suppressors and the general noise of the crowd were combining to hide what was going on in close proximity to the podium, he shoved his earpiece back in, just in time to hear Mitch swear.

'Exit door to roof is locked,' he shouted.

Dan heard David curse loudly, echoing his own thoughts.

He wanted to activate his comms piece to ask what had happened to the gunman on the stairs but couldn't without alerting the second sniper to his presence.

Thankfully, at that moment, David confirmed the kill.

'The clown's dead,' he confirmed.

'Huzzah,' said Mitch.

'Accessing the stairwell now,' David said, ignoring him. 'Mitch – shoot that lock out. To hell with it; he's going to know we're nearly onto him.'

'Copy that.'

'Dan – where's the PM?'

'About to step out of his car.'

'Shit.'

The comms link went silent as each man concentrated on the task at hand.

Stop the sniper. Don't let him shoot the Prime Minister.

Dan's head shot up as the vehicles stopped in a line in front of the podium, and then the security team moved towards the back door of the middle car.

His stomach lurched, and he began to elbow his way through the dense mass of people who lined the cordon, their bodies packed into the small space.

Most appeared to be tourists, mobile phones and expensive-looking cameras held aloft as the back door of the car was opened, and the Prime Minister stepped out.

The man turned and waved to the crowd across the roof of the car, turning from side to side to make sure all the television cameras and reporters got an opportunity to capture the moment.

Dan clenched his fists and took one look at the security team surrounding the leader of the country and then at the deputy who stood next to him.

'Here goes nothing.'

***

Mel adjusted the volume on the speakers next to her computer screens, tuning out the voices of the rest of the team.

'What's wrong?' asked Sarah, looking up from the document she'd been examining.

'I'm not sure,' said Mel. 'Hang on.'

She concentrated on the chatter filtering through her earpiece from the police channel, and then frowned as her mind processed what she was hearing.

'Shit,' she muttered, before reaching across the makeshift desk and punching in a series of numbers on the computer, the frequency changing to a relatively unknown one.

Her breath caught at Malikov's name, and then her heart lurched.

'There's *another* operation underway,' she said.

'What?' Sarah crossed the room in a heartbeat. 'Why didn't they tell us?'

'Good question.'

The space hidden within the tunnel system seemed to contract, and Mel fought off the light-headedness that threatened to engulf her.

Mel swept her notes and reports from the desk and began typing furiously at her keyboard.

'No,' she murmured. 'No, no, no.'

She tapped her comms piece and then cursed as the signal dropped out.

Nothing.

She jumped in her seat as an alarm began to sound within the small room, her insides threatening to turn to liquid.

'The tunnel door's been breached. There's someone coming. We need to destroy all of this. Start shredding.'

Sarah moved across to the table and began gathering up the documents, then hurried across to a shredding machine that had been set against one wall.

Mel noticed the other woman's hands shaking as she fed the pages into it, then her gaze shifted to the monitors above her screen, and she watched in horror as, one by one, her carefully planted security cameras went black.

'What the hell is going on?' she muttered.

Her fingers moved over the keyboard as her eyes sought another way, another frequency she could use to reach the team to warn them.

'Christ, the whole system is dead.'

She pivoted on her seat and began the series of keystrokes she'd developed that would wipe all the information on her computer system, protecting David's mission from prying eyes.

She swallowed, her mouth dry as the sound of running feet on the metal walkways outside the secure door reached her ears.

They were out of time.

'They're here,' Mel said.

She hit the 'Enter' button on the keyboard and then covered her eyes with her forearm and turned away to protect herself as the door blew inwards.

Chapter 55

Dan shoved a teenager out of his way and moved quickly into the space next to a policeman standing with his back to him.

'Oi,' exclaimed the teenager. 'You're in my spot!'

'Piss off,' muttered Dan.

'I heard that.'

Dan ignored the tug on his sleeve, his gaze sweeping the layout of the raised podium and lectern, trying to form some sort of logical plan.

'Hey – I was talking to you,' the teenager said, louder.

The policeman glanced over his shoulder and arched an eyebrow at Dan and the teenager. 'Problem?'

'Yeah – he took my place.'

'You can have it,' said Dan and then pushed past the policeman with all his strength and launched himself at the parked cars.

As he slid across the bonnet of the Prime Minister's vehicle, he calculated he had seconds before the security men behind him caught up and their colleagues to his right realised what was happening. Gambling on the confusion that would delay their reaction, he sprinted towards the podium, where the Prime Minister and Porchester were shaking hands with members of the local constituency as they made their way up the short flight of steps to the stage.

'Talk to me, Mel,' he said. 'What's going on?'

Static reached his ears, and he cursed.

'Dan, stop!' David yelled over the comms link.

His voice was echoed by the security team, whose reactions were starting to catch up with Dan's progress.

He arched round to the right, ignoring the shouts behind him, a fleeting thought passing through his mind that the security team might shoot him if he didn't stop.

'Dan, wait!' David's voice increased in urgency, and he winced as the shouting grew louder.

As his long legs carried him up the steps, the Prime Minister turned to see what the commotion was, and his eyes opened wide.

'Dan…'

Porchester began to turn, and at that moment, Dan caught up with them.

'Get down!' Dan yelled.

He pushed Porchester into the Prime Minister, tackling the two men to the ground.

As he fell onto Porchester's legs, he saw a flash of red spray in the air above them, blood ejecting from the politician's body, and then a woman began to scream, closely followed by others.

He raised himself up onto his elbows, and then ducked at the sound of loud gunfire from the building where Mitch and David had been hunting the sniper.

In the split second silence that followed, he realised no more shots had been fired at the podium and rolled away from the politician.

'Shit.'

Porchester lay still, face-down on the stage. A large exit wound in the man's back bled profusely, covering the stage area with viscous dark blood.

Dan's gaze moved to the PM, who was sitting up, groaning. He watched in disbelief as the leader of the country began unbuttoning his shirt.

'A bulletproof vest?'

The PM's eyes met his, and he shrugged.

'Jesus Christ,' said Dan. 'Why didn't you tell us?'

A clatter of footsteps began to climb the wooden steps behind him, and Dan struggled to his feet, pulling out his gun from his belt as he stood, and spun on his heel to face the building where he'd left Mitch and David.

He ignored the commotion around him and pushed his earpiece into place. A burst of static filled his head, and he ripped the earpiece away, cursing loudly.

Then the security detail surrounded him.

'Down, down!'

'Drop your weapon!'

'On your knees!'

Dan flicked the safety on his gun, slid it across the stage towards the security guards, and then clasped his hands behind his head and dropped to his knees.

'Here we go again,' he muttered.

Chapter 56

Malikov hurried along the hallway, jabbed his forefinger against the panel for the security code to his temporary office, and pushed against the steel-framed door as soon as the locking mechanism deactivated.

Sweat pooled between his shoulder blades. He'd known it could come to this, had replayed the moment in his mind, but all the emotions were wrong in his dreams. He'd imagined anger, indignation, a sense of justice or retribution.

Instead he felt hollow, discordant.

He stalked across the room to the desk, its surface clear of any computer or telephone. He withdrew a set of keys from his pocket and then cursed as his fingers trembled while he tried to select the right one.

He exhaled, a vain attempt to release some of the pressure rising in his chest.

He finally found the key he sought and stabbed it into the small lock that was set into the drawers of the desk, twisting it counter-clockwise.

He wrenched open the top drawer.

The snub-nose revolver gleamed in the sunlight that poured through gaps in the closed blinds at the window.

Malikov ran his palms down his trousers, trying to lose some of the moisture, and then reached out with his right hand and wrapped his fingers around the weapon.

He checked the chamber and then flicked the lock back into place and straightened, his eyes turning to the open door.

Another spasm gripped his sternum, and he gritted his teeth, his left hand gripping the desk to steady himself.

He panted, waiting for the pain to subside, until it faded to a dull ache, and then set his shoulders and strode towards the door.

He didn't lock it behind him; there was no need now.

He checked his watch. The sniper hadn't called in, yet the television news channel that filled the screens in the living room as he passed confirmed his presence. Both the Prime Minister and Porchester had been rushed to hospital in what the press office was calling 'critical condition'.

Malikov swore under his breath.

He ignored the glances from the two guards as he began to climb the stairs, motioning to them to remain where they stood.

The taller of the two shrugged and levelled his weapon along the hallway towards the front door, anticipating the inevitable breach.

Malikov reached the landing, removed his shoes, and crossed the carpeted area to the first room.

He rested his forehead against the cool wooden surface and closed his eyes.

He'd never believed in a god; conversely, he didn't believe in a hell either, but his soul would surely pay for what he was about to do.

He took a last wavering breath and then turned the door handle and pushed.

The room was bathed in soft light from the summer sun as it crested the roof of the house, casting shadows into the corners of the room.

A simple double wardrobe stood against the wall to his left, while a single bed took up the length of the wall to his right.

He stepped over the threshold, his steps silent in his sock-clad feet as he padded closer to the figure in the bed.

She was lying on her back, headphones on, blissfully unaware of his presence as the hiss of escaping music reached his ears.

Her long blonde hair fell over her shoulders, one arm thrown over her shoulder as she lost herself in the pop tune.

She wore an old t-shirt and jeans that had holes at the knees, her bare feet brandishing bright pink toenails. Her chest rose and fell with each relaxed breath, a gentle hum escaping her lips.

It had been easy for Krupin and his men to snatch the willowy twelve-year-old as she'd stepped out of the car. After that, her mother had followed meekly, terror in her eyes as she'd tried in vain to calm her hysterical daughter before they'd been transported to the house in the country.

Malikov wiped his brow and then cocked the revolver.

He crept closer to the bed, hoping she didn't open her eyes, knowing his resolve might shatter otherwise.

She snuffled, and he nearly dropped the gun. She hummed a bit louder, and then her breathing returned to normal.

Malikov swallowed.

Don't think. Just do it.

He shuffled closer until he was within touching distance of her and then reached over and snatched up the second pillow that had been discarded to one side.

He blinked, and then in one fluid motion, he pulled the pillow across her face, lowered the revolver, and turned his head away as his forefinger squeezed the trigger.

He fired once.

The blast ricocheted around the small room, and he sensed the life pass from the still form beneath his grasp.

He blinked, left the pillow where it was, and tried not to think about the blood that spattered out from under it.

Doors slammed throughout the building, running feet pounded up the stairs, and confused shouting filled the air.

One voice rang out, cutting through the others.

'Emily? Emily!'

She was coming closer, her room at the far end of the house near enough to give her an advantage over the guards climbing the stairs.

He heard her panicked breathing moments before she staggered through the doorway, her eyes wide in terror.

Her gaze met his and then lowered to the gun in his hand and then to the prone figure on the bed.

She dropped to her knees, a keening wail beginning in her chest before its crescendo filled the room, moments before she started to scream.

He advanced on her slowly and raised the gun.

Her attention snapped from the dead child in the bed next to him, and he knew then what pure hatred looked like.

'She was innocent,' the woman hissed, tears streaming down her cheeks. 'You promised you wouldn't hurt her if we came with you. You said...' Her mouth worked, but she seemed unable to find any more words.

'Her father made a deal,' said Malikov, steadying his grip. 'And your husband broke his word.'

He pulled the trigger, and Lily Porchester, ex-Mrs Malikov, slumped to the floor.

Chapter 57

Dan sat on the back seat of a heavily guarded car, fuming.

His requests to speak to David had been ignored, the Prime Minister's security detail going out of their way to make him as uncomfortable as possible while they'd frog-marched him towards the nearest vehicle.

He'd ducked at the last minute, narrowly avoiding hitting his head on the door frame as he'd been pushed onto the back seat. He'd twisted as he fell, to avoid landing awkwardly on his wrists and breaking them, swearing under his breath.

The door had slammed shut moments after he'd tucked his feet into the foot well, and then the car was locked, and he was left alone, staring alternatively between the blacked-out windows and the glass that separated him from the front of the vehicle.

A cordon surrounded the car comprising a mix of the Prime Minister's security team and several police officers, their backs to the vehicle.

It took a moment for Dan to realise what they were doing, but when he did, he was grateful. They were sheltering him from the prying eyes of the assembled television cameras, reporters, and general public. His mind turned to the sniper's intended target.

After he'd been dragged away from the podium, he'd twisted between his captors' grip until he could see over his shoulder.

The Prime Minister was nowhere to be seen, and a sickness surged through Dan.

What if he'd been too late?

What if the sniper had managed to take a head shot and killed the PM?

Why the hell hadn't they been told about the plan for the PM to wear a bulletproof vest?

He leaned down and wiped the sweat from his brow onto his shoulder.

With Porchester dead, would anyone believe them?

He forced down the urge to panic and instead tried to reason with himself. He closed his eyes and fought the exhaustion that now threatened to engulf him.

His head jerked up at the sound of the front door to the car opening, and Mitch slipped into the driver's seat.

He caught Dan staring at him in the rear-view mirror. 'Don't say a word,' he murmured. 'We're not out of danger yet.'

He slung a long item on the passenger seat next to him, wrapped in his jacket. As it landed on the leather upholstery, a polished grey metal flashed briefly into sight, and Dan realised it was the sniper's rifle.

'Why have you got that?'

Mitch glared at him in the mirror. 'We had to get to you,' he hissed. 'We couldn't leave it behind for someone else to find, could we? Now shut up.'

Dan forced his gaze away, and stared out of the window instead.

Mitch turned the ignition key, released the handbrake, and eased the car through the security cordon that surrounded it.

As the vehicle moved, the security cordon moved with it, the men keeping pace until Mitch had steered them out of the square and onto the street.

A police motorcyclist cleared a path through the traffic ahead of them, leading them away from the centre of the city until the rider steered away, holding his hand up as the bike powered to the right and disappeared.

Mitch's foot nudged the accelerator harder as they joined a busy dual carriageway, and then they were free of the capital and onto the motorway that led south-west.

Neither man spoke, each lost in their own thoughts as they tried to process the events of the past few hours.

A few miles later, Mitch turned off the motorway and took a series of turns before finding a quiet country lane. As soon as he was able, he pulled over and climbed out.

Dan waited until the back door opened and then climbed out.

Mitch reached out to steady him and then held up a small key. 'Let's get those off you.'

Dan flexed his wrists gratefully as Mitch tossed the handcuffs into the back of the car and glanced at the rifle.

'You got the sniper?'

Mitch nodded. 'David got him, but obviously not before he could get that first shot off and killed Porchester. You did good. We got the clown, too.'

'Is the Prime Minister okay?'

'A bit shaken, but yes.'

'Where's Sarah?'

'With Mel. David will explain.'

'All right, what's the plan?'

Mitch shrugged. 'David told me to get you as far away from London as I could within half an hour and then phone him on this.' He held up a mobile.

'Okay, let's do it.'

Mitch put the phone on the car roof, dialled a number, and made sure the speaker setting was on.

David answered before the first ring tone had ended.

'Are you safe?'

'Yes,' said Dan. 'Thanks. What's going on?'

'Apart from the Prime Minister having to admit his error in insisting on an extremely public press conference you mean?' David sighed. 'We're in damage control here.'

'What's happened?' Dan looked at Mitch and raised an eyebrow, but the other man shrugged and shook his head.

'MI5 were running an operation of their own to try to draw Malikov out, to see if he made a mistake. They failed, so they waited to see if our plans worked. They infiltrated the bunker and confiscated Mel's computers about an hour ago. Mel and Sarah have made formal statements. They're not going to be charged, but our investigation has been taken over by MI5.'

'Shit.' Dan met Mitch's eyes over the expanse of the car and noticed the same shock that he felt register in the other man's face.

'There's no easy way to tell you this,' David added, his tone grim. 'Hugh Porchester's wife and twelve-year-old daughter had been kidnapped by a rogue Russian group based here in the UK, led by Malikov,' he said. 'In order to keep them safe and get her back, Porchester had been made to agree to overthrow the PM's attempts to stay in the EU and help the Russians sabotage the government's fracking project.'

'Are they okay?'

There was a moment's pause at the end of the line. 'Malikov executed them both,' said David. 'MI5 think he realised it was the end for him, so he shot them before the house could be breached.'

Dan staggered and reached out to lean against the car. Next to him, Mitch put his hands on his head and turned away, swearing profusely.

'Jesus.' Dan ran his hand over his face. 'Why weren't we told of this before, David?'

'Because people outside of the EPG decided to use us as bait.'

Dan's head jerked up, and he saw the same confusion as he felt cross Mitch's face.

'They did what?'

'It wasn't just a case of waiting to see if we were successful,' said David. 'It seems that Hugh Porchester was willing to help the Russians up to a point. We were right about that. When you started getting too close to the truth, he tried to back away from whatever deal he'd struck with Malikov. And it appears that MI5 knew all about it.'

Dan felt bile rise in his throat. 'So, if I hadn't kept the pressure on him, his wife and daughter would still be alive,' he said.

'We don't know that for sure,' said Mitch. 'Isn't that right?'

Mitch glared at the phone, waiting for David's response.

'No, we don't,' agreed David. 'There's something else you should know, too. Lily Porchester was Malikov's ex-wife.'

Mitch slammed the palm of his hand on the roof of the car. 'This just gets better,' he snarled and turned away.

Dan concentrated on keeping his breathing calm, knowing that if he lost his temper, David would be reluctant to divulge any more information. He held up his hand to silence Mitch.

'David? What did you mean, we were used as bait?' he said. 'What's been going on?'

'I'll keep it brief,' said David. 'I don't have much time. Essentially, from what I've been able to gather since Porchester was shot, is that there's a rogue element within the Russian government that are extremely worried about the effect EU sanctions are having on their country.'

'That's a good thing, though, isn't it?' said Mitch. 'That's the whole point of the sanctions being in place.'

'It is, if it makes the Russian government back down,' said David. 'The problem is, this rogue element doesn't believe that's ever going to happen, not with the current leader they've got, and that's what's had MI5 so concerned. Malikov and his backers decided to take advantage of the British leadership's stance on the UK's place within the European Union and persuade them to use those negotiations to ease away from the EU restrictions on Russian gas exports.'

'But he could only do that if Porchester persuaded the Prime Minister to include that in his negotiations,' said Dan. He frowned and rubbed his chin. 'That's what Heatherington was driving at – the cost of gas without Russian imports is going to increase due to an ageing population.'

'Right,' said David. 'But the Prime Minister doesn't want to lose his vetoing powers within the EU, so he was reluctant to even put that on the table. Instead, he decided to press ahead with the Northumberland project to prove to the public that fracking for gas was a more viable option.'

'So, Malikov arranged for the theft of the isotope in the hope that he'd force the Prime Minister back to the negotiating table,' said Mitch. 'He sabotaged the development programme.'

'How did Porchester get involved with that?' asked Dan.

'We're helping with the investigation now,' said David. 'Mel's working with the other security agencies, and it seems that Porchester may have approached the Russians first to test the water about the possibility of a new gas deal with them before the party in-fighting started. Once the air cleared and he found himself in a better position of power, it looks like he tried to back out of those negotiations.'

'And the Russians didn't like it,' Dan finished.

'Exactly.'

'What was in it for Porchester, though?' asked Mitch. 'Before his family were kidnapped, I mean.'

'Probably a place on the board of any UK company Malikov set up to manage the gas import business here,' said David. 'He was too damn greedy to settle for life as a public servant. Mel's finally been given access to the other files she was trying to trace; it looks as if Malikov was providing a monthly sweetener to Porchester on the side, provided he continued to play his part, of course. Once Porchester realised that his plans might be uncovered and tried to back out, Malikov kidnapped his wife and daughter to force him to see the plan through.'

Dan shook his head. 'I can't believe how arrogant this Malikov is,' he spat. 'He just thinks he can force this government to abide by his rules.'

'Money talks,' said Mitch.

'True,' said David. 'And the only way to ensure their plans didn't go wrong was to make sure the key members of the Energy Protection Group were well out of the way. At the end of the day, it was Porchester that handed over your mission details to the Russians, no-one else. He did that voluntarily. Malikov's men only took Porchester's wife and daughter to make sure he didn't back down once he realised how close you were to ruining Malikov's plans.'

'What's the Prime Minister doing now?' asked Dan.

David cleared his throat. 'He's advised everyone here that he's going to meet with Malikov.'

'What? Why?' Dan stepped closer to the phone, unable to believe what he was hearing.

'I'm presuming to try to clear this up in such a way that the public don't find out that their government was nearly ousted by a Russian-backed coup,' said David.

'Where's he meeting him?' asked Mitch. 'Surely he wouldn't bring him back to London with all the press focus there?'

'A team have been sent to collect Malikov from his house. They'll take him to the PM's country residence,' said David. 'The PM wants to speak to him in private.'

'He fucking used us,' snapped Dan. 'He knew damn well what would happen. It's kind of convenient he's managed to keep Malikov alive so he can talk to him, isn't it? Thanks to us.'

'We can't prove anything,' said David. 'And be careful you don't broadcast that point of view anywhere outside of the EPG.'

'It's true, though, isn't it?' said Mitch. 'The Prime Minister didn't want us near Malikov. Why?'

Dan snapped his fingers. 'He's going to make a deal with him.'

A silence fell while Mitch and David let his words sink in.

'Jesus Christ,' Mitch murmured eventually. 'That's it, isn't it? Get rid of Porchester and start off on a clean slate with Malikov – or his contacts back in Russia.'

Dan nodded. 'It'll give the PM a back-up plan, just in case the European Union issue him with an ultimatum – stay in or get out and fend for yourselves.'

'Hang on a minute,' interrupted David. 'This is all just conjecture. You've got nothing to prove that's the case. So, in the meantime, we support the PM. Is that understood?'

'Jesus,' murmured Dan and rubbed his hand across his face. 'What happened to Malikov's men?'

'They were all killed during the raid,' said David. 'Although they probably had links to other groups based here in the UK. MI5 are going through the data now.' He paused. 'Hang on.'

Dan glanced across the roof of the car at Mitch, and then turned up the volume on the phone.

Someone else had entered David's office and was speaking to him, their voices muted as if they were deliberately talking out of range.

Dan decided to press on, ignoring the interruption.

'How did they manage to get so close to Porchester's family?' he asked. 'Surely Porchester's daughter would have been watched.'

'Sadly with the number of terrorist threats MI5 have to deal with, keeping an eye on the Russians was well down the list,' said David. 'And unless you're the Prime Minister, you don't qualify for the sort of high-level protection that was needed in this case.'

'What happens now?' asked Mitch, his face pale.

Their boss's tone changed. 'Whichever way we look at it, Dan, you pushed Porchester in front of the PM, and because of your actions, he was killed by a sniper,' said David. 'I realise you were acting on the information we had at hand, but we've got to deal with that.'

Dan looked at Mitch, and both men shrugged.

'So, we face another Parliamentary committee hearing?' asked Mitch. 'I'd better dust off my suit.'

'Not exactly,' said David. 'The story being given to the press is that a man is being held for questioning by police in relation to the shooting of Hugh Porchester.'

'What?'

'Hear me out, Dan. It's for your own safety,' explained David. 'It's going to take a while to gather all the evidence so a Parliamentary enquiry can take place. You will get your name cleared, but we need to play by their rules for now.'

'So, what do you want me to do?'

There was a slight pause at the other end of the line before David spoke. 'I'm sure you'll think of something. We'll have a complete debrief when you get back to base here. There are a few people that would like to talk to you.'

Dan frowned and looked at Mitch.

The other man shook his head and put a finger to his lips, before leaning closer to the mobile phone.

'Understood,' he said, his voice doing little to hide his frustration. 'We'll head back as soon as we're done here.'

Dan raised an eyebrow, but Mitch shook his head again.

'Before you both go,' said David. 'The Prime Minister asked me to convey his gratitude for your work today. His actual words were "tell them they were outstanding".'

'I should hope so,' Dan growled. 'I've put my bloody life on the line for him.'

'I hope so, too,' said Mitch. 'We've got his car.'

Chapter 58

Mitch ended the call and looked at Dan and then frowned. 'What?'

'You tell me. David obviously isn't telling us everything,' said Dan. 'Why didn't you want me to say anything to him?'

'Because he wasn't alone and probably wanted you to be careful what you said,' replied Mitch. 'Otherwise he wouldn't have pulled the whole "people would like to talk to you" line, would he?'

Dan tugged at his ear. 'You think someone else is in charge now?'

'You want to know what I think?' said Mitch and then continued without waiting for an answer. 'I'll tell you what I think. I think the minute we walk in that office, you're going to be arrested. They'll put you in a military prison, and they *might* let you out in a year or so, once they've got all their stories lined up and ensured their arses are covered.'

Dan felt a cold chill across his shoulders, despite the warmth of the end of the afternoon.

He swore and stepped away from the car.

He rubbed his thumb over one of the scabs that still clung to his chin, and touched the indentation underneath that would surely leave yet another scar on his body.

As he ran through the conversation with David in his head, he began to understand Mitch's concerns. David had a habit of being cagey at best, but had never dodged a direct question before. Ever.

What do you want me to do?

I'm sure you'll think of something.

Was David trying to warn him?

Or was he trying to give him another sort of message?

He lowered his head and glanced at Mitch.

The other man had his back turned to him, hands on hips, staring at the lowering sun over the tree line at the edge of the field beyond where they'd parked the car.

I'm sure you'll think of something.

Dan swallowed then turned and made his way back to the vehicle.

'Three lives, Mitch,' he said as he drew closer. 'Why the hell didn't any of us realise he was being blackmailed?'

'It didn't start off as blackmail,' said Mitch. 'You heard David. Mel had the evidence to prove Porchester had taken Malikov's money willingly to further his career.'

'And by the time he realised what Malikov was really capable of, it was too late to back off,' said Dan, pacing beside the vehicle. 'But how did the security services find out where Porchester's wife and daughter were being held so quickly?'

Mitch's eyes opened wide. 'He *knew*. The PM knew they'd been kidnapped.'

'So, why didn't he do anything to help them?' Dan stopped. 'Christ, he was *using* them as well.' He stared at Mitch. 'He knew where to find them, but he didn't order the rescue until he knew Porchester was out of the picture. He didn't want to alert Malikov that MI5 were onto him.'

'And then it was too late to save them,' finished Mitch. 'And now, the PM is going to arrange a meeting with Malikov once he's in custody.'

Dan raised his gaze to the horizon, lost in thought for a moment, before he exhaled.

'This stinks.'

He shook his head and concentrated on the traffic passing over the motorway bridge above their heads. He checked his watch. It was too early for commuters. Less traffic compared to what there would be in, say, an hour from now.

'We need to move,' Mitch said and gestured to the parked car. 'You heard David. We have to report in, make formal statements.'

'Malikov will get away with it,' murmured Dan and then blinked and fixed his stare on Mitch. 'If Malikov ransomed Porchester's family, who's to say he hasn't blackmailed other politicians?'

'You're not making sense,' said Mitch. 'Get in the car. Let's go.'

'No.'

Mitch sighed and rubbed at tired eyes. 'I took a big risk getting you out of the shit back there. David needs our help, so, please,' he finished, gritting his teeth, 'get in the damned car.'

'I can't, Mitch, sorry.' Dan held up his hands and took a step back.

'Wait,' said Mitch. 'What are you going to do?'

'You heard David. A transfer team is going to collect Malikov from his house,' said Dan. 'I remember the building being listed in one of those financial reports that Mel had. It's a big eight-bedroom place near Ashford. The hit squad will be winding back their involvement at MI5's request, and the transfer team are on their way to a simple pick-up, right? All the other bad guys are dead.'

Mitch's eyes narrowed, and he folded his arms. 'And?'

Dan told him.

Mitch spun on his heel and stalked away, a string of curses exploding from him as he paced the pockmarked asphalt. Finally, he calmed down enough to walk back to Dan.

'Are you fucking kidding me?' He stared at Dan for a moment, and then realisation reached his eyes. 'No, you're not.'

He began to pace once more. 'You've lost your bloody mind.'

'You're not helping.'

'Are you fucking serious?'

'Listen to me.'

'Of all the stupid ideas I've heard from you over the years, Taylor, this is the dumbest.'

'*Mitch.*'

Dan waited until the other man stopped pacing and turned to him.

'You're not coming with me.'

'What do you mean?'

Dan reached out and squeezed Mitch's shoulder. 'You're sitting this one out.'

'No way.'

'You haven't got a choice.' Dan's eyes flickered to the lull in the traffic above.

'Is this going to hurt?'

'Probably.'

'Don't leave a scar, okay. It'll just –'

Dan swung his fist, punching the air from the other man's lungs, and then landed a stun blow to the back of his exposed neck.

Mitch crumpled to the ground, out cold.

'Sorry, mate,' said Dan, dragging Mitch's body towards the car, 'but this is for your own good.'

He unlocked the trunk of the car, emptied the space of the paraphernalia associated with the head of British politics, and then hefted Mitch's dead weight into the confined space, before removing the tail light to improve air circulation, and slammed the lid shut.

He jogged round to the driver's door and glanced at the bundle on the passenger seat.

He reached across and lifted the material, the soft glare of the sniper's rifle glinting in the subdued light.

Mitch had emptied the chamber and placed all the rounds in a plastic evidence bag next to the weapon.

Dan exhaled and dropped the covering back into place, gunned the engine and released the handbrake.

There was no time to lose.

Chapter 59

Dan parked the car behind an old horse trailer, out of sight from the road, and then climbed out and peered across to the farmhouse.

It appeared to be deserted, its curtains drawn, and no noise emanated from either of the large corrugated iron sheds that had been built to one side of it.

The place seemed to be more of a hobby farm, a smallholding, rather than a commercial venture.

After waiting for two minutes, during which time he didn't even hear a dog bark, Dan checked his watch and then leaned into the car and pulled out the sniper rifle.

He slung it over his shoulder, put the rounds in his pocket, and locked the vehicle.

By his calculations, he had a twenty-minute head start on the transfer team, and he intended to make the most of that advantage.

He jogged towards the woodland that bordered the farm and Malikov's property, knowing he was taking a gamble that the Special Forces team would have already cleared the area.

He tried not to think about what would happen if he were wrong in his assumptions.

He'd be up against the best soldiers the UK could throw at him, and he wasn't sure he'd survive a direct encounter with one of them.

Dan reached the first line of trees, carefully pulled apart the lines of barbed wire fence that ran at waist and knee height, and climbed through the gap.

He crouched down, rubbed his hand in the dirt, and smudged his face, paying attention to his cheekbones, nose, and forehead. It wasn't the best camouflage, but it would have to do. It would, at least, break up his features once he was closer to the property.

He tested the weight of the sniper's rifle in his grip. He patted his pocket. He had enough rounds. Only one of those needed to count.

Dan picked up his pace, resisting the temptation to check his watch. He had to hurry, but there was no point in raising his heart rate too high, only to have to wait for it to settle once more before taking the shot.

There was also the risk that the hit team would still be patrolling the woodland. He'd reasoned with himself that once Malikov and his men had been killed or apprehended, the team would retreat, and the woods would be deserted.

He erred on the side of caution, though, stepping through the dense undergrowth with as little sound as possible.

After a few minutes, he noticed the trees thinning and dropped to his knees. He slung the rifle over his shoulder, made sure the ammunition was safely tucked in his pocket, and then crawled on his elbows and knees towards the perimeter.

He lay for a moment, getting his bearings.

On the driveway, outside the house, were two black four-wheel drive vehicles, an ambulance and a dark-coloured panel van.

Dan flagged the two four-wheel drive vehicles as belonging to the last members of the hit team, so he guessed there to be a minimum of eight men still active around the property.

The dark panelled van was surrounded by long black plastic bags, body-sized, and Dan figured the local coroner's team would be having a busy night.

He wiped the sweat from his forehead and glanced once more at the ambulance. Two men were rolling a covered stretcher across the gravel driveway from the house towards it, their movements almost reverent in their care of the fragile body as it was loaded into the back of the vehicle.

Porchester's daughter.

Dan's jaw clenched, and he slid the rifle from his shoulder.

His thoughts were clear as he loaded a round into the chamber, his actions precise and methodical as he lined up the sight with the waiting cars.

Once he was ready, he brought his wrist up to his face and checked his watch.

Any time now.

He let his body relax into the undergrowth, the musty smell of bracken and rabbit droppings rising up from the earth as the air cooled.

After twenty minutes, the sound of two cars powering through the nearby lane reached his ears.

He exhaled, concentrating on slowing his breathing, fighting down the adrenalin that would explode through his veins if he didn't retain control.

The cars' engines quietened as they slowed to turn into the Malikov property and then appeared at the top of the driveway, forming a single file as they approached the house.

Dan closed one eye and peered through the scope. If he was running the handover, he'd have Malikov escorted out, with men at the front and rear to prevent a last-minute escape attempt.

The Russian would probably be handcuffed, too.

On cue, the front door opened, and two of the original hit team descended the low marble staircase to the driveway, their weapons at their side. They each took position at the point where the stone staircase met the gravel driveway and waited.

The cars slowed and followed the natural arc of the turning circle in front of the house before coming to a standstill.

The drivers remained behind the wheel of each vehicle, while the men in the passenger seats climbed out.

Two men climbed out from the back seat of the lead car, their heads turning left and right as their gaze swept the grounds.

Finally, the last man climbed from the passenger seat of the rear vehicle and spoke to the others.

Dan swore under his breath as the man stretched, turning his face towards the woods.

Neil Evans.

Dan fought down his anger. David and the team being kept out of the loop until the last minute made sense now. The PM would know they would never agree to a Russian criminal being given a chance to do business with the government.

The current leader of the EPG yawned and then spun on his heel to face the house.

As he did so, a figure was half-pulled, half-pushed through the open door, his wrists cuffed in front of him.

Malikov.

His shirt and trousers were dishevelled, his hair a mess; blood covering one side of his face seemed to have congealed around a bruise under his eye.

Evidently the oligarch had refused to give up easily.

Dan frowned as the man shuffled awkwardly over the threshold, before realising that ankle cuffs also bound the Russian.

His captors weren't taking any chances.

Once on the steps, two guards each grabbed one of Malikov's elbows and began to march him down towards the waiting cars.

Two more men hovered at the doorway, their stance suggesting they were watching the tree line, not their captive.

Dan exhaled, knowing that if he didn't take the shot within the next few seconds, he wouldn't get another chance.

He steadied his grip on the stock of the rifle, his right forefinger resting gently on the trigger.

The two men in front of Malikov took another step forward, putting them at a lower level to their prisoner behind them, and exposing the Russian's chest.

Dan squeezed the trigger and held his breath.

Almost.

A shot rang out from Dan's right, and he jerked his eye away from the sight of the rifle in shock.

Malikov's body arced away from his captors at the force of the bullet striking his torso, a burst of red showering the men around him, before he slumped to the stone steps and fell still.

Dan's head snapped to his right, the sound of a person moving through the undergrowth next to him reaching his ears.

He turned back to the house at a shout.

The two men beside Malikov dropped to the ground, their comrades falling to their knees as they brought up their weapons, sighting them at the perimeter of woodlands surrounding the property.

Evans stood, facing the woods, and then cupped his hands to his mouth and shouted.

'Taylor! Give yourself up now!'

Dan held his breath and remained rigid until their gaze swept past him and then shuffled back on his elbows and knees, dragging the rifle with him.

What the hell?

Who shot Malikov?

And how did Evans know I was here?

Once concealed within the undergrowth, he raised himself up into a squatting position and disassembled the rifle, tipping the unused rounds into his hand, before stuffing them into his pocket.

Raised voices carried on the wind from the direction of the house, and he jerked his attention back to the property.

The team were good; they'd already worked out the trajectory of the kill shot and were pointing towards the woodland in Dan's direction, weapons raised.

Dan began running at a crouch, knowing that the stance would slow his progress, but desperate to get away without being seen.

He also wanted to find out who'd killed Malikov before he'd had the chance.

He zig-zagged through the fallen pine needles and bracken, sliding across damp leaves until he could see the perimeter fence that separated Malikov's house from the farm.

A shot rang out, and Dan ducked as the tree trunk next to him exploded and then swerved left and right once more to try to avoid the gunman's line of sight.

Evans's team were onto him.

He slowed as he reached the barbed wire fence separating Malikov's property from the farm, pulled apart the top and bottom lines of wire to climb through, and then jerked his head to the right at the sound of branches snapping.

He swore as the wire fence fell back into place, whipping against his jaw, and instinctively reached for the scratch that now bled freely.

His eyes found the Prime Minister's car, the vehicle unmoved from where he had left it. He discarded the idea of taking it again. Evidently a location tracker had been placed somewhere on the vehicle, which was why Evans had guessed he'd been there. He needed something that wouldn't be tracked, that wouldn't be reported stolen as soon as he'd escaped.

He sensed movement to his left and spun in time to see a man running in the opposite direction, a rifle similar to the one Dan held slung over his shoulder.

'Hey!'

The man kept running away from the farm property and up towards the lane.

Dan checked over his shoulder and swore.

If he tried to catch the killer, he'd be captured, and somehow, he didn't think that was a good idea. Not if Evans believed him to be the killer.

He turned back to the direction of the lane. The other gunman had disappeared from sight, but then the sound of a motorbike starting up reached his ears, and Dan realised he needed to concentrate on his own escape.

He grunted in pain as something slammed into his shoulder, a fiery force searing his muscles, and then stumbled forward, falling to his knees.

He raised his gaze to the trees beyond the barbed wire perimeter and knew he was out of time.

Chapter 60

It was twilight by the time Dan reached a small fishing village and parked the stolen four-wheel drive behind a chandler's office.

The business was closed for the day, its windows floodlit to show the scant collection of boats for sale.

He sat for a moment, pain flooding his shoulder. He lowered his chin until he could get a better look at the skin above his chest and then gritted his teeth.

It was a bloody mass of tissue, torn away by the bullet as it had exited his body.

He poked his finger through the hole in his jacket, tracing the scarred edges. He'd been lucky – if the bullet had lodged in his shoulder, his situation would be a lot worse. As it was, he would have to seek help as soon as it was safe to do so and hope the wound didn't get infected in the meantime.

He'd been fortunate that the farmer's beat-up vehicle had been left unlocked, forgotten perhaps in the haste to leave the property. Mud and fur covered the back seats, and the distinctive aroma of damp dog permeated the interior.

Dan opened the door and eased himself from the vehicle, ignoring the blood-stained upholstery, and craned his neck until he could see the far end of the quay, towards the lifeboat shed hugging the algae-covered concrete wall.

A gust of wind tugged at his collar as he glanced over his shoulder.

A small trawler had rounded the end of the harbour wall. Once white, its hull was now a dirty cream colour, its wheelhouse a dull blue. Nets and machinery filled the back section towards the bow, while aerials and a small flag post leaned with the boat as it rocked in the waves towards him.

Dan checked his watch, calculating the time it had taken him to reach the small seaside village. He lowered his arm and squinted into the distance, back towards the main road that skirted the top of the heathland, and dropped down the hill towards the village.

He reckoned he had a head start on the transfer team, now his pursuers, if he was lucky.

And they would know he had been shot. The trail of blood that he'd left at the scene would be a clear indication that he needed medical attention.

No headlights swept along the coast road towards him; the only noise that carried across the harbour echoed from the one pub that stood on the edge of the main street between the quay and the first row of houses; no doubt full of the local residents comparing sizes of catch that day and planning on early nights to be up before dawn the next day.

Dan exhaled, exhaustion seizing him. He turned as the sound of the approaching trawler reached his ears over the waves crashing against the concrete jetty.

The vessel appeared deserted, except for the captain, who steered the boat expertly alongside the quay. Dan heard him put the engine in neutral, and then he stepped out from the wheelhouse.

A large man, his face obscured by a large brown beard with flecks of grey, moved with precision across the deck, a cigarette dangling from his mouth. He hurried to the stern and grabbed a coil of rope, tossing it towards the quay, his eyes full of expectation.

Dan dropped his hand from his shoulder and grabbed the line, holding the boat steady as its fenders bumped gently against the reinforced concrete, and then used one hand to tie it off and waited while the captain switched off the engines. When the man emerged from the cabin once more, Dan called down to him.

'What's it like out there?'

'Perfect,' said the man. 'You heading out now?'

'Yeah,' said Dan. 'Figured I might.' His hand found his shoulder again, and he grimaced as a fiery spasm shuddered through his body. He pulled the jacket closer so the fisherman wouldn't notice the gaping wound in the fading light. His fingers rested against the bloody skin, sticky and warm. 'I should probably get a move on,' he managed.

The man raised his hand. 'Might see you when you get back, eh?'

'Maybe.'

Dan nodded in farewell and hurried along the quayside. He'd spent enough time stalling.

He slowed as he approached the boat at the end of the row of vessels.

He ran a practiced eye over the cream-coloured fibreglass hull and cabin and noted that only day-to-day grime clung to the surface.

She looked abandoned, and Dan wracked his memory to try and recall when he'd last taken her out.

He blinked in surprise when he realised it had been several months ago, and crossed his fingers that the local reputation of the harbour as being a safe one with little fuel theft still held true.

'Guess I'll soon find out,' he murmured.

He crouched down and loosened the ropes that held the vessel to the quay and then stepped over the low lip of concrete that bordered the quay and dropped to the deck of the vessel, landing on both feet with soft *thump*.

Dan hurried to the rail and gathered the ropes, coiling them onto the deck where he wouldn't trip over them, before running his hands across the roof of the cabin until he found the loose flap of metal that concealed the keys.

He unlocked the cabin and pushed his way into the small space, inhaling a mustiness that hinted at the months of neglect since his last visit.

He'd never told anyone about the *Seahorse*. His father had bought her several years before his death, and Dan savoured the times he spent on her in between missions.

The vessel gave him a sense of normality and a way to relax.

Not tonight, though.

He patted the wheel.

'Guess we'll be spending quite a bit of time together,' he said and then turned his attention to readying the boat for departure.

He ran though his preparations with the sixth sense of someone who was comfortable at sea, habits born from school holidays spent with his father on the boat, scooting around the south coast of England during the winter months, with the occasional foray over to France during summer holidays.

He exhaled, trying to work through the pain in his shoulder.

Somehow, he didn't think France would be far enough this time.

Maybe not Spain, either.

He inserted the key into the ignition and listened to the engine, trying to gauge whether it was going to run without issue or whether he was going to have to abandon his plans and steal another car. He crossed his fingers and raised his gaze to the fuel indicator.

Still full.

Satisfied the engine wasn't going to leave him cast adrift in the busy shipping lanes of the English Channel, he turned to shut the door of the cabin and froze.

Car headlights were descending the narrow lane from the main road along the ridge towards the village, and whoever was driving the vehicles wasn't hanging around.

His heart lurched painfully, galvanising him into action.

'Dammit, Mel.'

Somehow, somewhere on his clothing, Mel had planted another tracking device.

And it had worked.

He pivoted on his toes, reached out, and eased the throttle open, powering through the other moored vessels as fast as he dared.

He reached up and switched off all the lights, squinting in the dusk, and steering his way out towards the breakwater.

He risked a glance over his shoulder.

The cars had reached the village, had passed the pub at the far end, and were speeding towards the start of the quay.

Dan gritted his teeth, swung the boat past the last vessel in the harbour, and opened the throttle.

The craft bounced over the swell of the waves, the engine humming as it powered through the current and out past the harbour wall, the tiny village receding quickly.

Dan finally allowed himself to breathe, switched on the running lights, and rubbed at his eyes.

He had enough fuel to reach the Spanish coastline. After that, he'd need to refuel and move on, in case the British authorities decided to alert Interpol to his exploits.

Somehow, he suspected they wouldn't, that they'd deal with their issues out of the prying gaze of their European counterparts, especially given the Prime Minister's agenda, but he'd have to be careful until he knew for sure.

He pulled out the mobile phone from his jeans pocket that Mel had given him, the one she'd assured him couldn't be traced as it had no GPS capabilities, and hit speed dial.

'It's me.'

He closed his eyes as Sarah's voice washed over him, her initial anger turning to concern and fear as he quickly told her what had happened.

'I have to go away for a while,' he explained, coughing to try and conceal the break in his voice. 'I don't know how long.'

He wiped angrily at his eyes and then sniffed. 'I'll call you, okay? It might take me a while to sort things out, but I'll call you. I promise.'

He ended the call and then punched in another number. David answered before the phone could ring twice.

'Is it done?'

'It wasn't me.'

'What happened?'

'There was someone else there. He took the kill shot.'

'Who?'

'I don't know. He got away by motorbike. Did you know Evans was going to be there?'

'He announced he was going to accompany Malikov back here, yes.'

'Who else knew about Malikov's involvement?'

David was silent for a moment. 'I couldn't tell you at the time. We suspected the Kremlin might have a team in place.'

'But you still let me go, knowing they were there?'

'Would you have reconsidered if I'd told you?'

Dan clenched his jaw before he exhaled. 'Probably not. Are the others still with you?'

David paused. 'No. No, they're in the next room.'

'But you can't be sure they're not listening, right?'

David sighed. 'We were told you've been shot. Is that true?'

Dan peered down at the blood that was beginning to congeal on his shoulder. 'Yeah. I got shot. One of Evans's team got me when they went after the sniper.'

'How bad is it?'

'Bad enough.'

'We need to get you to a medic,' urged David. 'How soon can you be here?'

Dan held the phone away from his ear and glanced over his shoulder at the receding coastline.

'I'm done, David,' he said eventually.

A silence stretched for what seemed an age before his superior spoke again.

'What do you mean "done"?'

'Innocent people lost their lives today.'

'Porchester wasn't an innocent,' said David. 'He got greedy.'

'It doesn't change anything.' Dan made a slight correction of the wheel, his knuckles gripping the metalwork harder than was needed. 'I can live with trying to kill Malikov, even if someone else beat me to it. What I can't live with is what we've become. We were put together to protect the UK's energy industry,' he added. 'Now it feels like we're back in the bloody army, taking orders from politicians with their own agendas.'

He swallowed. 'I used to *save* lives, David. And I was good at it.' He sighed. 'Besides, having me around at the moment probably wouldn't do the Prime Minister any favours, right?'

'I'm not sure he'd agree, but you've got a point. What are you going to do?'

'Keep my head down for a bit.'

'Is that a good idea?'

Dan heard the concern in the other man's voice. 'It's the only idea I've got at the moment.'

'Where are you?'

Dan couldn't help smiling as he imagined David sitting forward in his chair at his old desk, brow furrowed.

'Best you don't know.'

'Deniable, you mean.'

'Something like that. You still want a career, right?'

'Is there a way I can reach you?'

Dan closed his eyes. 'This number should work for a while.'

'It doesn't look good, running like this,' David persisted.

Dan shivered. 'I'm not going to a military prison while they argue over whether I'm right or wrong regarding

Porchester's death or for going after Malikov,' said Dan. 'The man deserved it. That's good enough for me. I'll let you and Evans decide if you want to pursue the Kremlin over that one.'

'I can cover for you this time, but if you run, I can't protect you. You'll no longer be part of the EPG, understand?'

David's voice was gruff and Dan could tell the man was trying to keep his emotions in check.

'Understood.'

'Where's Mitch by the way?'

Dan's mouth twitched. 'Where did you locate the Prime Minister's car?'

'What do you mean? You know where the bloody car was,' snapped David. 'Still at the farm. We've ordered a tow truck to transport it to Hendon for forensic analysis. Why?'

'You might want to check the trunk first.'

'Wh –'

'Yeah. Tell him I'm sorry, but it was the only thing I could think of to keep him out of harm's way.'

'He's not going to be happy,' said David, vainly trying to keep laughter from his voice. 'I may send someone else to go get him.'

'That's probably wise,' agreed Dan. 'Will he be okay?'

'Yes,' David assured him. 'You overpowered him, right? Resisted arrest, as it were?'

'Yeah. Yes, I did.'

'Then he'll be okay.' David's voice had turned serious once more. 'Stay in touch, all right? You'll contact me if you need help, right?'

'Right,' said Dan. 'I'll be seeing you.'

He ended the call before David could answer or try again to coerce him back to London. He checked the boat's heading and then slid open the cabin door and stepped out onto the deck.

Spray from the swell beside the hull splashed his jeans, puddles of water forming at his feet as he stood still, his arms at his side.

Dan swallowed, the reality of his situation hitting him hard.

'I'm a bloody fugitive,' he murmured. 'Shit.'

As the moon crested the horizon to his left, he swung his arm in a wide arc, releasing the mobile phone from his grip. He watched as it spun in the air before dropping into the deep water, and then he stripped out of his clothing and threw his boots into the water, just in case Mel had fitted a tracking beacon on those as well.

He wouldn't put it past her.

'You're not going to find me, David,' he muttered and hurried back to the cabin, slamming the door behind him.

He knelt, reached under a bench seat, and pulled out a canvas bag. He unzipped it and unfolded clean clothes. A fresh pair of boots was the last item he extracted before he kicked the bag out of the way and returned his attention to the helm.

After he pulled on his jeans, he checked the boat was still on course and then pulled out a drawer set under the wheel and picked up the first aid kit that he'd always kept on board for emergencies.

He cleaned and dressed his shoulder as best he could, pushed the first aid kit back into the drawer, and then leaned on the wheel and pointed the boat south.

Dan peered over his shoulder, unable to take his eyes off the coastline as England slowly slipped over a darkening horizon.

'I'll come back,' he said, as the last glimpse of land dipped out of sight. He clenched his fists.

'One day, I'll come back. I promise.'

THE END

ALSO BY THE AUTHOR IN THIS SERIES

WHITE GOLD

A conspiracy to destroy alternative energy research... a global organisation killing to protect its interests... and a bomb that will change the face of terrorism forever...

Would you know who to trust?

When Sarah Edgewater's ex-husband is murdered by a radical organisation hell-bent on protecting their assets, she turns to Dan Taylor – geologist, ex-soldier, and lost cause. Together, they must unravel the research notes Sarah's ex-husband left behind to locate an explosive device which is circumnavigating the globe towards London – and time is running out.

In a fast-paced ecological thriller which spans the globe, from London to Brisbane and back via the Arctic Circle, Dan and Sarah aren't just chasing the truth – they're chasing a bomb which, if detonated, will change the future of alternative energy research and the centre of England's capital forever.

ISBN: 978-0-646-57340-3

UNDER FIRE

An explosion rocks a Qatari natural gas facility… a luxury cruise liner capsizes in the Mediterranean… and someone has stolen a submarine…

Are the events connected?

Dan Taylor doesn't believe in coincidences – all he has to do is convince his superiors they are next in the terrorists' line of fire.

As Britain enters its worst winter on record, Dan must elude capture to ensure the country's energy resources are protected. At all costs.

In an action-packed adventure, from the Middle East through the Mediterranean to London, Dan and his team are on a quest which will test every choice he makes. Assisted by the exotic Antonia Almasi, Dan realises he faces an adversary far greater than he ever imagined, and not everyone is going to survive.

ISBN: 978-0-992-26850-3

ABOUT THE AUTHOR

For more information about Rachel Amphlett, and to sign up to the readers group for exclusive book news and giveaways, see www.rachelamphlett.com

Lightning Source UK Ltd.
Milton Keynes UK
UKHW03f0628180418
321252UK00001B/228/P